SHERLOCK HOLMES: TO A COUNTRY HOUSE DARKLY

In this collection of twelve brand-new cases, Sherlock Holmes and his long-serving biographer and companion Doctor Watson face a wide-ranging criminal fraternity. Adventures include a one-time Baker Street Irregular jailed for violent robbery, a devious squire at a country house in Berkshire, the terrible secret of an antique which is only revealed when put up for auction at Sotheby's, and a bemused clergyman haunted by a singing nun.

N. M. SCOTT

SHERLOCK HOLMES: TO A COUNTRY HOUSE DARKLY

Complete and Unabridged

LINFORD
Leicester

First published in Great Britain

First Linford Edition
published 2019

A catalogue record for this book is available
from the British Library.

ISBN 978–1–4448–3985–2

Published by
F. A. Thorpe (Publishing)
Anstey, Leicestershire

Set by Words & Graphics Ltd.
Anstey, Leicestershire
Printed and bound in Great Britain by
T. J. International Ltd., Padstow, Cornwall

This book is printed on acid-free paper

For Amanda & Sylvia

Contents

Contents

1

To A Country House Darkly

Mr Sherlock Holmes and I were travelling to London on the Cathedral's Express one dreary afternoon in November, a low-lying mist rolling off the Malvern Hills. My companion, who had consumed two pipefuls of tobacco, took out his leather pocket book and began making notes with his propelling pencil.

'Would you care to browse over the obituaries, old man?' said I, about to fling a somewhat crumpled and creased copy of the *Times* newspaper up onto the rack above.

'No thank you Watson, I've already read the short pieces on Canon Mitchell and Professor Kemp. Pass me the matches, will you.'

Holmes continued with his jottings and we smoked our pipes agreeably and, comfortable in each other's company, did not talk again for some time.

Travelling across the river at Worcester I glimpsed the spire of the Cathedral through the fog and, when our train pulled into the station, I noticed a small group of passengers milling about. How glad they must have been to forsake the damp, chilly platform for a warm compartment. We were joined by a couple of delightful ladies — a mother and daughter, Mrs Lamb and Pru — and it turned out there had been a choral concert promoted at the Cathedral that they had attended that same afternoon and Mrs Lamb was more than enthusiastic about the conductor of the choir, whom she had met briefly during the tea interval.

'A talented church organist, a budding composer — what was that young man's name again, Pru darling? It's on the tip of my tongue — Edward somebody or other.'

'Edward Elgar, mama,' replied the daughter, her eyes sparkling with merriment.

'Yes, Elgar — mark you, gentlemen,

that young man shall go far. I have seldom witnessed such a rapt audience for a first-time work, and such a polite and well spoken, unassuming fellow. I hear he is an accomplished violinist and plays the bassoon. His father owns a music shop in the town, apparently.'

Mrs Lamb's consummate praise of Edward Elgar, the new talent, was interrupted by a loud rap at our compartment window. A pale, anxious face peered in at us. I grabbed the leather strap and down came the window with a thump, allowing a good deal of unwanted cold air to circulate. We were confronted by a man of middle years; a lean, wiry individual wearing his salt and pepper hair heavily Brilliantined and centre-parted. He wore a dark coat and a bright tie. 'Mr Sherlock Holmes?' he gasped, 'of Baker Street?'

'I am he,' answered my friend in a kindly way, leaning forward upon his cloth-covered seat and giving the fellow his full attention.

'The consulting detective?'

'Certainly.'

'And you, sir, I take it, must be Doctor Watson.'

'I am.'

'Look here, Watson, you're an old University of London man. I am Roderick Heston, Director of Music at Royal Holloway College.'

'Good Lord, I attended the opening ceremony of the college in '86. Her Majesty the Queen was present. Don't tell me you were the organist chappie conducting the choir of undergraduates.'

'Just so.'

'May I enquire why you wish to make my acquaintance?' asked Holmes good-naturedly. 'The train is about to leave, you know.'

'I am being followed, sir, hounded at every turn!' he exclaimed. 'Please take this folded note, Mr Holmes. You must contact Sir George Daymond of Buckinghamshire straight away. You must promise, for he is in terrible danger. I am sure he will comprehend the urgency of the matter and furbish you with all necessary details you require. We were at school together. I can't say much more. There's the dratted whistle, the train will be moving out shortly. I must dash. Good evening, gentlemen, and you too ladies.'

'Mr Heston,' trilled Mrs Lamb, unable to compete or make herself heard above the departing whistles and shunts of steam and smoke as the engine now prepared to depart. 'You did enjoy the choral concert, I trust.'

But the manic gentleman was nowhere to be seen. He had rushed off into the fog. I heard muffled footsteps and the slam of a carriage door.

'I should say that man is in some sort of trouble, wouldn't you, my dear?' enquired Mrs Lamb of her daughter, who was powdering her nose.

'He seemed very agitated, mama,' she agreed. 'Oh, do let us see that note, Mr Holmes. You know how we ladies love a mystery,' she added coltishly.

My companion unfolded the piece of paper, studying it minutely with his magnifying lens before passing it round for general view.

RODERICK HESTON
ARNOLD TRIBBS
GEORGE DAYMOND
PONSONBY CROFT

'Is that all? Golly,' said Pru, peering intently at the writing, shifting the notepaper under the meagre glow emanating from the hissing gas mantle. 'I imagined an epistle written in blood, a cry for vengeance, else a blackmailer's demand for money. Instead, why it's just four boring old surnames underlined in red ink. What are we to make of it, Doctor Watson?'

'Very little,' I conceded, offering Mrs Lamb my last boiled peppermint from the bag. 'There are no directives, no address. Who is this Sir George Daymond he talked of, I wonder?'

'All very vague,' admitted Holmes, relighting his briar-root pipe and creating a fug of smoke in the compartment, of which the ladies did not approve. 'But I shall not ignore his entreaties. Mr Heston spoke in earnest. What did he say — he was being followed — hounded? Most singular.'

'A rather nervous, jittery fellow, I thought,' said Mrs Lamb, nodding to her daughter, who acquiesced.

We spent the remainder of our railway journey chatting and basking in the mother and daughter's charming conversation and easy humour, particularly enjoying hearing Pru recount her various antics as a student, for she was enrolled at the Guildhall School of Music studying piano composition. The journey to London passed all too swiftly. Oxford and Didcot flew by and we were soon rattling past Royal Oak into Paddington Station, falling over each other as we reached up to the rack for our hats and coats and bundled-up luggage just before the train drew into the buffers.

'If you're Marylebone way, do pop into our digs — Mrs Lamb, and you, Pru — 221B Baker Street. Got that? The Metropolitan line runs there.'

'I've already noted your address, Doctor Watson, and both Pru and myself should be honoured to visit the London address of that most famous consulting detective, Mr Sherlock Holmes. It has been a most agreeable journey. Now, Pru darling, do help me onto the platform, it looks an awful long way down.'

We were walking smartly up beneath the rounded cast-iron shed along the main concourse, when all of a sudden came confused, harassed shouts and a flurry of activity — slamming carriage doors and the echo of hastening footsteps.

'Someone's been stabbed!' called out a porter. 'We need a policeman. The poor devil's had it, run through good and square. There's blood on the compartment floor. Jim Bentley the guard's got it on his trousers. Go to the office; get the ruddy stationmaster Mr Hadley. Quick!'

Holmes did an about turn and dashed past the group of concessions, the small bar, tobacconist shop, gentleman's barbers and waiting rooms. The carriage was not hard to locate for a crowd were gathered on the same platform we had alighted from earlier. By the time I caught up I was considerably puffed out.

'Is it Roddy Heston?' I called out,

fearing the worst.

'Run through — just look at this, Watson,' cried Holmes, leaning into the open compartment, taking full advantage of all the confusion and hoo-ha before the official police arrived.

'Heston's still got his dratted pipe in his mouth. The dagger's impaled him to the back-board, plumb through the seat.'

We were seriously confounded, though lacking any form of tact or decorum in the face of death my colleague was quick to begin his calculations and assessment of the scene.

Seizing his magnifying lens and pocket tape measure, despite the horrified glances of onlookers mustering on the platform, he began an intense if minute search of the interior of the compartment and only when he was finally satisfied did we make haste to the main concourse laden with luggage, our winter overcoats folded over one arm. After we handed in our tickets and were heading for the cab rank, others — by that I refer to a number of uniformed constables and Scotland Yard officials, one of whom I recognised as Inspector Bristol, a passably competent policeman who had come up through the grades and owned the steady if unadventurous mentality of the so-called 'plodder' — were entering the station.

'Ah, Bristol, you are in charge of the investigation, I take it?' remarked Holmes.

'I am, Mr 'olmes, and I ain't got time to stand 'ere scratching me 'ead theorising. There's practical police work to be attending to. What got you here so quick? Tipped off by a bookie, I shouldn't wonder. Odds on the bloke's been stabbed with a knife. Out me way.'

As our hansom rattled through crowded London along Praed Street through the fog, we could not help but discuss the murder of poor Roddy Heston, the nondescript note he had earlier entrusted to my colleague now of the greatest significance.

'Do you recall, my dear Watson, did we make many stops before Oxford?'

'Indeed, Holmes. I remember clearly we came up the bank of the Cotswold escarpment, and at the summit our train steamed into Chipping Campden, a small rural station.'

'A box and crossing gates.'

'The fog delayed our train for some ten minutes before pushing on to Moreton Marsh. There was a signal box and a gated level crossing, certainly.'

'We are clear that Heston was murdered by an opportunist killer between Worcester and Paddington, but was it a fellow passenger or could the murderer have been lurking on the platform at Chipping Campden, I wonder? Taking advantage of the fog and the delay, the victim was taken unawares, I grant you.'

'The train was not crowded. Heston was more likely alone and sat next to the window, close to the carriage door, huddled in a corner of the compartment.'

'The door is opened and, 'voila' — the assailant plunges the dagger in fearfully hard, impaling his victim to the backboard, then simply slams it shut and runs off into the fog which should have been very thick at the summit of that escarpment. This I think, Watson, offers us the most likely possibility. That said, it is imperative we contact Sir George Daymond. Ah, I see our cab is approaching Marylebone Road. I trust Mrs Hudson's delicious supper shall appease our appetites somewhat. The events of the last hour or so have left me absolutely ravenous. A plate of cold partridge else curried fowl accompanied by a bottle of fine old Burgundy shall go far to assist our reasoning faculties concerning this most promising of cases.'

★ ★ ★

I confess I was glad once more to be sat comfortably before a cheery fire burning in the grate, ensconced in our rooms at Baker Street, after having appreciated a first rate supper.

My companion was lounging in his armchair opposite wearing his shabby old purple dressing gown and slippers, his long, lanky legs stretched out in front of the hearth considering the aforementioned note while puffing on his long pipe, our front sitting room permeated by the reek of the oily, black shag he preferred.

'Four names, one struck off,' said I, chucking my journal of medicine aside and reaching for a cigar from the coalscuttle.

'Just so. Roddy Heston can be crossed off our list and that leaves Tribbs, Daymond and Croft, all of whom I am assuming were educated at Houghton, one of the top public schools in the country. You recall, my dear Watson, the late musical director at Royal Holloway College in passing told us he had been at school with Sir George Daymond. I made a note at Paddington that Heston was wearing an old school tie, purple and green diagonal stripes bearing a crest and school motto 'Our learning maketh us wise'. I consulted our tatty copy of the Old Schools Directory and found a reference to Houghton.'

'Houghton it is then,' I conceded, lighting my cigar with a Vesta. 'I have been fairly industrious, Holmes, applying myself to looking up Sir George Daymond.'

'And . . . Pray, what did you find?'

'He is a landowner with a large farming estate in Buckinghamshire and resides at Stoneycroft Grange on the borders of the county.'

'Well, Watson, I can tell you,' said he, having listened gravely to all I said, 'Sir George shall be receiving a visit from ourselves at the Grange tomorrow morning and I shall be bally anxious to get to the bottom of this note. The names must obviously mean something to him and I concur his life is in grave danger if Roderick Heston's anything to go by. Pass me that Bradshaw's will you. Buckinghamshire it is then.'

★   ★   ★

Honestly expecting to be back by supper time, we bid our redoubtable housekeeper Mrs Hudson adieu and took a cab to the station where we caught the 9.06 service, which arrived at our destination, Stoke Woodley, at midday.

Dressed comfortably in our tweed suits and cloth caps, a first class

14

compartment to ourselves that inevitably filled rather quickly with a thick fug of tobacco smoke, pipes being lit and re-lit, we made do with a bundle of morning editions, swopped repeatedly, and avidly perused for the duration. Some time elapsed before our train achieved Bucks, and thereafter, chuffing along the rural branch, eventually Stoke Woodley, a picturesque railway station built in the country house style with a tile hung upper storey and incised plasterwork.

Mr Penfold, who operated a 'For Hire' waggonette on the forecourt, agreed to take us the remainder of the journey. Thus, after clattering along un-metalled, bumpy lanes for quite some twenty minutes or so, we passed through a set of granite gates and, our waggonette trotting round the curve of a rhododendron bordered gravel drive, we caught our first glimpse in the weak winter sunshine of Stoneycroft Grange, an old Georgian style country house. Nearby were a group of thatched farm buildings.

I perceived a series of terraces led down to the garden consisting of topiary and shrubs interspersed with a lawn, the Buckinghamshire hamlet of Stoke Woodley with its little parish church, the square clock tower visible beyond the trees.

At the front door an elderly retainer summoned Sir George and after we had made our business abundantly clear and showed him the note of four names, without any preamble he accepted us into his house and had further places set for lunch.

The squire, in company at least, appeared both amiable and easy going. Ruddy of complexion and plump of stature he would issue on occasions raucous bellows of laughter and I observed a frothy spittle formed at the corners of his rather wide, rubbery lips whenever he dwelled upon some estate topic — a gamekeeper's new covey, where a best trout might be caught. His preferred attire was a dark swallow-tail coat with brass buttons, a light waistcoat, breeches, top boots and a white cravat.

Throughout lunch, served on a fine refectory table, the squire appeared attentive to his wife, patting her hand, occasionally running fingers through her ringlets of jet-black hair. The beautiful creature was patiently fed her meal by the nurse in attendance and afterwards led like a somewhat confused, stranded child, to her favourite armchair beside the fire, content with her familiar routine and surroundings. Evidently some illness of the mind, I suspected, being responsible for her fragile condition.

'Sir George,' said Holmes over port and cigars, 'so, we can begin to make some headway and bring to justice a very clever and devious killer who is presently at large and well able to strike at a time and place of his own choosing. What have you to say for yourself? I understand there is a link with Houghton Public School, of course.'

'Well, gentlemen, I read about Heston's murder in the papers — Paddington Station of all places — so public, so full of milling crowds, discovered alone in a train compartment of the Cathedral's Express. Terrible, terrible. The morning editions were full of it.'

'Sympathetic platitudes are not what I

wish to hear. I require facts, hard facts that you alone can furbish. Come man, everything you say will be treated in the strictest confidence. I and Doctor Watson are not here to judge or condemn you. What's important is we may be able to save your life. Let us return to our one solid link. Houghton Public School. It's in Lancashire, isn't it?'

'You are not going to like what you hear, Mr Holmes. There is something in my past that you should know about. We four, and each name is identified correctly on that note, were responsible for killing a form master, a Latin teacher. Before you hold up your hands in protest I should make it clear he was a sadistic brute who over a number of terms made our lives a misery, goaded us in the classroom, beat us constantly and would brook no mercy.'

'Killed a master? Murdered him?' I said incredulously.

'It is incomprehensible, I know. I had myself almost forgotten what came to pass that long summer term when Ponsonby Croft, now a professor at

Oxford, myself, Tribbs and Heston decided enough was enough and we would no longer tolerate the clever teacher's mental torture, the unfair thrashings, the bullying. For one night in July, after first bundling Mr Pike semiconscious in an eiderdown, we carried him downstairs from the dormitory and wheeled him across the playing fields in a barrow before tipping him, half alive, into a lime kiln pit. They were carrying out a burning for slake lime, you see. The form master had been previously paralysed by a powerful sedative supplied indirectly by Ponsonby's father, whose speciality was medicine at Cambridge.

'While Pikey slept, he was unaware a boy crept across to his bed delivering a quick acting serum expertly into his spine. The drug took immediate effect. Croft from an early age was interested in medicine. All his vast knowledge of pharmacology derived from probing letters sent back and forth to his father at the Cambridge faculty. Myself and Heston were both strapping young fellows who provided the muscle power. Our sports training was put to good use that night of the lime burning, I can tell you.'

'Good gracious!' I ejaculated. 'You kill a chap as though he were nothing more than a laboratory rat or a toad in a school biology class.'

'Doctor Watson, I have had ample leisure to dwell on the past and yet I cannot find it in me to be in any way critical of our endeavours.'

'Until now,' said I, stubbing out my cigar before reaching for the port decanter to refill my glass. 'For it appears you had not covered your tracks quite as effectively as you thought. A simple schoolboy prank is one thing, but this, sir!'

'Yes, the time for recriminations appears to be in order,' agreed my colleague re-lighting his cigar.

'Look, gentlemen, we covered every eventuality. I admit us boys were young, but we had plenty of brains between us.'

'The perfect crime, committed all those years ago. Seamless, no hitch, until now that is. Well someone's close on your heels and, by jingo one person is already dead.

Have you no inkling who could possibly be out to murder you and the others, Sir George?'

'None, I am at a total loss. If I knew, if I only had a name, I would be the first to communicate whom I suspected, Mr Holmes.'

'Could it possibly be one of the four, or at least one of the three remaining?' queried Holmes.

'Absolutely not! We had an unshakeable bond of trust.'

'But you yourself must realise that you all went your own ways. Were you not four separate individuals? Cannot attitudes change?'

'We were one. We swore upon an oath. All of us hated Pike to the last. No, no, a traitor in the camp is inconceivable.'

'If I may change tack slightly,' said Holmes, seriously, 'both Doctor Watson and myself were earlier impressed by your remarkable wife. May I venture to suggest she suffers from a rare medical condition that leaves her rather 'other worldly' in appearance? Like a beautiful waxwork, she does not seem aware of her own great beauty or able to communicate emotion. For all the time I saw her she was immobile — and said not a word. This is of course mentioned in complete confidence and I do not mean to pry else cause offence.'

'And none taken, sir. I well understand your curiosity, gentlemen. Others have likewise remarked upon her angelic disposition, her likeness to a holy statuette created from the finest alabaster out of a mould. Alas, my wife was simply the victim of a nasty accident that occurred on our honeymoon in the Lake District. We were both young then and followed outdoor pursuits. We were keen on sailing.'

'A boating accident you refer to?'

'Precisely. We were a newly married couple at the peak of our happiness, the future spread before us, so much to look forward to, so in love. It was a beautiful calm day; we were surrounded by crags and fells, skimming along the water in our sail boat with not a care in the world. And then my wife lost her footing. I believe the sole of her plimsoll slipped on the wet deck. With a little gasp, she fell backwards and cracked her skull on the tiller. That's all it took. The resulting brain injury robbed her of all her long-term memory, left her wholly unaware of her previous life. Her wonderful sparkling personality, her beautiful nature and noble feelings all vanished. She became as you see her now, a sensationally pretty waxwork, wholly bereft of feeling or emotion.

'Believe me, all the money and wealth I possessed were of no value in the case of a severe brain injury, this despite consulting the most eminent foreign specialists from many continents. Unaware she is one of the most beautiful women in creation, I have even had a great artist like Whistler wish to paint her, but I cannot bring myself to allow such requests. She left the church as a blushing bride in a flower bedecked landau and returned to Stoneycroft Grange from our honeymoon in a horse-drawn ambulance, ushered discreetly through a side entrance upon a sheeted stretcher, only a few trusted servants aware of the tragedy that had befallen the happy couple.'

'I could not help but notice the bottles of tablets, Sir George,' said I with a good deal of sympathy. 'Are they of any real use in a serious case such as this, when the brain is badly affected?'

'They are crucial to her wellbeing, Doctor Watson. A regime of physic to help reduce harmful fits, a violent reaction to her illness that must be carefully administered.'

'Perchance, has she ever been lucid since the boating accident, able to respond — to talk or express herself?'

'We live in hope, Mr Holmes. I am assured by her eminent Swiss specialist that in certain cases the human brain, the damaged cerebellum, can, over time, heal itself, but I confess I have seen little change or improvement in her condition these many years.'

★　★　★

I confess the squire who had taken his leave, concerned with the day-to-day running of his estate office, left us in something of a moral quandary. Upon one side of the scales, whatever the plausible excuses of the psychoanalyst, the valid compassionate arguments of the psychologist, as a schoolboy he was guilty of a heinous crime. Upon the other, here was a conscientious husband who obviously adored his wife despite her persistent brain illness, and more importantly was at great pains to look after her. 'In sickness and in health, till death us do part' sprang to mind. Anyhow, Holmes had already decided upon a plan. He proposed we act as his protectors and that perhaps it would be prudent to stay a while at Stoneycroft Grange. To this, over our port and cigars, the squire readily agreed.

'Well, my dear Watson, what do you make of these latest revelations? A group of schoolboys implicated in a sensational crime of murder at Houghton. That Latin master, Pike, thrown half alive, poor devil, into a lime kiln pit where they are carrying out a burning?'

'The method is astounding,' I conceded. 'But you are right, our place is by the side of Sir George. Perhaps, like some magnetic force, we shall be able to attract this clever assailant who murdered Heston and apprehend him here at the Grange. Is that your idea?'

'Exactly, Watson. A risky strategy, I know. Now, that queer wife of his interests me. Not such a waxen dummy as he would have us believe.'

'Oh, why do you say that?'

'Because I detected the faintest flicker from her eyelids when I mentioned the name of Roderick Heston. I cannot be sure, but she appeared to register something of what I said. It was only the briefest impression. I could of course have been mistaken.'

'The brain is a damned complex organ, Holmes. As an army doctor I know of cases in my old regiment, the Berkshires, where wounded soldiers have remained hale and hearty, despite having a piece of shrapnel or a bullet embedded in the soft tissue.'

Holmes went off to seek the village post office and after making enquiries, completed telegraph forms forthwith and returned to the house in jubilant mood, The counter clerk had proved very helpful in certain matters and he was confident an important meeting could now take place the following morning, the nature of which he chose not to disclose.

Later that evening, after a game of billiards while Holmes, assisted by the butler, made himself familiar with every nook and cranny of the old place, being supplied with the necessary pyjamas and toiletries, I was for an early bed.

★　★　★

I awoke to a dull, overcast morning, the garden shrouded by autumnal mist clinging to the shrubbery, cedars and mulberry trees. By the time I was dressed, there was the comforting sound of crackling, burning leaves and I saw from my bedroom window the gardener had lit a bonfire and could be observed raking the lawn.

I went downstairs to the dining room. Holmes was already at breakfast consuming a plate of ham and eggs, as was Sir

George himself. I went across to the sideboard and helped myself from the heaped dishes. About to return to the dining table, my plate piled high with all manner of delicious meats, the old retainer, a fellow whom I only knew as Grieves, came in and introduced two smartly attired gentlemen, who it turned out had recently arrived from the station.

'Ah, you got my wire I see.' My companion dabbed his chin with a napkin and leapt from his chair. 'Watson, may I introduce Professor Ponsonby Croft and Mr Albert Tribbs. This is something of a school reunion I think, eh Sir George? Do stand easy gentlemen; the post office clerk gets all the credit for locating your addresses. My name is Sherlock Holmes, by the way. I am a consulting detective and this is my good friend and colleague Doctor Watson. Of course, Sir George, although a little older and wiser, requires no introduction. If you studied your papers you will know of the murder of Roddy Heston. I am naturally anxious a second death does not occur. I will not apportion blame at this juncture, but if you value your lives you would do well to cooperate. Do I make myself clear?'

'Perfectly.'

'Understood, Mr Holmes,' replied the shorter and more stout of the two gentlemen.

'Be good enough to go over the events of that summer term — the night when you removed Mr Pike the Latin master from his bed, took him downstairs from your house dormitory and placed him in a wheelbarrow.'

'We were so extremely bright and intelligent and had created a strategy for murder,' considered Tribbs.

'A strategy for murder,' said I incredulously. 'You talk as if even as pupils you were an authority on the subject.'

'Before implementing our plan, Doctor Watson, for example the lime kiln burning, the timing had to be precise. The hour between two and three o'clock of the morning when the whole school would be sound asleep. The route across the playing fields must be close to the hedgerow, to the tree line. The wheel of the barrow was of primary concern. It

29

must be well greased to achieve fairly silent momentum from A to B; no squeaks or unnecessary noises from rusty parts.'

'Croft effectively paralysed the form master,' explained Tribbs. 'It was his father, you see, always writing letters to one another, discussing points of interest regarding drugs and their various effects. Samples were often forthcoming, packaged in Ovaltine tins. That's how we received the glass syringe and the fast-acting sedative as yet untested (on humans at least), a serum for paralysing the central nervous system. Ponsonby wrote to his father saying he should like to experiment on the school cat, but of course we had other ideas.'

'Mr Pike, you mean?' said I, rather brusquely.

'Indeed, for we realised once the form master was 'neutralised' then the rest of our scheme could be implemented fairly easily.

'Bundling old Pikey in an eiderdown we carried him down the back stairs of the block housing the dormitory. We kept a lookout for each other. I've never been so scared, yet exhilarated in all my life, Mr Holmes. The risks did not bear thinking about should we have been found out. The reputation of our school should have been put in jeopardy and, despite being only juveniles, we would have stood trial and been incarcerated, probably for life, as mental incompetents.'

'So the four of you now find yourselves reduced to three. Look, I mean a bad teacher is to be reprimanded or dismissed,' said Holmes, 'but to murder a fellow just won't do. I'm frankly surprised you managed to get away with it, I really am. But now it appears you have your comeuppance, somebody wants you all dead.'

'What conclusion did the school authorities reach? Were there questions raised? A teacher does not so simply vanish overnight,' I enquired.

'We enquired into his personal history. Pikey was a confirmed bachelor. Both his parents were dead. We forged a sealed letter. Accordingly everything gave the appearance of him having fled the school in a hurry to begin life anew on the continent, a sudden, impulsive running away if you will. A scandal was broadly hinted at. Both Heston and Tribbs came forward and claimed certain improprieties and as we rightly assumed, the board of governors and the headmaster, not wishing to risk the considerable reputation of the school being sullied, the matter was conveniently brushed under the carpet.'

'Gentlemen,' said Sir George excitedly, 'might I suggest a glass of sherry? Do you remember our tuck shop, Tribby? All those lovely buns and fizzy pop, and the bosomy matron, Miss Dryce, whom we were all madly in love with?'

'Perhaps we should toast our continued survival,' suggested Tribbs nervously.

'The ghost of Mr Pike may yet still strike,' laughed Ponsonby Croft, accepting a proffered cigarette from Holmes, who leaned over and lit it for him. But thereafter my friend delivered the following broadside:

'I propose, Sir George, that the dagger used to kill Roddy Heston I am fairly certain came from a display case in your gun room. I observed a certain gap last night in your collection. The remaining daggers, which have uniquely carved antler handles, match the one I saw poking out of Heston's chest. The one used to skewer him so effectively to the back of the compartment seat. Originally a set of six, you now have but five daggers displayed under glass. Have you anything to add?'

'I-I had absolutely no idea. Are you certain, Mr Holmes? I confess quite candidly I hardly ever visit the gun room these days, except to wash the dogs. I had no inkling a weapon of the Civil War period as used by Roundheads — cavalry officers, that is — has been mislaid. You'd best speak to Grieves or my housekeeper. Perhaps they could help.'

'Nonetheless, it is curious coincidence, is it not. As Watson will concur, I am possessed of a keen eye for detail and rarely miss anything. That singular indentation in the felt lining of the display case causes me to be wary of light fingers amongst your staff, perhaps?'

'I shall not hear a word said against my domestics. I pride myself on choosing and interviewing everyone from scullery maids to cook, to head housekeeper personally. They are beyond reproach. I trust you are not undermining my vested authority as squire. If so, it's a dashed impertinence and I shall require you and your colleague to leave my house this instance!'

'My dear Sir George, you misunderstand me. I was merely pointing out certain possibilities and in no way did I intend to cause offence.'

'Humph, I should hope not. A Civil War dagger missing from my gun room, you say. Well, well, I can't understand it. I am sure it will turn up somewhere in the house. I recall the antler handle, certainly.'

'I fear our absentee knife is presently in police custody and will be useful as evidence should the perpetrator of Heston's train murder ever be brought to justice. That said, let us quickly move on. Has any member of your staff left your employ recently? I mean, for another situation, not necessarily because he or she has been dismissed.'

'I am reminded of my faithful estate manager Mr Stevens, who had been with us for many years. He became gravely ill with influenza and passed away suddenly last month. He is buried over at the churchyard. Such a damn pity. He was well liked and dependable. I trusted him like a son. He shared my estate office and assisted collecting tithes and so forth. Trust you to dredge up such a sorrowful event in my life, Holmes. I can feel tears welling in my eyes at just the thought of his genial presence. Why are you looking at me like a dratted crow about to peck at fresh carrion? Have you no sense of discretion when dealing with affairs of the heart?'

'I am foremost a consulting detective, Sir George. The estate manager Stevens's first name, if you please.

'Henry.'

With a flourish of his propelling pencil, my colleague noted the estate manager's name on the sleeve of his shirt cuff for future reference.

'I shall detain you no further, gentlemen. Ah, the sherry tray beckons. Is your wife present, Sir George? I have not seen her sat in her usual chair of late. I trust she is in passable health?'

'The nurse normally prefers Jane to sit in the conservatory amongst the ferns and potted plants of a morning — finds it soothing, I imagine.'

After sherry Mr Tribbs and Professor Ponsonby Croft bid us good day, the one to catch a connection for Oxford, the other an express service on main line metals back to London, the former gentleman living in Wandsworth.

'I'll have the four-wheeled chase sent round if you want,' Sir George barked, striding across the sitting room to give the fire a poke while Grieves, the elderly butler, after replacing the sherry decanter on the sideboard, gathered up the tray of glasses to take them out to the kitchen to be rinsed. He returned shortly laden down with assorted hats, coats and sticks.

'I can get my stable lad to harness the horse. You've got a good hour before the stopping service. My groom can take you to the station.'

Mr Tribbs accepted this offer of a ride. However, the professor, the more energetic of the two, declined, informing us he would be walking to the station to enjoy some good country air and a brisk trudge by way of exercise. The interview with these two old Houghton public schoolboys had proved most advantageous, the reunion providing an excuse for my colleague to emphasise the seriousness, for despite the incident involving the death of a school teacher having happened many years past almost to be a distant memory, ugly retribution was close at hand and both men had better guard against complacency.

We ourselves set out for a stroll, visiting the tiny hamlet, taking in the Parish church, the Green, surrounded by a most charming group of thatched cottages with neatly maintained gardens, mostly dormant at this time of year, but still resplendent in autumn colours, with the fallen carpet of leaves and an abundance of nuts and berries visible in the hedges and yew borders thereabouts.

After an hour or so it began to rain, and Holmes and I departed for Stoneycroft Grange, where, enjoying a light tea, we sat watching from the comfort of the sitting room the garden outside — the drenched topiary, paved walkways and shrubbery glassy with a sheen of pouring rainwater. The late post arrived which caused my companion to rush into the hallway and seize a letter from the butler that had arrived addressed specifically to him. He hurried up to his room and when he came down to dinner that night I recall my old friend looked pensive and moody.

★ ★ ★

At bedtime, Holmes was quick to usher me into his room, closing the door behind him and securely locking it. The oil lamp upon the dresser gleamed softly. The rain had stopped and a clear starry night was in progress. The lamp glass cast a cheery glow about the chimney piece and old oak furnishings. My colleague snatched his long pipe from the stone mantelpiece before indicating I should plump myself on the edge of the bed, the mattress of which was very hard; an intricately carved, gloomy four poster of dark wood, a relic from the times of Queen Bess, I supposed.

'This bed's surely only fit for a slumbering ghost,' I remarked, 'preferably a spectre wearing a ruffle, doublet and hose and holding its head under one arm.'

'My un-sprung bed is the very least of our concerns, dear boy. By the by, I made some useful inroads regarding the character assassination of Mr Pike, the Latin master at Houghton, so much maligned of late,' said he.

'Deservedly so, in my opinion. That scoundrel,' I thundered. 'You know how I detest those brutes who infiltrate our public school system, Holmes. Why, at times I almost find myself sympathising with that murderous group of schoolboys back then.'

Wrenching open his travelling bag, my friend drew out a post-marked envelope, already slit along one edge with his trusty pipe knife.

'A letter — do you want me to read it out loud?' said I. He gave me an amused and tolerant smile.

'Not this particular epistle, Watson. I think upon reflection it would be prudent to remain silent upon its contents. But, pray, by all means tell me what you make of it.'

Unfolding the headed letter with its official Houghton School crest and motto at the top, I was aghast. I digested the contents of the neatly typed document. The letter recently received and addressed to Mr Sherlock Holmes personally from the bursar.

Dear Mr Holmes

Thank you for your enquiry. I can confirm that Mr Alfred Pike was indeed a teacher of languages at Houghton and much loved by a generation of pupils and staff alike. A mild-mannered scholar, a man of the utmost integrity, it is with great regret that he left us suddenly and quite unexpectedly towards the end of summer term 18 —

According to my files he suffered a breakdown brought on by nervous depression and sadly made a difficult decision to quit teaching altogether and begin life anew on the Continent. I hope this is of some value in your tracing your distant relative.

Yours sincerely

Patricia Gatty — Bursar

'This is all wrong, Watson. Mr Pike 'a mild-mannered scholar much loved by a generation of pupils and teachers alike?' Really, does that sound remotely like a brute, a teacher with a violent and uncontrollable temper dishing out corporal punishment and instilling fear in the classroom?'

'Unlikely,' I conceded. 'Drat it all, Holmes, if it is a blasted lie. Sir George and the other two are being economical with the truth. Are they extemporising? Or indeed is the school simply covering up?'

All of a sudden my colleague dashed across to the latticed window and waved the long stem of his cherry wood pipe in the direction of Stoke Woodley church, a dark silhouette, the clock tower just visible beyond the shrubbery and clump of mulberry trees at the end of the garden.

'By Jove, that's where we're headed next, my dear Watson. I have a neat little theory that shall require some patient spade work, if you catch my meaning!'

'Dig up a corpse? You're not serious. Whose coffin do you intend to break open, anyhow?'

'Why, that estate manager chappie, Henry Stevens of course. He was, according to Sir George, suddenly taken ill, and then dies rather conveniently, if I may say so, and is buried over there in that churchyard. Last month in fact. Do you not recall the squire's fondness for him?'

'An impromptu exhumation, without

proper permission? What do you take us for — a couple of blasted grave robbers? We should be arrested and put up before a magistrate. You can see for yourself the lights blazing over at the rectory. Are we to be overseen, found out by the vicar or his sexton? I fear your wits have deserted you at long last, Holmes.'

'On the contrary, I am completely clear upon the point. The churchyard it is. We shall wait until every lamp is extinguished and thereafter set about producing a couple of spades from the garden shed round by the glass houses. The grave soil I'll wager shall be fairly loose and there's no frost to speak of. Why, I quite fancy a little fresh air and exercise, Watson. Don't look so down in the dumps. No doubt the church clock upon that handsome thirteenth-century Norman tower shall have struck one chime before we make our move. Take up your pipe, dear boy, and charge it with tobacco. You have a stash of your usual Arcadia mixture, I trust. We shall smoke for a while and keep a keen eye on that rectory over there.'

Carrying a coiled rope and spades fortified by a large brandy we trudged warily beneath the lychgate in the direction of Henry Stevens' relatively recently filled in grave, which was easy enough to locate due to scatterings of jaded flowers and tired old wreaths atop of a mound of heaped soil.

It took a good half hour of digging to a depth of five feet or so before we struck solid wood. Such was Holmes' impatience that his spade splintered through the elm lid, damaging the very coffin we were intending to re-open.

'Steady,' said I. 'I know you're not a religious chap, Holmes, but show some modicum of respect for the dead. This is a Christian burial, an Anglican plot, after all.'

'Dead — a corpse you refer to — really, Watson, have you perchance observed the damp sand adhering to the blade of my shovel? We can dispense with 'undertakers etiquette' upon this occasion. I can assure you it is NOT

Henry Stevens who is buried down here but a brace of sandbags heaped inside to approximate the weight of a body. Time to tidy up, there's no need to delay any further, I've got what I came for. Evidence that the last fatal illness and funeral of this estate manager was a cleverly manipulated sham, aided no doubt by a confidante of Mr Stevens, no less than the medical practitioner who has his brass nameplate screwed to the door of that charming cottage we saw on the outskirts of the village when taking our morning constitutional. A Doctor Madden.'

* * *

'Good morning,' said Holmes the following day, helping himself to a generous plateful of devilled kidneys from the heated dishes upon the sideboard in the dining room. 'I trust you slept well. There's nothing like good Buckinghamshire air and a little healthy exercise to warrant a sound night's sleep.'

'I slept like a top,' said I, taking my

place at table and helping myself to toast and marmalade.

'Well, gentlemen, I confess I sleep uneasily these days with a pistol beneath my pillow and a loaded shotgun leaning against my bedroom door. I am growing more anxious by the hour that we shall soon have an unwanted intruder lurking in the grounds of my house, spying out the land, waiting for an opportune moment to strike.'

'Henry Stevens,' remarked Holmes, tucking into his breakfast with relish. 'Your departed estate manager was familiar with your house — the rooms and passage ways, and so forth.'

'Certainly, as I mentioned before, he was a much liked and trusted individual. He shared my estate office and we would often chat and discuss agricultural matters in my study. Why do you ask? I told you, Mr Holmes, the fellow is dead, for goodness sake and nothing will bring him back, worse luck.'

'Yes, dead persons are harmless on the whole, unless returning as a malignant spectre concerned with hauntings and other mischief.'

'Poltergeists, that is the proper name for impish spirits. Are you inferring you have heard unexplained noises in your room, repeated knockings and thumps in the middle of the night? I can assure you that's the water pipes. Does my old antique four-poster rock of its own accord? Other guests remark there is an uncomfortable presence lurking in the mattress, a restless ghost who does not like sharing the bed with the living. I have never myself seen or heard anything remotely untoward. Ghostly footsteps on the stair, the clanking of a suit of armour.'

'Ghosts and spirits aside, Sir George,' said Holmes, dabbing his chin with a napkin. 'Our own antagonist — that person responsible for murdering Heston, is a real flesh and blood entity, a malignant human specimen certainly, and undoubtedly a ruthless individual set fair on a determined course. Would you mind passing the coffee pot, my dear Watson?'

Later that morning our host was required to visit a Mr Dempsey, a gentleman who farmed thereabouts, on a business matter concerning agricultural machinery, and left us to ourselves. We were sat in our armchairs, when I heard the rustle of skirts and saw a gentle feminine hand tug timidly at the sleeve of my colleague's frock coat. Like myself, Holmes twisted round in his armchair to be faced with Sir George's wife, more waxwork than alive, staring down at us from on high. Yet upon this occasion, the holy alabaster statue actually spoke and made intelligible sense.

'I am captive,' she said in almost a whisper. 'I know you to be both noble and kindly gentlemen, Mr Holmes, and you too, Doctor Watson. Do not breathe a word of our conversation to anyone in the house. My nurse believes me to be resting. We have very little time and limited privacy. My husband must be kept in total ignorance of our meeting. He is presently visiting Mr Dempsey, an old friend of his.'

'Your brain has begun to heal itself, your long term memory and personality restored. But your husband remains ignorant of this,' said my colleague, taking both of her frail, little hands in his.

'And must be kept so. George is clever and seeks to use powerful sedatives to control my behaviour and chain me to a life of confinement. The boating accident was no accident. My husband deliberately pushed me, hoping to shove me overboard so that I might drown and he would take possession of my immense fortune. Instead I sustained a terrible injury to the base of my skull, which, as you will by now realise, left me severely brain damaged for many years. You are right — my brain is in recovery. I am once more aware of who I am'

'But where on earth have you been, madam? We have not seen you for quite some time. I asked after you often,' insisted Holmes.

'Recently he has begun to keep me for long periods under lock and key with his mother and father downstairs in the basement. What dreadful company they are, to be sure. So lifelike I sometimes imagine they chit chat to one another.'

'Your husband's parents kept imprisoned against their will?' said I, completely misunderstanding.

'They are embalmed, Doctor Watson. The work was carried out at grievous expense by clever Russian chemists. My husband adored both his parents and could not bear to be parted from them. The corpses were made to sit in cottage chairs, either side of a table. His mother, wearing a bonnet, plump and jolly, busy and industrious at her embroidery. He, the father, smoking a clay pipe with a glass of stout in his hand. Every inch the archetypal English gentry, a brace of pheasants and a large game pie set before him.'

'The parents embalmed. Why, that is surely rather drastic, allowing for grief. A period of mourning certainly, but — embalming!'

'It's disgusting! Two rejuvenated corpses that should have been properly buried in a Christian way and allowed to decompose, kept fresh and lifelike in a specially sealed, pressurised glass-sided cabinet. But hush, I hear footsteps. I shall pass upstairs to my bedroom by means of a hidden staircase. Not a word to anyone, Mr Holmes. Remember what I have told you. Out on the lake it was no accident. He is mad. If he had his way he would place me in one of those awful embalming cabinets like a trophy. He is a compulsive liar and capable of immense duplicity.'

The recovering mistress of the house, so svelte and light of foot she might have been a visiting shade passing through a wall, left our presence, the butler Grieves entering the dining room to clear away breakfast things. We behaved as though nothing out of the ordinary had occurred. Both of us took out our pipes and, in a casual manner, stood before the immense fireplace, a log fire hissing and spitting in the grate, we smoked and generally made small talk.

'Is everything to your liking, gentlemen?' asked the butler politely. 'The billiard room is at your disposal. Can I fetch you anymore coffee?'

'A pot of coffee wouldn't go amiss, but the gun room is more to my taste,' said

Holmes, somewhat caustically, beckoning Grieves, the elderly retainer, to come closer. 'Do you perchance know what became of the Civil War cavalry dagger normally kept on display in the glass case?'

'Bless my soul, sir, I have no idea.'

'Because there are now two daggers missing. I checked earlier.'

'Dear me, I'm sure they will turn up. Perhaps one of the kitchen staff has taken them out to be cleaned and polished. I shall enquire on your behalf. Will that be all, sir?'

'I am obliged to you, Grieves. Your efforts are much appreciated. By the by, were you familiar with Henry Stevens?'

'The estate manager — oh yes, always joking and teasing the girls, a real card. It was a shock when after such a short illness he was taken from us. I attended the funeral. Henry was like a son to Sir George, you know. Mr Stevens died at home at his cottage, you see, with only old Doctor Madden in attendance, who was prepared to sign the death doings and got him confined very respectful.'

'Doctor Madden, you say. Well, well, he sounds a good country surgeon altogether, a most caring and compassionate individual. I should like very much to meet him. He attends your mistress?'

'On occasion, sir, but there is an eminent Swiss specialist who is in charge of her long-term care and sends boxes of medicine regular to the nurse — also a foreigner — from his clinic in Lucerne.'

'Well, one thing is for certain,' I laughed, once the old butler had hurried off to fetch us a pot of coffee. 'This Henry Stevens chappie is alive and lacking and most assuredly above ground, as our sandbags will testify. Do you think he and Mrs Daymond may be linked in this case?'

'I do Watson. I take my hat off to Mrs Daymond. She's certainly a truly brave woman, deserving of our praise and sympathy. If anything can come out of this topsy-turvy tissue of lies and fabrications, I hope with all my heart that she may once more become well and able to enjoy her privileged place in society and the considerable fortune that is rightfully hers, although I dare not think how much of her wealth has been squandered by Sir George. Ah, the squire returns. We must remain on our best behaviour.'

★   ★   ★

After a good lunch, the squire, appearing passably convivial because he had that very morning taken delivery of a new-fangled machine for harvesting swedes, turnips and other root crops which would save much time and labour costs, invited us to take some exercise and walk the dogs to work off the roast beef and sherry trifle consumed earlier.

My companion Mr Sherlock Holmes kept up a light-hearted banter. To be perfectly honest, despite his sinister proclivities, the fact Sir George was an out and out rotter for the despicable way he sought to control his wife Jane, he proved surprisingly lively company and our afternoon walk progressed without incident.

That is until we reached a five-barred

gate further along the lane, nestled among hedgerow trees where one could pause to smoke a pipe and soak up the Buckinghamshire scene, with its rolling hills, an autumnal November sky, steel-grey and full of starlings, the tiny hamlet of Stoke Woodley with its beguiling little church and jumble of cottages.

Suddenly, one of the gundogs, a Labrador, bounded over to a patch of nettles and began sniffing around with its muzzle in a drainage ditch much clogged with fallen leaves and stale rainwater. The dog, a bitch called Molly, a favourite of Sir George began barking for all its worth.

'Come away! Do as I say, you bad, bad girl,' shouted the squire, by now exasperated but unable to bring the dog to heel.

'There's something in that ditch,' cried Holmes, running over to take a closer reconnoitre, swishing about with his cane until the quizzical expression on his long and gaunt face said it all. The second of the missing cavalry officer's daggers was evidently found!

'He's lying face down in the ditch, Sir

George, but poor old Croft's caught it in the back I'm afraid. He must have been walking down here on his way to the station when he was set upon.'

The squire looked on in disbelief, his previous jovial countenance drained out of him, replaced by a sombre and more contemplative demeanour.

'The dagger's embedded to the hilt,' said I. The poor fellow caught unawares stood no chance. He would have collapsed like a sack of potatoes into the ditch beside the road. He was smothered in leaf debris, I'd guess deliberately.'

'Well, Sir George, that's two of you gone, which, if my arithmetic is correct, leaves two surviving. We had better apprehend this villain quickly. Your murder club at Houghton public school is severely depleted, I think.'

'Don't say that, Holmes — 'murder club'. There never was a dratted murder club at Houghton. You can cut that sort of nonsense out right now — do you hear?'

'Whatever. Professor Croft is no more, the police must be informed promptly. You do recognise the antler handled dagger, presumably?'

'Of course I recognise the blasted dagger, don't rub it in so. I'm at my wits end over this. Do something for God's sake, Holmes. You're the consulting detective.'

'I shall be brutally frank, Sir George. Your gun dog's discovery of the Professor indicates to me the killer is not far off; he may even be lurking in the grounds of Stoneycroft Grange as we speak.'

'That had crossed my mind, Mr Holmes.'

'Well, let us have the presence of mind to stay calm. To panic or act rashly at this stage could scuttle any chances we have of catching this villain,' The squire nodded agreement.

'Alright, alright, I'm with you. I think a large whisky is in order. We'd better return to the Grange. I'm in need of a blast of fire. As we head into December the weather is turning decidedly parky. C'mon dogs, let's get back and give you a bath and a rub down. We'll take the footpath.'

Regarding the police — I'd say that

chap of negligible intelligence — old Constable Baines, isn't it — from the police house, and Doctor Madden, the local physician, shall be our best bet for the time being,' remarked Holmes dourly. 'Of course Scotland Yard will need to be informed, Bristol will want to bag this murder investigation for himself. He won't want anyone treading on his toes. Mark you, he'll be down by special from Marylebone before the night's out.'

★　★　★

Many hours having elapsed since our walking the dogs, Inspector Bristol of the Yard was indeed down from London and spent his innings with a Home Office surgeon supervising the examination of the crime scene.

By eleven o'clock, the body of Croft had been despatched to the nearest town for autopsy and, the night being bitterly cold and damp, our munificent squire sent out a generous invitation for Bristol, Doctor Madden and the others to come back to Stoneycroft Grange to clean up, thaw out and get a good hot meal down them.

'Well I'm blowed, Mr 'olmes,' said Inspector Bristol, taking liberties slapping my colleague on the back as though they were intimate chums, after having sat down with the others to a substantial meal of game pie washed down by liberal amounts of ale. 'Yet another of them bloomin' daggers, eh — cripes! Like as not they're popping up all over the shop, ain't they, sir. I've examined the two used to stab Mr Heston and Professor Croft respectively, hoping to glean some useful fingerprints. Did I, by 'eck? They was as clean as a whistle. Gloves, Mr 'olmes, gloves was used each time, see. Daggers stolen from a display case in the gun room, the squire now tells me. Very sneaky, very clever. We're dealing with pure devilment, sir, a servant at the Grange being the obvious suspect. The murderer is a member of the squire's retinue — mark my words.'

'Doctor Madden,' said Holmes, somewhat irritated after his encounter with the pugnacious detective, aware Bristol was about to play a match of billiards with Sir George, hesitating until they were safely out of sight before taking the elderly physician aside and offering him a cigarette from his case. 'Might I have a brief word?'

'Dear me, sir, it's normally quiet in our little hamlet, tucked out of the way in the provinces, then murder strikes! Constable Baines, poor fellow, finds himself somewhat out of his depth; locals just don't know what to make of this body in the ditch. You are a consulting detective, I hear?'

'Indeed,' my friend riposted.

'Let me put in my two pennies' worth. I am of the opinion the person who stabbed this poor gentleman while he was walking to the station to catch a train was a bovine sort, an agricultural labourer, very strong, heavily built, local.'

'Keenly and sharply observed all round, although I have known a woman murderess of diminutive stature who could cleave a head clean in half by a vicious swipe of an axe. However, I shall not quibble. A strong male it is then.

Might I change tack slightly, Doctor Madden? Perchance is Mrs Daymond the squire's wife on your books, a patient of yours, I mean?'

'Well, as you will be aware, I am a country surgeon and I reside in our little hamlet, so yes, to a point I could be regarded as Mrs Daymond's physician. However, although I deal with colds and flu and minor ailments, she remains in a state similar in some respects to a catatonic trance due to an accident long ago. An eminent brain specialist from Switzerland is in charge of her case and I should not dream of usurping his authority. There is a nurse, as you know, in constant attendance. I'm afraid her long-term brain injury is really out of my province.'

'You can be straight with me, Doctor Madden. I am completely on your side and Mrs Daymond's welfare is upper-most in my concerns. Everything you say will be treated in the strictest confidence. You must trust me.'

'I'm sorry, I don't quite follow.'

'I propose that for some time now you

61

have been aiding Mrs Daymond's recovery; this, at great risk to yourself, I might add. You rightly consider yourself her ally and friend and thanks to your valiant efforts and her brain's resurgence, she is at last becoming more herself.'

'Go on.'

'The estate manager Henry Stevens sought to help Mrs Daymond. He at once realised her plight and the difficult situation she was under. He approached you and explained the terrible truth — that — apart from the brain injury, now in remission — she was being transformed into a living waxwork by a constant usage of a powerful sedative, supposedly to control fits, the supplier of those pink tablets none other than that wretched Swiss quack in Lucerne who sees Mrs Daymond as nothing less than a passive guinea pig. I put it to you Doctor Madden; it was you who agreed to assist Mr Stevens by preparing what in modern pharmacology is termed placebos. Thus, Mr Stevens, while up at the Grange could empty the bottles of the dangerous contents and surreptitiously make a swap.'

'Watson, old fellow, you will recall during one afternoon we were watching the dreary rain falling on the topiary in the garden from the French windows when out of sheer boredom I went over to the table where Mrs Daymond normally sits and unscrewed her medicine bottle and sampled the contents. I was pleasantly surprised when I discovered the bottle contained harmless sugar sweets. This alerted me to certain possibilities.'

'Good grief, you are correct, Mr Holmes, there's no use denying it,' the kindly old physician answered. 'I have come to love, if that is not too strong a word, the dear brave lady as a daughter. You see, Mr Holmes, I am a simple country surgeon and Henry and I worked closely together to help wean Mrs Daymond off those powerful sedatives and thereby allow her to re-establish her own life and begin to regain control over her considerable inheritance — a vast fortune of capital and shares passed on from her late coal magnate grandfather when she was but twenty.

Henry Stevens remains committed to help bring this about and works stolidly on her behalf, behind the scenes as it were. We thought it prudent to fake his death so that he might the easier serve the lady whom he has grown to love dearly. The sums of money involved are colossal, Mr Holmes, and to think Sir George may have his clutches on much of it. If you want to learn the measure of the man, just consider this. He attempted to murder his own wife on their honeymoon. How's that for sheer wanton greed?'

'Yes, Mrs Daymond informed me of the details,' confided my colleague.

'I regret to say there has been an escalation,' said I, cutting in. 'Her husband appears fascinated by the preservation of bodies, perhaps an inability to accept the finality of death, and fears grow that he may one day place his wife in a glass fronted cabinet, a hermetically sealed container, so that she will be exhibited with his embalmed parents downstairs in the basement.'

'Were you not aware that recently he has begun shutting her away for long periods in the basement, Doctor Madden?' asked Holmes querulously.

'Sir George's parents embalmed. I'm afraid you have the advantage of me, sir.'

'So it's true, there are secrets that even you and Mr Stevens were unaware of, eh? I see the squire returns from the billiard room, our conversation must of necessity conclude, Doctor Madden. Thank you again for all your kind confidences. Goodnight and a safe journey back to Stoke Woodley. Watson, I think it prudent we retire to our rooms. I see Inspector Bristol has left and they are locking up Stoneycroft Grange for the night.'

★　★　★

That night I tossed and turned and found sleep elusive. In the early hours a hard gale was blowing across the county, rain lashing furiously against the casement window. I could hear the wind howling, whistling, changing pitch, gusting about the eves and chimney stacks, rattling the

65

slates on the roof. If a dratted spectre had wished to make an appearance, I shouldn't have been the least surprised. My fire was smoking in the grate and the oil lamp upon my chest of drawers become extinguished.

I should say the severe storm reached its zenith between the hours of four o'clock and half past five of the morning when it seemed to die down and it so happens during this lull when one's senses are acutely heightened and you become aware of gurgling drains, overflowing guttering and cascading sheets of rainwater pouring down the window pane that I heard a gunshot, a distinctive muffled bang from somewhere downstairs and my first thought was that Sir George Daymond was now definitely dead and that his past had finally caught up with him. I heard Holmes moving about across the way, a door being wrenched open.

'Holmes,' I cried, tying my dressing gown together and rushing out to join him on the landing. 'You heard it too.'

My colleague tore down the staircase,

leaping the last four steps before landing squarely on his feet at the bottom. I followed as swiftly as my old war wound would allow, seizing the banister rail for support.

'Hurry, Watson,' he bawled back. 'It's the devil's own work all right. I fear we may be too late to save Sir George's life. Our clever assassin has struck for the third time and there is a sort of inevitability about all this. How can you keep an old rambling house secure? A loose window catch, ill-fitting frame of a pantry door, and to top it all, the screaming gale — perfect for approaching the house by stealth. Steel yourself, dear boy. Mark you, the squire's corpse is close by, I am sure of it.'

'Really, Mr Holmes,' said Sir George Daymond haughtily, stepping out from his study, a shotgun held under his arm. 'Give me some credit, at least. Do I look like a corpse? The body's in there, I heard noises earlier and crept downstairs. The intruder was rifling through my papers look into it for me, will you Holmes? I'm off in search of a whisky.'

'Did you perchance recognise this person?'

'Never seen him before in my life, but he had a weapon alright, one of those Civil War daggers from the gun room. Where's Inspector Bristol when you need him? Over at the inn fast asleep in bed, I suppose.'

I bounded into the squire's study and flung back the drapes. Dawn was breaking over the tiny hamlet of Stoke Woodley and by the better light I was able to see what had occurred. The circumstances of the victim's death were not hard to envisage.

'Good grief, he's done for, Holmes. Shot at point blank range through the chest cavity,' said I, making a preliminary examination, satisfied this was a lost cause and that the bearded fellow before me, sprawled out in front of the squire's desk like a rag doll slung aside in a slovenly, untidy way by a petulant child was beyond help. The deceased wore shabby tweeds and a pair of lace-less hobnail boots. The force of the gun blast had thrown him off his feet. I shifted over to allow my colleague to shine a globe lamp he had procured on the face of the victim.

'Tut tut, this is a poor show indeed,' he muttered, shockingly tugging at the gum-adhered bushy beard and ripping it off with a flourish, revealing a clean-shaven chin and gingery side-whiskers beneath. 'You will additionally perceive, my dear Watson, the fellow's wild curly hair is in fact a wig — false and unedifying.'

Hardly had he spoken than a piercing scream issued from another part of the house and frantic running footsteps. My colleague tossed aside the hairy wig, peering into the hallway.

'You know, Watson,' said he, seizing my arm and helping me get to my feet, 'the fairer sex do possess an uncanny intuition where matters of the heart are concerned. Mrs Daymond knows, of course.'

'Knows what? What are you driving at, Holmes? Don't talk in such confounded riddles.'

'That it is he — Henry Stevens — who has been fatally shot, and that it was her husband who just blasted him with a shotgun. Alas, our elusive estate manager will be shortly returned to the grave, but this time there will be no reprieve. I fear this will badly upset her.'

'They were lovers — is that what you infer?'

'To do her every bidding, prepared to pit his life on the line time and time again and risk prosecution and being sent to the gallows. If that can in truth be called love, then, yes, I suppose they were.'

'On her behalf he systematically went about eliminating each of those responsible at Houghton for the death of old Pike, the Latin master, you mean?'

'Mrs Daymond must have somehow got wind of the conspiracy and, using all her newly developing cleverness, realised this was the best way to get back at her husband — the genius of the scheme being that over a long, protracted period he would be forced to watch his old school chums be eliminated, one by one.'

'Mr Pike, the school master, was but an innocent,' A woman's voice softly moaned as the mistress of the house, the beautiful

Mrs Damond, came from out of nowhere circling round us, her eyes glittering in a simmering fever of mania. She wrung her hands piteously. I noticed the flouncy white muslin dress she wore, gathered in at the waist, revealing her ample bosom, decorated with gorgeously intricate silver ferns, appeared to be spotted with coppery stains.

'Those despicable, cruel-hearted children, Croft, Heston, Tribbs and my husband, spiteful and endowed with all the very worst traits of the psychopath. It was they who were the brutes, Mr Holmes, they who murdered him for sport, you see, as a wager, a bet that they could get away with the crime — as I believe you will have worked out for yourself by now.'

'That was my conclusion exactly, madam. You do realise Henry Stevens is dead? I'm so sorry; this will be a wrench for you. Shall I fetch Doctor Madden, he will I am sure do everything in his power to ease your sorrow at this time of trial.'

'First, let me speak plainly, Mr Holmes. One night when I was confined to the basement with his dead parents, my husband came down the steps in a morose depression. I believe he had been drinking heavily, and his reason was affected. I recall he slumped in a chair and began talking out loud to his father, as if that stupid corpse could somehow come alive and converse ordinarily. He remained as I and dearest Henry preferred — totally ignorant that I could perceive once more and think for myself and was not the inanimate waxwork or statuette he imagined. I heard every horrid word, gentlemen, a rambling philosophising discourse in which he expounded upon certain incidents in his life, which horrified my sense of decency and left me in little doubt the man was a degenerate monster.

'While in this state of melancholia, he confided to his father's corpse everything about Houghton — names and details, the wicked way in which, for a bet, a wager amongst themselves, the four children murdered a poor, defenceless Latin master, slinging him, half alive, down into a lime kiln pit where were heaped layer upon layer of coke, shards of wood, and lime.

'Upon that night the burning would be at its peak, well able to consume and reduce a body to ash and charred bone most efficiently. The human skull, unable to withstand the pressure, explodes, gentlemen, in a labyrinth of white hot flame, dissolved by the slaked lime and later to be spread upon the agricultural landscape, a compound used to enrich soil and encourage a higher yield of crops. Such was the poor form master's resting place. I vowed there and then on behalf of Mr Pike to take revenge upon each of those deceitful individuals.'

Grieves the butler, wearing his cloth slippers and a nightshirt and cap, came rushing down the hall in an absolute panic, causing Mrs Daymond to press a concealed panel and pass through the wall whence a bookcase conveniently opened and shut behind her.

Rushing headlong towards us, Grieves cried out, 'The squire, my governor. Oh do come through to the drawing room, sirs. Something truly terrible has come to pass.'

'Calm down, Mr Grieves,' said I. 'Lead us to your master and then have the good sense to fetch a bottle of brandy. I fear we are all of us in need of a glass or two to settle our nerves.'

What a sight awaited us. As if one corpse was not enough, it was now our misfortune to be confronted by still more violent death. The storm outside may have abated and blown itself out over the surrounding hills, but within the confines of Stoneycroft Grange, circumstances could not be more perilous.

I cast my gaze upon a sabre, discarded on the carpet, the blade's tarnished, razor-sharp edge glistening with blood.

A hunched figure in a leather club chair sat nursing a whisky. It was Sir George and he was decapitated, passably beheaded, a wide arc of blood upon the ceiling and drips from the cut glass chandelier bore testimony to the quantity that should have eddied from his severed neck. By following the butler's trembling outstretched finger it was easy to trace the trajectory of the head as it flew off, rolling squarely along the carpet to beneath the bay. The face, drained of blood, bore a chalky-white expression of confused bewilderment.

'By Jove, Watson, it is the wife's doing. That's a clean strike. Her displeasure at Henry's death must have given her phenomenal strength. She surely swung the sabre about her and executed the squire while he nurtured his whisky — all this done shortly before she came to see us.'

'If you don't mind, gentlemen,' said Grieves, looking very pasty, 'I shall fetch the brandy and serve drinks in the dining room.'

'An excellent idea,' said my colleague, lighting a cigarette from his case and passing me one. 'Where is our lady of the lake, anyhow? We have her sword at least.'

'Holmes,' said I, 'listen, what if in her current state of frenzy Mrs Daymond decides to take her own life? Is that a possibility?'

'Distinctively so,' he agreed. 'By Jove, Watson, I've got it, dear boy. That basement she talked of, where the squire kept his precious mummies. A confounded cabinet, wasn't it?'

'A hermetically sealed container. My God, Holmes, you're right. Grieves!' I called out. 'Leave the brandy for now, old fellow. Can you lead us down to the basement?'

By following a narrow winding stairwell, stooping low and entering a stone-flagged passageway, we were able to see Mrs Daymond had broken into the room where Sir George's mother and father were stored and, I might add, we arrived in the nick of time to witness the destruction of the thickened plate glass fronting the specially constructed cabinet containing the embalmed couple.

The empowered woman took a mighty swipe, but on the first occasion her axe bounced off. The second attempt proved more fruitful, as the axe blade wielded by the petite lady struck home with a satisfying crack, not unlike the sudden noisy snapping of ice upon a frozen lake. This was but a prelude to the loosening of India rubber sealant surrounding the glass-viewing window. Thereafter a sultry green gas began to seep out round the edges, tendrils of pungent vapour seemingly reaching out to ensnare the beautiful, distressed creature who, despite escaping gas, a result of those clever Russian chemists and their secretive concoctions used in the preservation process a decade or so earlier, raised her axe for a final triumphal strike.

'I am healed, Mr Holmes,' she shrieked joyfully. 'I am myself again! It appears these morbid events, this frenetic activity, have roused all my passions. Now sirs, let us bid the old dead couple a fond adieu.'

'Mrs Daymond,' Holmes shouted, a hanky firmly gripped to his nose. 'Jane, my dear, they will kill you — the embalming gas, it is currently engulfing the basement. Leave that wretched container for now to its own inevitable destruction. The old mummies are already beginning to deteriorate.'

The homely scene of man and wife contentedly sat there in cottage chairs at table had become a grisly charnel house tableau fit for hell itself. 'Come away, I

77

say, before it is too late!'

Fortunately the mistress of the house was acceptable to my companion's entreaties and, stumbling awkwardly, her breathing compromised, she made her way to the door.

'The grievous gas is enveloping the basement,' I gasped, choking back the fumes.

Rushing back out into the low-ceilinged stone-flagged passage, our group was desperate to escape up the spiral staircase, supporting each other as best we could, the butler and my colleague Mr Sherlock Holmes keeping their arms tightly wrapped around the fragile little lady, always cajoling her, spurring her on, all of us doing our damnedest to seek a dose of life enhancing fresh air out in the garden.

At the top of the stairs we were met by other servants and a general pandemonium ensued. Coughing and gasping, the basement door firmly shut and locked behind us, the green corpse gas left to lurk in the central cellar where the winter coke and stacks of split logs were kept and stored, I understood the poisonous fug far too heavy a vapour to rise into upper areas of the house.

★　★　★

'Oh, Doctor Watson, what a narrow escape from the dreaded green vapours,' exclaimed Mrs Lamb, helping herself to another cup of tea from the pot. 'Darling, be a good girl and pass the sugar, will you?' she asked her young and vivacious daughter Pru, who coquettishly smiled and did as she was asked.

We were presently sat in our front sitting room at our digs in Baker Street, enjoying afternoon tea, just having recounted our adventures at Stoneycroft Grange. The ladies had been enthralled from start to finish and hardly allowed me a moment's pause, else time to relight my cigar. Mr Sherlock Holmes, himself in good spirits, sat at his desk with a gum brush pasting a number of recent newspaper cuttings into his voluminous scrap book. It was now drawing towards the middle of December, the lamplighter at his rounds, the weather of late alternating between thick fogs and showers of sleet. As it grew dark, freezing rain dashed against the windows, peppering the pane. Our globe lamps were emitting a gently audible hiss and a merry fire crackled in the grate.

That afternoon, ensconced warm and comfortable in our front sitting room, we were in convivial company for Mrs Lamb and her daughter Pru had arranged to visit us and catch up with all our latest news.

'How queer that this poor woman you speak of, Mrs Daymond, should have been almost 'liberated' if that is the right word, set free if you will, by a set of seemingly impossibly horrid circumstances. The brain is a curious organ and we so little understand its complex function. That aside, does a consulting detective of your standing, Mr Holmes, normally have to endure such a range of morbid excitements? Are there not calmer moments to enjoy a more placid and ordinary existence? Are one's nerves continuously wired so tautly?'

'My dear Mrs Lamb.' My colleague broke into convulsive laughter, glancing up from his scrapbook. 'Doctor Watson and myself are not every day subjected to such heightened levels of excitement, I can assure you, but the murder of Roddy Heston on the Cathedral's Express from Worcester, after appreciating a fine choral concert of music conducted by this new fellow Edward Elgar, and that business of the note listing four seemingly innocuous names, could not be ignored. One cannot just stand by and do nothing, can one? On the whole I confess I rather enjoyed the fray, particularly the fact that Inspector Bristol of the Yard gained so little headway, proving once more the official Metropolitan force is seriously wanting. Their capacity to fail to grasp the finer points of these murders frankly leaves one marvelling at such bungling incompetence.'

'Now, now, Holmes,' said I, becoming slightly irritated. 'Don't crow so, our lady friends I am sure are not concerned in the least with the workings of Scotland Yard, incompetent or otherwise. Have another slice of this delicious seedcake, old chap.'

'I shall, Watson, I shall, and another cup of tea if I may.'

'Mrs Lamb baked it specially and I have seldom tasted finer. You must tell us the recipe.'

'Oh, Doctor Watson,' laughed Pru, beside herself with fits of giggles, 'you are an accomplished flatterer, sir! And mama laps it up, don't you, dearest? No wonder that Mrs Hudson downstairs seems to have a soft spot for you.'

'Really,' said I, frankly embarrassed, cutting us all another slice of cake each, 'she is of Scotch extraction and can on occasions be as hard and intractable as nails. Neither of us likes to get on her wrong side. Holmes is on the whole the worst offender with his infernal week-long stinks caused by his chemistry. That really gets her going, but I am no saint either.'

'Gentlemen, to return to the vexing issue of Stoneycroft Grange,' said Mrs Lamb, pouring out my esteemed colleague a second cup of tea and passing it over to him. 'What will become of poor Mrs Daymond? A large part of her fortune I understand was misappropriated by Sir George, the squire?'

'Mrs Daymond will hang, mama, the Daily Sketch and Evening Standard say so,' exclaimed Pru with all the certainty of youthful exuberance but little actual knowledge of, else interest in, the court case, for her music studies were at present consuming all her time. 'She's queer, just too queer for words.'

'I think not,' answered Holmes kindly, sipping his tea before placing the cup and saucer on his chemistry desk. 'That ill-sparking brain of hers is come to her rescue.' He elaborated further: 'As you are aware, Mrs Lamb, the trial continues, but there is every likelihood she will escape the noose, for many eminent continental specialists, medical experts and surgeons, have stepped forward to verify she was indeed suffering from a long-term brain injury. There will be doubt amongst the jury that she, a beautiful young woman afflicted by such grievous concussion, should be capable of plotting the murders of Heston and Croft. It is of course far more likely Stevens, the estate manager, shall bear the brunt of the accusations. He was after all the actual perpetrator of the crimes. The late squire comes out of this business very poorly. The fact when alive he attempted to murder his wife while on their honeymoon in the Lake District, latterly caused her to be confined for long periods in that basement, brings into question his sanity. No, I prefer to think there will be a happy outcome. After all, she is not a poor woman and still has private means. Already her counsel has indicated there are plans afoot for Mrs Daymond to make a short tour of the Antipodes and that Doctor Madden, who has as you will be aware, stands by her throughout the trial, fully intends to make it his duty to care for her and accompany his charge upon the requisite long sea journey abroad to Pacific climes. No, Mrs Lamb, fear not. I think we may look forward to a more positive outcome to the trial.'

2

The Curio

I shall now do justice to a startling episode relating to that portly, brilliantly minded individual whom we have overlooked until now, Holmes's elder brother Mycroft. Denizen of the Diogenes Club, a canny political analyst, strategist, and policy advisor retained by Her Majesty's Government no less, and consulted upon many matters pertaining to state security and the running of the country, there was even rumour he was to be knighted in the New Year's Honours List.

I recall not long after our hearing of that delightful concert of Elgar at Worcester my companion received a short note indicating we should visit his brother at once.

Mycroft was then inhabiting an exclusive bachelor flat in Pallmall along with his devoted man Rodrigo and very accomplished French cook, Mariette Champney, who did house for him and catered for his every culinary indulgence.

Alas, by this juncture his physique was failing and, dare I say this, Mycroft's love of port, cigars and fine wines, his epicurean tastes, had finally got the better of him. He reminded me at best of a giant species of inflatable slug, grossly over-weight and confined to a reinforced wheeled chair for much of the time.

Stubborn to the extreme, he would brook no argument put forward by either myself or his personal physician promoting a more healthy diet or exercising regularly, say, a good brisk daily walk accompanied by pipe or cigar, believing erroneously that a modest reduction in food and alcohol would suffice and be beneficial to his overstrained constitution; say a little less port, a modicum less of brandy, a slightly smaller portion of dessert pudding which he consumed with so much relish during those famously long lunches at the Diogenes Club with his Whitehall cronies.

Predictably, we found him wheezy and

pasty-faced, fatter than ever, ensconced behind his desk, his apartment study graced by cabinets of fine porcelain, rare antiques of many descriptions and his library of calf bound stamp collecting albums he coveted so zealously.

'Sherlock, you are aware I have been allocated a lot number at Sotheby's and a description appeared in their latest catalogue. Prominent advertisements have been placed in various dealer publications announcing the up and coming sale of my interesting little curio 'The Hand of Vladimir Chekovich.''

'Indeed, you mentioned something about that upon the last occasion we met,' said he, snatching his pipe and tobacco pouch from his pocket. 'You rarely remove it from its wooden box. I believe I saw it once, but Watson here will I am certain never have had the privilege of viewing your precious artefact.'

'Quite so, Sherlock. Well, I shall remedy that at once. Have the goodness not to touch if you please, either of you. What do you make of it, Doctor?'

An inlaid teak casket was nudged by

chubby fingers across the study desk.

The lid was unlocked and yawning open. What lay inside displayed upon a rich maroon velvet lining was a beautifully crafted silver gilt artificial hand that gleamed bedazzlingly in the sunlight. The detail was really quite exquisite, delicately etched fingernails, skin texture remarkably reproduced in precious metal.

'I am most impressed,' said I, leaning forward before having my wrist firmly slapped by Mycroft, being wholly unable to resist reaching out to touch and caress the fine workmanship.

'And responsible for the extortion of vast sums of money from many wealthy and privileged young ladies residing in Moscow and St. Petersburg,' remarked the epicurean drily.

'One of the most devious and efficient criminal implements ever to have been devised,' pointed out Holmes, lighting his briar-root pipe and engulfing the room in rank tobacco smoke.

Hastily snapping the lid shut and re-locking the casket, Mycroft placed it back in his safe.

'And highly dangerous to handle, I might add,' he gravely asserted, re-positioning his wheeled chair before the desk once more.

'Dangerous?' I laughed. 'An artificial hand? I mean it undoubtedly has its uses, certainly for some unfortunate amputee. In this case I'd venture to surmise, a very wealthy Russian personage with some means.'

'A stimulating hypothesis, but entirely erroneous, my dear fellow,' remarked Holmes, an amused expression written large upon his hawk-like features.

'But how can you possibly justify its criminal association?' I enquired, a trifle heatedly.

'I shall provide you with a brief history and all shall be made clear.' Mycroft lit a cigar and shifted his vast, lardy bulk upon the creaking, reinforced basketwork seat of his wheeled chair. His brightly intelligent eyes twinkled with excitement, betraying the boundless enthusiasm of a serious collector. I confess for the next five minutes or so I neglected to relight my own cigar and was forgetful of the glass of malt whisky placed before me earlier by Rodrigo.

'I must begin by saying that to shake hands with Vladimir Chekovich's masterpiece in silver, his falsified left hand to be precise, was not always to be recommended. As Sherlock here will confirm, he was not only a master of disguise but foremost a ruthless and compulsive fraudster. He was, however, a genuine amputee whose hand was severed in a winter sleighing accident as a boy.

'Chekovich's method was both audacious and astoundingly clever. He chose to appear at some prestigious charity ball, else society café or exclusive restaurant frequented by the rich and famous posing as a gallant cavalry officer heroically wounded in some campaign. His heartfelt, sincere manner, his efficacious charm swiftly gained the sympathy and attention of rich and gullible young ladies of society and invariably at the end of conversation he would clasp their dainty hand in his. Unbeknown to the carefully chosen victim, the slightest pressure applied to the lifelike fingers of the artificial hand by means of a compressed air chamber allowed a miniscule needle in a fraction of a second to be activated, delivering a barely noticeable pin-prick jab before withdrawing once more into the hollow metal palm, a glass ampule of serum being also concealed in a tiny compartment of the hand. A few hours passed before that poor young lady, due to the quick action of the serum, would become feverish and ill, and confined to her bed.

'But a day would pass before the symptoms became so extreme and confusing to diagnose the victim was pronounced dangerously close to death.

'In the meantime, of course, before the crisis was reached, an anonymous letter would conveniently arrive detailing the symptoms exactly and politely offering an equally fast-acting and efficient antidote serum for the price of 100,000 roubles, cash to be placed in a bag and deposited at a discreet location, no questions asked, no police.'

'And he got away with this monstrous subterfuge?' I asked, sampling my glass of malt whisky.

'Many times. In fact, he amassed a considerable fortune, although eventually unmasked for the villain he really was, by an extraordinarily bold and intelligent woman, a banker's daughter residing in St. Petersburg, who point-blank refused to shake his hand and thereby helped requisition an arrest.'

'Tell me more.'

My colleague thereafter took up the reigns of the story.

'My dear Watson, fortunately for womankind in Russia, this young banker's daughter Tatiana Serov, sharing a table outside a venue near the Summer Gardens, became suspicious of the overtures of glory being foisted upon her by the dashing military gentleman opposite, believing him to be bogus, a fantasist.

'When he grew insolent because she once more refused to shake his proffered hand, Tatiana summoned her coachman Ivan, a very tough and dependable fellow, and a heated scuffle ensued outside the café.

'Chekovich was laid out flat on the

pavement and later, in police custody, was uncovered the peculiar silver gilt hand attached to the stump of his left arm, its devious mechanism later analysed. He eventually died in prison I believe, as did his accomplice.'

'Ah!' exclaimed Mycroft, stubbing out the remains of his cigar. 'We must now allude to Chekovich's cousin, the accomplished silversmith Surikov. Neo-classical sugar basins, the ice pail, the tea urn, candlesticks and sconces, soup tureens with covers were not the only test of his supreme workmanship, for it was he who took on at his manufactory a commission from his nefarious uncle Vladimir to produce a mechanical silver hand. Thus, with hammer and punch, the chasing, embossing and repoussé of precious metal, he produced surely his most profound piece.'

'And went to prison for his trouble.'

'Indeed, the hallmark, the stamp of the maker, was a foolish egoism that cost him dear.'

'But how did you obtain this Russian curiosity, Mycroft?' I wanted to know.

'The artefact was presented to me over a rubber of whist at the Diogenes Club by the Russian diplomat Argunov in gratitude for a favour bestowed. I managed to avert a scandal, a sordid affair that should the press hounds have got hold of would have harmed relations between our two countries — government-wise I refer to, of course. So it represented a sort of gift. He was inebriated at the time, however.'

'But surely it is a valued Russian antiquity. Won't they want it back? The mechanism is unique in the annals of global crime.'

'Then if all goes to plan they shall have to pay me a considerable sum at auction,' chuckled Mycroft, his huge belly quivering. 'A very substantial sum of money indeed, Doctor Watson, so that it may be presumably housed in the Kremlin's Black Museum for perpetuity.'

★ ★ ★

Upon the morning of the catastrophe, I was browsing somewhat disinterestedly through my copy of the *Lancet*, seated before the extinct hearth, bright bars of summer sunshine cast upon the mantel-shelf where was kept our rack of pipes and tobacco slipper. But a week had passed since our last meeting with Mycroft, breakfast barely finished.

Imagine our surprise when at half past nine, Rodrigo, Mycroft's valet, came rushing into our rooms, half-crazy with hysteria. Even after being ordered to sit down and offered a large glass of medicinal brandy, he kept bursting into tears at the drop of a hat, no doubt his passionate Latin temperament inflamed by recent events.

It turned out his master had been taken ill that very morning in his flat, collapsing in front of his study desk, and was now lying abed unconscious. Indeed, his old Diogenes cronies, Professor Tomkins and personal physician Doctor Phossey, summoned without delay, were presently in attendance at his bedside but uncertain as how to exactly diagnose their patient's sudden and dramatic decline. His heart remained robust, although his immense weight was an added complication. Their best shot was that he had somehow ingested a virulent poison into his bloodstream. The next twelve hours were crucial to the patient's recovery — nay, survival!

But there was another pressing matter. Rodrigo, upon entering the study, had observed the safe to be wide open and the 'hand of Vladimir Chekovich' nowhere to be seen — missing, believed stolen. The French cook Mariette Champney was likewise absent.

'By Jove, that dratted French house-keeper Mariette seized her opportunity alright,' fumed Holmes, pacing up and down before the fireplace like a caged beast. 'An opportunist if ever, but it was my brother Mycroft gloating over his prized trophy who, presumably forgetful of its dangerous propensities, must have accidentally triggered the device, injecting himself with historic dregs of the serum, thus allowing our wily thief to strike while he lay unconscious. An antidote must be found — and found deuced quickly!'

A loud rap at the door and Mrs Hudson announced, of all people, a demure little lady — a Miss Grint. The woman was a senior librarian at Marylebone public library that was just up the road from us.

Despite the fraught atmosphere, the inconsolable valet still stretched out upon the sofa, I confess she managed to introduce a note of calm to proceedings. I was intrigued as to why she should have searched out our rooms that morning.

'You have the advantage of me, madam.'

'So very sorry to intrude, Mr Holmes,' she sighed, being offered a fireside chair, looking timidly about her. 'But it's most queer, most peculiar and I'm certain there's a pattern.'

'Could you be more brief and to the point?' said Holmes irritably. 'What precisely is queer and peculiar?'

'The way the library books in our fiction section have been placed out of order on the shelves.'

'Indeed.'

'Deliberately left sticking out, the spines protruding an inch or two to draw attention to the titles for some reason. I noticed it, so did Miss Allen and Mrs Worth. We remarked upon it and, presenting the possibility of some sort of code, a rare puzzle, it was decided, being only a street or so away, I should make haste and seek out your lodgings, Mr Holmes.'

'By Jove, madam, it is thanks to you and your astute departmental colleagues that a life may yet be saved. Watson, hurry, Marylebone Public Library it is then. Miss Grint, lead the way!'

Upon entering the public library, a notable local landmark, we were hastily directed through its hallowed portals to the relevant section of that most architecturally pleasing of edifices. Encompassed by sturdy, well-arranged shelves devoted to general titles, a group of librarians clustered round as with magnifying lens, my colleague took it upon himself to minutely examine the vellum-bound spines poking out at intervals from the rest of the books.

'You will observe, my dear Watson, the titles themselves I think represent a far too lengthy and complicated route. The authors' names, however, offer us every possibility. Your pocket book and pencil at the ready. I shall work along this row first and then the next.'

Dabbing the tip of my pencil with my tongue, I prepared to take down whatever was relevant to decipher what came to be called 'The Library Book code'.

Here is an accurate facsimile:

DICKENS AUSTEN NESBITT GASKILL
ENGELS RYDER-HAGGARD HENTY
OLIPHANT LE FANU MAYHEW ELLIOT
SHELLEY DICKENS RYDER-HAGGARD
KEATS ELLIOT AUSTEN NESBITT
BRONTË AUSTEN RYDER-HAGGARD
TENNYSON SHELLEY
MAYHEW USHER KEATS HENTY
ELLIOT NESBITT ADDISON

What great good fortune befell us that morning. But for the zealous eye of that group of lady librarians Mycroft would surely be long dead and gone. The reality, I am glad to report, was that Doctor Kean, a notable chemistry lecturer at

Barts, did indeed prove his worth by producing, along with his students, a highly effective anti-toxin and despatching the serum that same afternoon, modern day lab equipment and a much greater understanding of blood poisons playing their part of course in Mycroft's full and swift recovery.

I can report at the time of writing both Madame Champney, alias that clever planted foreign agent Mukhena, as well as 'The Hand of Vladimir Chekovich' are believed to be back in Russia.

3

The Folly Upon Gibbet Hill

There exists upon Gibbet Hill in Derbyshire a tall stone turret erected to celebrate Nelson's victory at Trafalgar by Lord Stimpson of Wellby Hall, containing a narrow, winding staircase leading to a small room at the top, windows providing a panoramic view of the surrounding landscape common to that district.

Visited by an Inspector Sturrock from that same county at our rooms in Baker Street in the blowy month of March, it soon became evident my esteemed colleague's considerable talents as an uniquely independent consulting detective, whose fame and reputation were now far-reaching and much in demand, being something of a celebrity in the capital, was required urgently to solve a pressing case of murder near the Derbyshire village of Ruggton. A Mr Thornbury of

Mortley Cottage, an ornithologist of some repute, a man dedicated to netting, shooting and the close observations of all manner of bird life, a well-received author besides, had been found upon the east slope of Gibbet Hill, his body violently beaten about.

The local force were convinced the brutal attack had taken place on the evening of March the fourth, the assailant, being in possession of a hefty cudgel, had rained down blow after blow on the poor, defenceless fellow, leaving him for dead to be discovered early the following morning by a gentleman out walking his dog. The traumatic nature of his injuries meant Mr Thornbury would have expired at the scene.

We travelled up by train, changing at Derby before following the branch to Tembech where we engaged a horse and trap that took us direct to the small Derbyshire village of Ruggton, dominated to a degree by this so-named Gibbet Hill. Inspector Sturrock was quick to lead us to the village hall where the body had been temporarily stowed. Drawing back the rubber sheet from the reclining remains of Mr Thornbury laid out on a trestle table, it was not difficult to comprehend the severity of the attack. The state of rigor mortis only enhanced the traumatic state of his external injuries.

'Good gracious,' said I, glancing at my colleague whose hawk-like features appeared grim and pensive. 'The skull is stove in, bones fractured, and the bruising pretty extensive.' He merely nodded while the detective hurriedly replaced the sheet covering the corpse.

'A senseless attack, gentlemen; the motive is unclear,' said the detective with a shrug. 'But you know he was an enigma. By all accounts a fairly timid, reclusive individual, he rented Mortley Cottage and lived there for a number of years. It's a rather secluded spot at the base of the hill; pretty, mind, but devilishly isolated.'

'Amongst his clothing was found a brass naval telescope you told us earlier on the train.'

'Yes. His possessions at the time of death appear scant — no purse or wallet or loose change to talk of — simply a tobacco pouch, corn-cobber pipe and a box of Vesta matches, a key to his front door, a cheapish silver plate pocket watch and fob that were the combined contents of his pockets, the brass telescope being also discovered by my officers at the scene.'

'I should like to visit Mr Thornbury's home if I may, inspector. I wish to gain a better understanding of the individual in life; a corpse can only reveal so much.'

'Of course, gentlemen. The cottage is but a ten-minute walk from the main village, approached by a footpath popular with dog-walkers.'

Upon our way up the steep slope we encountered an enormous man, well over six feet tall, equipped with a tarpaulin hat and huge leather overalls and leggings. A gun was held across his left hand ready for use, and a rough black and white dog followed at his heels.

'Mr Gresley, good morning. May I introduce Mr Sherlock Holmes and his colleague Doctor Watson, who are up here from London helping us try to find whoever murdered your tenant Mr

Thornbury. Gentlemen, it was this chap who first found the body and reported the matter.'

We all shook hands most agreeably and Holmes passed round his silver cigarette case so we could help ourselves.

'Glad to meet you, I'm sure. I must confess I was not particularly close friendship-wise or on social terms, but we shared a common interest in ornithology and I would often shoot specimens for him, which he would then send onto Derby to be stuffed. Thornbury was a negligible talker, rather abrupt and taciturn, but once you got to know him, why he was warm-hearted and a sincere and gentle sort of fellow. No enemies I can think of, a decent sort who buried himself in his work, his love of birds.'

'Was there anything in his past that might be useful in assessing the man's character?' enquired my companion, lighting a cigarette.

'Come to think of it, there was that railway accident. He was involved in Mr Holmes, a tunnel collision just outside Tenbech in which thirty three people died and many more were injured when a passenger service collided with a heavy goods. Having to witness the aftermath, the maimed and the dying and the mutilated, meant for the rest of his life he underwent a battle inside himself.'

'Battle? To what to you infer?' said I, accepting a light.

'A battle of conscience, sir, common amongst survivors of these very public tragedies. He just never came to terms with the fact he came out of it with a scratch to his forehead, yet others as he explained to me — pretty, debonair women, children, hard-working young men with all their lives to look forward to — killed and maimed horribly in the train crash. He always regarded himself as of not much consequence, a mere scribbler blessed with some means inherited from a wealthy aunt. I put his hopeless attitude down to too much brooding on the past, a basically selfish, inward-looking bachelor. But, bless me, he insisted he was badly affected by that frightful accident. It affected his reason, made him timid and overly suspicious of others, I think.'

'So bird watching proved a sort of escape?'

'I would say yes, it did. When he first came to live here in Ruggton, he was rather poorly and still visibly shaken by his train smash experience. I, by the way gentlemen, live at 'The Gables'. My house is in the village and I am the lessor of Mortley Cottage and collected rent as such. Because of our shared interest in ornithology, I loaned him my precious expensive copies of Hewitson's British Ooligy and Yarrel's British Birds with their beautiful colour plates, and we got on splendidly, but from a distance, so to speak. I respected his wish for solitude, for privacy, but from time to time we went out together collecting birds' eggs, observing the local bird life, netting and shooting specimens with my dear old gun-dog here.'

'Would you thus term Mr Thornbury 'an obsessive'?' asked Holmes, eagerly.

'Undoubtedly; his myriad notebooks and journals testify to his obsession. Writing was also of great importance to his maintaining a balance of sanity. He was a published authority on birds of this locality of course, and his dozen or so books are well received in Derbyshire. When you visit, you shall no doubt bear witness to his crammed study filled with books, the stuffed fieldfare, bunting, linnet, mistlethrush, white owl and so forth, all kept under globes of glass displayed throughout the cottage. I shall miss him, I really will, though I doubt whether a single other human person alive shall care much for his sudden and violent passing.'

'My colleague Doctor Watson and I, along with Inspector Sturrock, most assuredly care a great deal, Mr Gresley. His murder shall not upon any account go unpunished and I shall pursue enquiries reverently.'

'I'm extremely glad to hear it.'

'If I might change tack slightly,' said I, 'were people really hanged up there?' I enquired, leaning heavily upon my stout ash stick, glancing up towards the summit of the hill, 'or is it merely local historical hearsay?'

'Well, sir,' Mr Gresley laughed, leaning

down to pat his affectionate collie, who shook its tail and grinned canine fashion, 'the church records do indicate that in the late eighteenth century a number of felons met their end up there, hung in chains and left to rot, sheep stealers amongst them, and a certain bold highwayman, Thomas Cuff, who was fond of robbing stagecoaches. A gibbet was certainly erected and presumably dominated the hill for a number of years as I suppose a warning to other local miscreants.'

'And now that we have grown much more civilised I observe instead of our timber method of dispatch we now have a rather splendid folly,' remarked my colleague, throwing aside his spent cigarette.

'Lord Elias Stimpson oversaw and paid for its construction. After Nelson's victory at Trafalgar up it went. Interestingly, there is a little brass plaque attached to the rocky base, all faded and green with metal corrosion, upon which is etched an engraving of Nelson's ship HMS *Victory*. The present Lord Stimpson, Roderick, still inhabits Wellby Hall and owns much of the lands and estates hereabouts.'

'Do you often climb the tower yourself, Mr Gresley?' I asked.

'The turret has been open to the public for many years. The view from the top is really panoramic and upon a clear day you can even see as far afield as the parish of Long Wharton, so it provides a useful purpose, anyhow.'

'And we can presume Mr Thornbury, who lived close by, often walked up the hill to view the bird-life from there?'

'The hawks in flight are truly awesome to behold, diving and swooping and turning so serenely so, yes, Mr Holmes, we were both regular climbers of those winding stone steps. The folly is of particular value to ornithologists.'

Nestled at the bottom of the hill, the old stone cottage presented something of a neglected and unkempt appearance. However, we were after all barely out of winter and with a lick of undercoat, a bit of sanding of those weatherworn, flaky window frames and the front door, a thick coat of lime wash applied to the walls, the place would be smartened up no end.

Upon first impressions, the interior was rather cramped and gloomy, a damp, mildew smell prevailing, hardly surprising, for since the untimely death of the tenant, the hearth and stove in the alcove remained unlit.

The front parlour led through to the study and a small back room used as a kitchen and workspace. We had barely a chance to gather our wits when a constable came hurrying along the footpath on his bicycle and began banging at the window and calling out frantically to Inspector Sturrock that there had been a second serious assault over at Deremitre and that a Mr Kennilworth, a local verger and accountant, lay fatally injured in a field four hundred yards or so from the parish church.

My colleague's steely composure was as always to be commended. Far from rushing headlong into another episode, he was exact and to the point, most forthright about what our own position was to be in this unfolding affair.

'There is no requirement at present for either myself or Doctor Watson to attend the victim at Deremitre. I propose instead we remain at the cottage for there is enough work to do here. Inspector Sturrock, perhaps you will remain also. I should place one of your officers, a senior fellow in charge at the scene. I have formed a rather dazzling hypothesis concerning Mr Thornbury's death. Could I bother you for the loan of a decently sprung bow, a quiver or sports-quality arrows, a ball of twine and a detailed map of the area?'

'I shall get cracking this minute, sir. The publican Mr Smith at The Three Bells is very partial to competing in archery contests at the village fete. I'll have a word with him; your map poses no problem.'

'Then we meet next upon the summit of Gibbet Hill, Inspector, to be precise the room at the top of Trafalgar Folly. Watson, have the goodness to join me over here in this untidy back room will you. What, pray, do you deduce?

'Well,' I answered, scratching my chin,

'you've got me completely stumped. By your bumptious attitude, Holmes, I'd say you're onto something. Confound it all, what do I deduce? Well, for starters, I see before me an untidy workbench, hardened paint brushes submerged in a jam-jar half full of solvent, rows of tools, a pot of congealed cow gum resting on a spirit stove, a partly prised open tin of wood varnish . . . '

'Not varnish, dear boy, but ship chandlers' resin, a sealant used for coating sails of schooners and yachts. When applied, the fabric, stretched out, also attains a rigidity and toughness and of course becomes weatherproof, and here where I am indicating with the tip of my cane we have most fortuitously a roll of sailcloth, do we not?'

'Granted, Holmes, but I also observe a tied together bunch of bamboo bean poles, lengths of dowelling and a couple of planks of two by two ply stacked against the far wall. Thus, I surmise the fellow was evidently rather fond of carpentry in his spare time, about to board up a cracked window pane or two, part of a spring tidy-up no doubt.'

'You have provided me with a fairly competent assessment, my dear Watson but alas, entirely erroneous.'

'I suppose you can do better,' said I, rather sullenly.

'Indeed I can. What we have placed before us, dear boy, is all the detritus of a clever inventor. I propose that the deceased was not merely an obsessive lover of birds, but far more crucially, from our point of view at least, obsessed with the art of flying itself, and this Mr Gresley was unable to impart to us earlier for he was entirely kept in the dark upon the matter.'

'Astounding, a deuced determined inventor at that! Icarus likewise was not so lucky in his endeavours. Thornbury built himself a pair of wings from outstretched canvas and ply using the bamboo rods for supporting struts, you imply.'

'To give him enough lift and buoyancy. Nothing is new under the sun, Watson. Believe me, it is even accounted in the eleventh century: Elmer, a monk, constructed wings for his arms and legs, although his manual flapping was a failure. He managed two hundred yards of flight before crashing and breaking both legs. Mr Thornbury, I'll wager, attained a still greater distance before being killed outright in the attempt. By Jove, Watson, just browse over this page would you. Really most queer.'

I should perhaps explain to the reader of this narrative that while Holmes had been postulating upon the subject of aeronauts, he had meanwhile shifted his attention to the cottage parlour, which represented the haphazard study of Mr Thornbury. While ambling amongst the crammed bookshelves and glass covered wild birds, he had been puzzling over a notebook which lay open on the ornithologist's desk. He had come across some interesting passages and copied out the relevant entries in my pocket book herein reproduced:

January 3rd
Sharp frost last night. Mr Kemp told me that John Beswick knocked down but lost a blackbird with a white

breast, possibly a ring-tailed ouzel.
Red lamp signal 2-1-3.

February 1ˢᵗ
Snow much deeper, bottom of my
gaiters frozen hard in walking to the
summit of Gibbet Hill tonight.
Another red signal 4-6-2.

★   ★   ★

Later as the light started to fade and
evening drew on in the little room at the
top of the folly, my colleague, with the
aid of bow and arrow unravelled twine
attached and a neat whitewashed stake
placed by Inspector Sturrock marking
the exact spot where Thornbury's body
was found, was able to determine by
approximation that the ornithologist,
after lifting off from the ledge of the
tower window, managed to travel some
three hundred and eighty four yards
possibly aided by a stiff breeze, alas
losing control and crashing to the
ground, being fatally injured by the fall,
not as was first thought, a strong person

bearing a hefty cudgel.

'But where's the evidence?' proposed the inspector. 'No broken canvas or bits of wood scattered about the hill.'

'You know, I thought at first the wind was responsible for dispersing the detached lightweight canvas and ply wings across a wide area of countryside, smashing them to pieces in the process. A stiff breeze blowing across the hill would be nature's way of disposing of the flimsy apparatus, but now I'm not so sure. Perhaps someone may well wish to keep these flying escapades a secret and have hurriedly gathered up the broken struts and rent canvas after Thornbury's crash.'

'What about the red lights mentioned in Thornbury's jottings?' I asked anxiously. 'The coded signals, Holmes.'

'Unconnected I think, a separate matter to our current investigation, but an intriguing conundrum nonetheless, Watson, that I shall endeavour to pursue.'

'So, Mr Holmes, you are of the opinion that Mr Thornbury's flight of three hundred and eighty-four yards from the top of the Trafalgar folly was being closely assessed by someone connected.'

'I am indeed. By a person of some wealth and influence I'll be bound, who wishes to keep his name and the true nature of the ornithologist's death out of the newspapers. Incidentally, these aeronautical endeavours are linked.'

'Endeavours? Linked? What on earth are you driving at, sir?'

'My dear Sturrock, surely you will have guessed by now. Your corpse, Mr Kennilworth, the verger found badly beaten about in a field over at Deremitre suffered exactly the same fate as Thornbury. He was attempting manual flight and failed.'

'Good Lord, leaping from the church tower!' I exclaimed.

'Precisely, my dear Watson. You have it in one!'

Holmes was adamant that as evening fell we should stay put for a while, keeping a close watch from the tiny room at the top of the folly for any red lamplights that should wink at us from the depths of the countryside, the hills and vales common to that region of Derbyshire.

I can report that at around ten o'clock we saw our first red light twinkle in the distance. Fortunately, there was that night a clear sky and visibility was good. Thereafter another light still nearer and yet a third red glow emanating further afield.

'The red lights. If we consider our map, most likely come from points such as St Martin's Church, the Norman Parish Church of Saint Barnaby's at Deremitre and that last one is signalling from far off Tenbech,' said Inspector Sturrock, returning the brass telescope to my companion.

'Signalling from the buttresses of church towers like in the old days when they lit beacons to warn of marauding armies,' said I. 'But to what avail?'

'You know when we first came up here to the Peak District I was reading my newspaper on the train and came across a pertinent article concerning cattle rustling and the stealing of horses hereabouts?' remarked Holmes, his heavy lidded features expressing a frown.

'The thieves represent a clever gang who have so far outwitted the police. The farmers complain bitterly,' replied the detective sombrely, 'but the local force seem incapable of determining their quicksilver movements.'

'Yet our cattle rustlers are able to strike with a degree of certainty each time, knowing full well the way is clear and they can avoid being detected. That's where our red lamps come into play so effectively — Tenbech! Isnt that where poor Thornbury met with that appalling railway accident?'

'The same. You will recall the branch runs through to Derby.'

'By Jove, I have it, Watson. The faraway red lamp, that's not a church buttress. Could it possibly be the steepled roof of that signal box here at the junction where the trains cross points? See for yourselves, I've marked the place on the map with my propelling pencil.'

While Holmes contentedly smoked his pipe, by the light of our hurricane lamp we perused the map, avidly consulting the unfolded railway routes, roads and landmarks shown.

'So you have, but where does that leave us, Mr Holmes? A signal junction box — so what?'

'Don't you see, the thieves are using the line to dispose efficiently of the stolen livestock. Railway employees are in their pay, Inspector, the cattle and so forth are sent to market via that route. No passenger service, I take it, runs along the branch after ten?'

'If my memory serves me correctly, the only train that runs during the night is a goods service.'

'Most providential, Inspector. The train would thus not stop at any rural stations along the line to Derby?'

'That is the case; stations along the branch would be shut at that hour.'

'But, Inspector, I put it to you, the goods train might conceivably stop at Tenbech junction box to await signals and therefore be delayed just long enough to load the cattle onto a wagon, else sheep or horses.'

'By heavens!' exclaimed the detective, childishly jumping up and down with glee, forgetful of his stature in the Derbyshire force. 'I believe, sir, you've hit the proverbial nail on the head. I must make haste at once. Your remarkable deduction presents a most feasible line of enquiry. Why, I'll get my officers working on it right away. Let's see, the goods will be due at Tenbech signal box at around quarter past one in the morning. That gives me enough time to mobilise a contingent of police officers and intercept and arrest the gang. I can't thanks you enough, Mr Holmes, I really can't. The Derbyshire force is indebted to you.'

★ ★ ★

The police operations did indeed occur that night and eight men were arrested and charged, a number of stolen cattle and horses in their possession. The guard in his break van, the driver of the train and the signalman were also detained, so Inspector Sturrock, upon Holmes's sound advice, had bagged the lot. He was in a jolly pleasant mood when we next met and Holmes insisted we interview Lord

Stinton. We headed the five miles or so from Wellsby Hall in a four-wheeled chase for the sole purpose of ascertaining certain crucial data.

We reached the Hall, a venerable old manor, at noon. It was I recall fairly cold but at least sunny and a glorious day to see the surrounding Derbyshire countryside. The Hall was open to us and the squire, a very concerned and attentive individual, was glad to make our acquaintance. He appeared to have recently broken a leg, which was encased in plaster, and thumped out to meet us, shaking hands warmly.

'Good morning, gentlemen. Lunch awaits. Our local constable alerted me to your calling today. I trust I can be of some assistance. These murders of poor old Thornbury and the verger Mr Kennilworth over at Deremitre are really quite appalling.'

'Accident,' corrected the detective with some emphasis, taking out his notebook. 'We the police prefer to view the deaths as accidental, your lordship; a loss of individual control.'

'Loss of control? Dear me, Inspector, you police fellows really are the limit. How can you possibly reach that conclusion? Accidental death? Why, I am informed both men received terrible injuries, were badly beaten about the face and body.'

'You yourself appear to have met with an accident, Squire Stimpson. Might I enquire if you are on the mend?'

'Thank you for your obvious concern, Mr Holmes. I stupidly, and my wife will attest to this, tripped over a box edging and landed awkwardly on the paved path. I was picking my first snowdrops at the time. What a numbskull, advancing years must catch up with us eventually, I suppose.'

'I believe you to be a most intelligent and somewhat gallant fellow, along the lines of riding out with the hunt and bravely charging your horse over tall fences and hedges. You were a champion fox hunter in your younger days I believe.'

'How complimentary you are sir. Now, however, you see I can barely hobble about my own sitting room, reduced to a housebound invalid. Sherry all round,' he called out to his attendant butler.

Holmes, quite unexpectedly, leapt up and gave the arm of the settee a good hard smack with his cane, causing a cloud of dust to be expelled from the seat cover.

'Dammit, reveal your true part in this affair! This must stop, Lord Stimpson.' He stared angrily at our shocked host. 'This, this absurd competition you launched, a good round sum of prize money for the aeronaut who first successfully covers so much distance in a single flight. Two people have already died in the attempt. You, sir, may be the next. Think of your poor wife left a widow, your tenants left grieving for a just and well-liked master. How many more contestants shall have to be scraped off the ground before you see sense? Your last man-assisted flight I see left you with a broken leg. Whatever next?

'Why, Mr Holmes, your allegations are scurrilous, unfounded. How dare you suggest I am responsible, how dare you imply . . . '

'I do most directly imply to your better

judgment, Lord Stimpson, leave off this dangerous pursuit of a record attempt. You and the remaining contestants, whoever they be.'

'Otherwise, we the police will curtail your reckless activities for you, your lordship,' said Inspector Sturrock with some gravity. 'I have enough evidence thanks to Mr Sherlock Holmes here, to implicate you most seriously. Drop your aeronaut competition, sir. This is a friendly caution, a warning, but next time you'll be arrested, I promise.'

'Your name emblazoned in all the Derbyshire newspapers, I shouldn't wonder,' said Holmes caustically, making sure the point was rammed home.

'Very well, it appears I have no choice in the matter,' said he, helping to pass round the sherry, 'but you shall never curb man's perpetual quest for flight. It is obstinate, fearless fellows like us who pave the way, gentlemen.'

'Oblige me if you will, your lordship, by erecting a small brass plaque to the memory of Mr Thornbury, something like: 'The aeronaut who flew three hundred and eighty four yards, beating Elmer's attempt by one hundred and eighty four yards.' It will do rather well at the base of the folly originally conceived by your ancestor Lord Elias.'

'Why,' said our host beaming from ear to ear, 'what a splendid idea, Mr Holmes.'

4

A Village Conspiracy

Consulting my journals for the year 1886, the month being November, I am intrigued to find us up in Yorkshire. My illustrious companion and I, bags packed at the request of the chief constable, had been asked to help solve the baffling murder of a Mr Sugden of Haworth. I should mention by all accounts he was a mild-mannered if eccentric personality who, acting independently, advertised himself as a Brontë expert, offering guided tours in his native home village.

It was thus upon a bitterly cold and damp afternoon we were met at Keighley station by an Inspector Ramsden, a bluff and forthright Yorkshireman who appeared most cooperative and indeed honoured to be sharing the case with my esteemed colleague, thus at first hand able to glean some useful insights into Holmes's somewhat advanced methods of detection.

Catching our stopping service, we travelled along the Worth Valley branch, five miles of line altogether, sharing the compartment of a little two-coach train serving Ingrow West, Damens, Oakworth, Haworth and Oxenhope.

While I smoked my pipe, in a leisurely way glancing out of the window at the rain, occasional homesteads of stone and slate tinged a mossy green passing by, the odd mill else small factory visible as we rattled along beside grazing sheep, the unfolding rural scene, the detective advised us on certain details pertaining to the recent murder of Arnold Sugden.

'It's 'owt a terrible business,' Ramsden admitted, filling his own pipe from a pouch. 'I'll tell you summat, Mr 'Olmes, I've never come across a worse.'

'We understood Mr Sugden was a tour guide in the village,' expressed my colleague.

'Aye, that he were, but some folks round here were that miffed. I mean, he were putting it about the Brontë family were long established vampires, I ask you. The fellow just had no idea the bad feeling he were fostering, 'specially because them's so revered as a family like. Brontë artefacts are on display at rented rooms above the bank in Haworth.'

'Hang it all, that is a bit below the mark,' said I. 'We're talking about a legend here — the popularity of the sisters' books I refer to.'

'Aye Doctor, and you can imagine why the vicar and Mr Kenley his sexton weren't exactly afavoured of the walking tour coming up the hill, stopping off at the church to ogle the Brontë vault, gathering round to hear him pontificate about how theys that were decently coffined inside were up and about on the moors of a night — a clutch of the undead what had over the years been able to slake their foul thirst by attacking sheep and cattle and feeding on their blood, but tiring of livestock were now about to turn their attention to the unsuspecting populace of the towns and villages of the Worth Valley. Whitby's the place for that sort of talk, not Haworth.'

'So presumably Sugden's premise that the Brontë family were in fact vampires undoubtedly provided an added frisson to his weekly walking tours.'

'Thou's got it in one, Mr 'Olmes. He even claimed in a letter to the Yorkshire Post that the council were affeared to open t'vault in front of witnesses, at his specific request, mind, cos the coffined remains showed little sign of putridness, not rightly decomposed. Pinkish complexions, wildly tussled hair, bodies unusually lithe and nourished, musky perfume of funeral lilies 'anging about the place. Utter fabrication, of course. 'Ow the 'eck were he supposed to know? The vault's been sealed for that many years and the sister, Ann, is buried in Scarborough anyhow.'

'We can thus conjecture,' attested my companion, puffing on his old briar as our two-coacher departed the platform at Ingrow West station, the locomotive blowing out clouds of smoke as the train entered a short stretch of tunnel, 'Sugden should have nurtured plenty of detractors, genuine Brontë admirers of Jane

Eyre and so forth who must have found his accusations and the Gothic theme to his lurid guided tour both offensive and done in very poor taste.'

'Well the father, Patrick, only passed away in 1861, and Charlotte, who predeceased him, hasn't been dead and buried long either, but a good earner though. Them walking tours is very popular, specially in the winter. Thou must give him credit, Sugden were a brilliant self-publicist, but you're correct, it were wrong to be making a packet from exploiting the Brontë name, given their obvious standing in the world of literature. Aye, there were plenty of hackles raised, half of Haworth wanted him out t'way. Well, we're approaching Damens station shortly Mr 'Olmes, you'll be wanting to examine the murder scene. Victim's body was left just as we found it. It's been that perishing cold up 'ere this week, there were no real need to shift Sugden to the mortuary just yet.'

'Excellent, and I trust your officers have been careful not to alter anything,' my friend mused, knocking out the bowl of his pipe on his heel as the train pulled in at the station.

'Nowt bloody likely. What do you take us Yorkshire bobbies for, bloomin' incompetents? Your metropolitans are the slackers, not we,' he chuckled.

★ ★ ★

At Damens, a modest country halt serving the village, we alighted, pausing to watch our little train steam off through the pouring rain along the branch to Oxenhope. Once the gated level crossing had swung into position, we three, brandishing our umbrellas to fend off the worst of the windy, inclement weather, headed up a lane until we arrived at the entrance to a mill, a 'For Sale' notice board attached to the gates. The inspector informed us it was a weaving mill for the manufacture of woollen garments, now closed and awaiting new buyers. There were a number of belt-driven looms in a shed nearby, but it was across the cobbled yard in the boiler house with its tall brick chimney stack where the murder victim,

Mr Sugden, lay very cold and dead. A number of police constables stood duty outside the entrance and with a nod in the inspector's direction allowed us to pass.

'In fact, gentlemen, it were fortunate Sugden were found at all. On Saturday afternoon the estate office gent, a Mr Barlow, were showing round prospective buyers, a Messrs Langton and Crowther who intend to re-open the mill, when as an afterthought they decides to come round 'ere to view the three coke furnaces and, by 'eck, were they in for a shocker.'

I was aware, as we stepped into the boiler house, of the resonance of Inspector Ramsden's gruff Yorkshire dialect reverberating off the thickly concreted stonework, the walls many inches thick, the vast boiler furnaces bricked into the structure. The coke furnaces were massive and should have required a good deal of stoking to maintain boiler pressure to keep the belt-driven looms working eighteen hours a day.

'Observe, my dear Watson, how the concrete floor is so scrupulously clean of coke dust, swept meticulously, and yet the furnaces themselves are filthy and half full of clinker. I'll wager this crime was premeditated; footprints and scuffs are entirely absent. This floor has been swept for a reason, other than factory cleanliness.'

'Never struck me as being important,' said Inspector Ramsden, scratching his chin thoughtfully.

Further across the room we were able to get a clearer view of the corpse, which lay stiffly spread-eagled, face up in the middle of the floor — a hideous expression writ large across the distressed features. Sugden's mouth wide open in a dying scream, his sightless eyes bulging with fear, trickles of coagulated blood seeping from both ears and the victim's nostrils. A big, strapping fellow by the look of him.

'Nowt a pretty sight, looks half scared out of his wits. See how the finger nails have bitten into the clenched palm of his hands.'

'The only marks of injury I can see appear to be upon the wrists and exposed ankles. He's evidently been tied securely to a bench or some such,' remarked Holmes, briefly leaning over to study the corpse to make an assessment.

'Indeed, there are no bruises or signs he was beaten about and yet it appears he has undergone some horrible, most excruciating torture,' said I, entirely puzzled.

'I concur, Inspector. This is truly a most remarkable death, and we can thus say with some certainty, whoever planned this murder did so with much fore-thought. This mill at Damens offers considerable seclusion from prying eyes and the boiler house is of such sturdy construction no one outside could possibly have heard the appalling screams of the victim.'

'But how was it done? Are thee not going to brandish that famous magnifying lens of yours, Mr 'Olmes?' exclaimed Ramsden with a disappointed glance towards my colleague.

'My dear fellow,' laughed Holmes, offering round cigarettes from his silver case. 'I can assure you our visit to the old weaving mill has proved most advantageous. That insignificant bowl of soapy water resting upon the furnace shelf, for instance, something you and your officers appear to have overlooked and neglected its importance.'

'Soapy water — doesn't impress me much.'

'Whatever, let us not tarry at the mill any longer. To overly concern ourselves with Sugden's corpse is futile; it is the living man that interests me. We shall learn a good deal, I'll wager, from a visit to his home in Haworth, for I am certain therein lies a clue to the why's and the wherefores of this singular murder and consequently its unique and baffling execution. Let us away to Damens station to catch the next train out. My, my, Watson, the rain in these parts appears eternal. It has not ceased for one minute altogether since our arrival in Yorkshire. Brollies to the fore!'

'We appear no nearer to identifying the killer then?' asked the detective doubtfully, gathering his coat about him and preparing to dash across the wet and gleaming cobbled yard.

'On the contrary, Inspector, we are a good deal nearer,' said Holmes with a perplexed frown.

★   ★   ★

While the swirling rain and biting wind did not abate, from Haworth station we proceeded along the street to a row of terraces built of the same hardy granite and slate much weather-worn and blotted green that I have already alluded to.

The inspector produced a key from his coat pocket and, upon entering the house, we found it a neat and tidy habitation. I personally felt much like a trespasser, vaguely uncomfortable about gloating upon a deceased man's treasured possessions gathered over a lifetime. The place had a familiar and comfortable atmosphere; well stocked with shelves of books and it was evident Sugden was widely read.

Whilst I surveyed the dining room, listening to rainwater gurgling from the guttering, my companion concerned himself with a shelf containing a row of exercise books to the right of the fireplace. In no time he had discovered some discrepancy.

'Numbers eight-ten and eleven are missing from the series of twelve volumes of jottings,' he murmured. 'Can anyone find a personal diary? Try upstairs, Inspector. Watson, the study over the way — be a good fellow and seek out any letters or postcards. Probably a roll-top desk worth a plunder before we leave.'

'Diary found!' shouted the detective from the upstairs landing, clumping hurriedly down the staircase to re-join Holmes.

'Nothing remarkable, leather-bound. Not much in the way of entries. You'll nowt glean any earth shattering clues from this, Mr 'Olmes.'

The inspector handed it over and paused, for he somehow sensed my companion was about to prove him wrong. Holmes began swiftly turning the flimsy pages, leafing through the diary with an anxious expression upon his wan, hawk-like features.

June-July-August-September-October-Nov . . .

'Ah, a most singular irregularity. See here, Watson, how certain pages have been roughly torn out, ripped away from the spine, not at all characteristic of our neat and meticulous Mr Sugden, who I am sure should allow the perforations to gently dictate the tear — not unconscious force.'

'Good heavens, you suspect someone has been rifling through his personal documents, and certain of these exercise books have gone missing, you say?'

Becoming more animated, my companion took out his strongest lens and began minutely examining the corner of a diary page devoted to calendar notes.

'Hallo — a mark, moist and recently done. By Jove, we have made serious inroads here, Watson. Inspector, I shall require a powerful microscope. Have it delivered to our hotel, could you?'

'I'll get a constable to fetch one from our police surgeon. You have discovered useful finger prints, I take it?'

'There is a deposit adhering to the paper, a greasy stain I wish to analyse. Not lamp oil, mark you, nor cooking fat, nor Vaseline, but a light cleaning agent perhaps, possessing a faint but not unpleasant odour. Bear with me, Inspector. I shall make my findings known to you before long. Watson, you poor chap, you look absolutely famished. Dinner is served at our hotel in an hour.'

★　★　★

The following morning proved wet and gusty, a bitter wind being blown off the rugged moors that surrounded Haworth, the pavement awash with rainwater. After leaving our hotel, while I visited a tobacconist, Holmes emerged from a music shop displaying various gleaming wind instruments in the window, where he had been speaking with the proprietor. Crossing the road, once more our trusty umbrellas held aloft, we made due haste up the steep hill to the parsonage for morning tea with the local vicar, the Reverend Hartley, who, it must be said, had arranged the meeting at short notice because my companion had need of certain information. The Georgian house with its neatly square chimney pots and frontage of nine sashed windows was Church of England property and surrounded by craggy, exposed moorland on every side.

We surmounted the stone steps of the porticoed front door and were invited in by the vicar's charming housekeeper Mrs Shaw. Best silver tea service and bone china cups, salvers and plates were already laid out in the drawing room and the vicar welcomed us wholeheartedly into his home, a roaring coal fire blazing in the grate, his two pet spaniels in keen attendance upon the hearth rug. The housekeeper bustled about pouring tea, offering serviettes and making sure we were comfortably seated before the homely hearth.

My colleague was nonetheless swift and to the point in his opening delivery. This was no mere social call but a means of expertly gathering data.

'Do you know of anyone who may have

done Mr Sugden a violence?' asked Holmes, sipping his Earl Grey. The vicar paused and thought for a moment, but he was more amused than confounded.

'Frankly, Mr Holmes, every one of us in the Brontë Society wanted to wring his neck,' laughed the vicar, offering round a plate of delightful iced fairy cakes. 'But seriously, we rent rooms above the Yorkshire Penny Bank and work extremely diligently to maintain the Brontës' reputation. The whole of Yorkshire and much of the world, it seems has fallen under the spell of their wonderful books. Additionally, we regularly receive visitors but, alas, no actual museum as yet.'

'Did you complain to the council about his tours?'

'The letter to the *Yorkshire Post* represented the final straw; publicly requesting us to open the vault pushed us into action. Dare I say this, he was actually gaining a following and becoming something of a celebrity in the Worth Valley. He was beginning to make a good income, all of it derived from the Brontës' name and reputation. I had personally written letters to Charlotte's publisher, Smith & Elder, and contacted our own solicitors to try and find some way of legally enforcing a ban upon his activities. Now of course that won't be necessary, thank goodness. Oh heavens, does that sound un-Christian, me a vicar and all!'

'Not at all. The crux of my enquiries into his death now centres upon a music shop in Haworth — Tuftleys.'

'Yes, I know it. Whatever for, Mr Holmes? I'm afraid I just cannot equate dear old Mr Tuftley, the owner of the shop, with a beastly murder. He plays church organ for us and is over eighty, you know.'

'Forgive me, Padre. In point of fact Mr Tuftley has assisted me greatly and may even have helped bring the guilty to trial. Be that as it may, I should like to enquire whether you could recommend a local brass band, popular with a group of regular players.'

'The Grimshaw Co-operative Mills Band play passably, not, I would hasten to add, always in tune, but much appreciated by us locals. They are Haworth men born and bred.'

'Their leader?'

'Fred Illingworth is their conductor. A charabanc takes a whole crowd of us as far afield as Hebden Bridge and Halifax to support their concerts.'

'Could the sound they create even be classed as discordant?'

'They have under Illingworth, it is true, attempted some rather experimental pieces but they normally stick to popular favourites which we all love: 'Jerusalem', 'Snowy Polka', 'The Shepherds Song' and the like.'

'And Mr Sugden attended these concerts also?'

'He did. A staunch enthusiast of their music. None of us in the society agreed to chat with him of course, or sat anywhere near him in the stalls, but yes, he was most certainly a regular.'

★　★　★

With a steely determination, and an energetic spring to our heels, Holmes, myself and Inspector Ramsden, together with a number of supporting officers, gathered outside a villa in Corby Street, a detached house brightly painted, the front door with its shiny, polished brass door knocker a glossy pillar-box red. How difficult it was to envisage this prim and pretty property as a meeting place for a group of conspirators bent on murder.

'Oh, Ramsden, it's you. Typical bloody weather we're 'avin oop here with the rain and gales. Come in, gentlemen. You were enquiring about the band, I 'ear. Can I fetch you a whisky or summat?'

'I'm arresting you, Mr Illingworth, along with other brass band members, on account of a murder at Damens Mill, the murder of a Mr Arnold Sugden of Haworth. I have a warrant here and my officers intend to make a thorough search of your property. Sergeant Rigby, do the honours and cuff the gentleman if you will.'

'Have you gone mad? Do you know who I am, Ramsden? I'm the conductor of the Grimshaw Co-Operative Mills Band; I'm a musicologist, a first-rate trombone player. I'm respected round 'ere.'

'And you put your trombone to infamous effect upon the night you killed that man, I'll wager,' snapped my colleague. 'You and your fellow bandsmen.'

'Who the hell are you — a southerner! We look after our own up 'ere. Sugden insulted the Brontë Society, making out the family were vampires. I shall contact my solicitor about this. Thee'll be struck off the force, Ramsden, you mark my words. You're finished, lad.'

★   ★   ★

'There are a number of points to be considered, my dear Watson,' said my esteemed colleague back at our hotel suite, relaxing, nurturing his whisky and splash, crossing his long legs before settling back in his plush armchair in front of the fire. He elaborated somewhat. 'You will recall, no doubt, how I first ventured into old Mr Tuftley's music shop at nine o'clock this morning.'

'I do indeed,' said I, lighting a cigar.

'Presenting my hypothesis regarding the page from the diary, I was instantly rewarded, for the old music shop proprietor recognised the perceptible fragrance from the deposit staining the paper and confirmed what I suspected all along — the smeared substance related to brass wind instruments. Baxter's valve oil was a possibility, Hobbs' slide cream another. Both are applied when taking the instrument apart for a thorough cleaning and washing, whether it be a trumpet, tuba French horn, brass trombone or whatever — mouthpieces, tuning slides, caps and valves all require careful attention.'

'That really is a most clever deduction, Holmes. I am astounded at your ingenuity,' said I, the flickering firelight, casting weaving shadows upon the walls and ceiling of our apartment. 'And thence you were led to make this crucial connection with the local brass band.'

'It is opportune, my dear fellow, that the missing pages corresponded to diary dates of the brass band's concerts. By trying to be overly clever and cover his tracks, in fact Illingworth 'criminated himself wonderfully. The missing exercise books which were retrieved from a drawer in his desk at his house in Corby Street by police this afternoon likewise mention write-ups of the band's various concerts. Therefore, we can safely deduce the conductor did not wish the name 'Grimshaw's Co-Operative Mills Band' to be linked to the murder.'

'But it was only you, my dear Holmes, who actually was able to discover a link. Poor Ramsden should have been out of his depth, I fear. No disrespect to the inspector, of course, for from the outset the case was practically unsolvable. I confess what baffles me most, however, is that tin bowl of suds you noticed resting on the furnace shelf?'

'I should prefer not to blow my own trumpet too loudly. It was only later I realised the true merit of the washing up bowl — Mr Tuftley assuring me that bandsmen use a flexible valve cleaning brush to unclog certain deposits in trumpets and trombones. Soapy water is ideal to rinse through, giving one's brass instrument a sweet sound and making it a pleasure to play.'

'And to think poor Sugden's final hours were spent tied to a bench in that enclosed boiler house, enduring an absolute agony of noise, being blasted by discordant notes of a certain resonance up close to his ears — screaming trumpet, bassoon, cornet, trombone — Illingworth's musical method of diabolical murder. Sugden strapped helplessly on a bench, powerless to cease the matchless din, his heart unable to cope with the shock of the noise,' said I.

'Indeed, Watson. Our Mr Sugden paid very dearly for dragging the Brontë name through the mud. Yes, I will have another top-up, dear fellow. Not too much splash this time, thank you.'

5

The Affair Of The Friendly Tramp

I recall one summer we were invited to stay at Figglesbury Manor, the Elizabethan house belonging to the explorer Sir Vivian Penworthy, that great African adventurer who was fortunate enough to discover gold deposits in the hills of the Sumboa region in '81. He was at the time of our visit in fact away in the Sudan but his wife, Becky, Lady Penworthy, was well known to us for she regularly attended lectures at the Royal Geographical Society in London and was aware of my friend's considerable reputation.

Anyhow, London was undergoing an insufferably close, uncomfortably humid heatwave so we were glad to be out of it for a while.

At the end of our stay, Sherlock Holmes and myself found ourselves jogging along in her large open carriage to catch our London-bound train from the branch station. The mistress of the house presented a most fetching picture of repose and loveliness, wearing her blue silk skirt and paisley shawl, the groom perched upon the wide box-seat up front steering the rains. We trotted along at a sedate pace, taking in the post and wire fence, grazing herds of livestock, and those little pink bindweed by the dusty roadside, lush green fields of flax, wheat and barley undulating in a gentle breeze beyond.

Of some note I recall that same morning, while we devoured our new-laid eggs and sampled honey in the comb, the sunlight falling in bright bars upon the wall of the breakfast room, Mrs Lester the housekeeper, for some reason, seemed out of sorts, not her usual jolly self. Being, it must be said, bachelors of long-standing, we have had our fair share of domestic ups and downs with our housekeeper, Mrs Hudson, not to realise something was amiss and my companion, the ultimate observer of human foibles was anxious to pry further into the matter.

'Oh, really, Mr Holmes, on the surface it appears so trite and insignificant. Mrs Lester is normally an absolute poppet, but I fear will work herself up into some fit or swoon, unless the matter can be cleared up quickly. Only yesterday, cook remarked that old Tom Yearling, the friendly vagrant from the workhouse over at Steeple-Magna had not made his usual visit round by the kitchen door. The first week in June, without fail, he journeys, pushing an old barrow, and will sharpen knives, sell old tat like matches and silk ribbons for a few pence else in exchange for ducks' eggs, cheese or half a loaf. Cook has gleaned intelligence from a Mrs Cobbs at the workhouse that he evidently set off punctiliously, but none has seen or heard word of him since he passed through the village of Upper Slaughter. Dare I say it, Tom Yearling is a well-known traveller of the road, a likeable character who will stop for a chat and smoke his pug pipe and share his baccy with anyone inclined to be sociable, making his nightly camp in the hedgerow. Talking of which, I must consult with Constable Pickles upon a curious matter of a nearby gypsy encampment at Buxley Heath, abandoned in a hurry.'

'Gypsy travellers, my dear Lady Penworthy, are hardly the most trustworthy or reliable of folk, indeed not particularly easy to keep track of,' said I, smiling warmly.

'But old Tom is habitual. Each summer in the second week of July, without fail he makes his pilgrimage by foot through the counties taking full advantage of the warm, dry weather. Oh, constable!' she called out as our carriage trotted round the corner and approached the police house, a cob and thatch cottage where at present the village constable with his beet red face and rolled-up shirt sleeves was outside in the front garden tending to his flowers with an upraised watering can. 'Constable Pickles, is there any word about Tom Yearling?'

'No, your Ladyship,' said Pickles confidently. 'I'se done everything you asked an' kept thee say an' keep my eyes peeled and ears open for any news in the villages roundabouts, but nothing of any consequence do I have to report, though I'd agree Yearling would pass this way shoving that ole barrow of his. I'd surely have seen by now of an early morning' them smelly old pair of hobnail boots of his poking out from the canvas and stick tent he'd erected in the beech trees where 'e normally camps, and the wood smoke from his fire rising among them, but not this July it seems.'

'Mrs Lester told me she was notified by Mrs Cobbs over at Steeple-Magna who recalls Tom taking time to explain his route on a grubby pocket map, indicating his stopping-off places, including us as Figglesbury Manor where cook, a most charitable and worthy soul, always makes sure to fill his billy-can with tea and prepare plenty of thick cut ham and mustard sandwiches and a slab of currant cake to see him on his way to the next village.'

'Lor', bless Mrs Lester for 'er kindness and thee, your Ladyship, for showing so much concern but Yearling, for better or worse, is a country dosser an' who's to say what becomes of such poor down and outs. Collapsed unseen in a wood, maybe dead for allus we knows, a meal for the 'ungry foxes 'n' crows peckin' at 'is corpse. Will that we all m'am?'

'Thank you, Constable Pickles, although I could have done without your macabre suppositions. Pray, have you enquired further about the gypsies who were encamped on my land?'

'The camp appears abandoned, certainly, 'astily doused fires, blackened sooty tea-kettles, pots 'n' cauldrons left lyin' about, which is out of character, but the tinkers' caravans are nowhere to be seen. No sign of any life or livestock either. They 'opped it alright though for what reason be unclear.'

'Nobody in the next village like Peter the smithy or Mrs Carter at the shop saw their caravans pass through?'

'No, ma'am.'

'Most queer. The annual horse fair is something of an event in the Romany calendar. That's where the gypsy folk were supposedly heading this weekend.

156

Considering how the men will, without fail, race, bet upon and barter their prize stallions and mares at these social get-togethers, where considerable sums of money change hands, how come they did not show up? Did no-one on the main road of a Friday or Saturday morning see anything of the caravans?'

'It appears not, ma'am. I'se shall venture forth to the manor on my bicycle the minute us police at a local level 'ears anything regarding the gypsy families or old Tom, who, knowing 'e cannot resist a good turn 'as probably got waylaid mending an old chair leg else sharpening cutlery for a cottager. Some such, any'ow.'

'Very well, Pickles, that will be all. Drive on.'

At a quarter to ten we eventually arrived at the station in good time to catch the down-line service to London. We had ten minutes to spare. I recall the young groom had previously hauled out our carpet bags and Holmes's little tin trunk from the rumble at the rear of the carried, and laid our belongings upon the

sun-drenched gravel of the station forecourt to be collected by the porter.
Thereafter, Holmes and myself were
about to step out of the open carriage
when my companion hesitated, seemingly
caught in something of a quandary.

'My dear Lady Penworthy,' he sighed at
length, 'neither Doctor Watson nor I can
possibly abandon you in your present
condition. You appear genuinely flustered,
upset over this old toad of a character
Tom, to say nothing of our vanishing
Romanies. Chin, up, I mean you are
surely not related or a close acquaintance.
Why become so hot and bothered?'

'Dear Mrs Lester will not leave off
pestering me about old Tom, the friendly
tramp, but in truth it is the Romanies I
am more concerned for. You see, Mr
Holmes, it was I after all who granted
them permission to camp on the heath
which forms part of our lands and estate,
my husband being away in the Sudan.'

'You feel a responsibility, yes, I quite
understand that.'

'It has always been the way at the big
house. My husband grants permission as

did his father and grandfather before him. Generations of travellers have proved both amenable and cause no damage to our beech woods and keep mostly to themselves. What I cannot for the life of me fathom is why the lucky heather ladies have not been out and about selling their wares as usual, and why, oh why, has Jem Faquar, the gypsy spokesman and leader of the group, a normally most polite and congenial fellow, failed to turn up at the estate office to thank us personally for allowing them to camp. You know, he offers us produce which we naturally decline.'

'Braces of woodcock and rabbits poached from your own fields, no doubt,' I chuckled wholeheartedly.

'But there's been no word, Doctor Watson. It's like the livestock, the womenfolk, the little urchins, the men with their earrings, colourful necker-chiefs and leather jerkins, both old and young with their curly, untamed hair, have just vanished off the face of our county. You see, they normally travel through the villages to reach the fair

— but no sign, no word.'

'Is there another farm estate nearby? Perhaps they parked on their land instead.'

'Why, certainly. Lord Crighton of Peabody Hall. He is our nearest neighbour, although our paths rarely meet. Both our estates have been hit hard by the poor harvests in the last couple of years due to unforeseen torrential rain lasting weeks at a time, a depression of unseasonal wet spells, if you will. Our grain crops and silage were decimated. Horrendous amounts of income lost. As a consequence, Lord Crighton, like many other farmers in southern England, was forced to economise. A number of agricultural workers lost their livelihood and were evicted from their tithe cottages.'

'All on account of the weather. We townies who spend our lives living and working in the metropolis are hardly aware of such things. Let us hope there is no repeat and the rest of the summer remains sunny and dry,' I remarked, giving my pipe a fill.

'Oh, a further bout of persistent storms and rain like last year and the year before shall mean many of our tenant farmers facing ruin.'

We now had less than four minutes remaining before our train arrived and the porter hurried over to buck us up.

'By Jove, old man, I suppose we can spare a day at least to solving this persistent problem of the disappearing tramp and so forth. But I must insist on our returning to Baker Street by no later than tomorrow evening, your Ladyship, for my brother Mycroft will be expecting me back at our diggings. He wishes to consult me upon a government matter concerning a Foreign Office mole.'

'So kind, Mr Holmes. My groom shall make sure your baggage is returned to Figglesbury Manor forthwith. Mrs Lester I am sure will be delighted and prepare your rooms.'

'But firstly,' insisted Holmes, lighting a fresh cigarette, 'let us make haste to the Heath. Thereafter we drive in your most charmingly quaint open carriage out to Lord Crighton's place. By the by, your

Ladyship, he and your husband are well acquainted. Do they share anything in common — members of the local hunt, or some committee or other?'

'Now you come to mention it, Mr Holmes, both Lord Crighton and my husband are keen agriculturists, always interested in the latest development of mechanical steam thresher, else modern aggregates, crop rotation, storage and silage. Farming and country pursuits such as fox hunting and shooting game birds are very dear to them.'

* * *

Upon arrival at the Heath, Sherlock Holmes leapt out of the carriage and concerned himself wholly with making a calculated survey. Brandishing his magnifying lens and wearing his countryside attire of tweed deerstalker, jacket and plus-fours, every briar bush, clump of hedgerow, acacias and the enormous copper beech came in for close scrutiny. I observed him pause to examine minutely the powdery ash and charred wood of the various camp fires, the sooty cauldrons still, he noted, containing the remains of bean and rabbit stew, blackened sooty kettles suspended on thick twigs positioned across Y-shaped wattled and split branches. After this he walked stealthily towards the far fence and paused upon the other side of the heathland for a moment to consider the immense pall of dark smoke ascending into the sky over in the far distance. From our carriage we had an excellent view of the billowing smoke intruding upon a perfect summer's day. An immense fire was evidently burning, presumably controlled and associated with some related agricultural work taking place in a field some miles always, although I surmised it was a trifle early for setting light to stubble.

Holmes strode back the way he had come, nimbly avoiding assorted cowpats and tough, hardy weeds amongst the wild grasses. Leaning upon the side of the open carriage, he said, 'You have every reason to be anxious about the Romanies, your Ladyship.' His wan, hawk-like features were riven with an intense and most serious expression.

'Violent and untoward behaviour has recently, I say very recently, occurred in this vicinity. Snapped twigs and branches, scuffed grass, signs of a struggle,' Holmes elaborated further. 'The smoke you see rising in the far distance I observed earlier, when I awoke, through my bedroom window. I spied the ash cloud beyond the village. That was at a quarter to six! I shall wager the fire has been raging for many hours, perhaps through the night, diligently tended and kept coaled by farm labourers, no doubt.'

'Rubbish burning, the blackness and intensity of smoke indicating many materials,' I remarked.

'Certainly. An astute observation, my dear Watson.'

'But upon whose land is this immense incineration taking place?' I queried.

'Why, Doctor Watson, it appears from our raised vantage up here in my carriage to be upon Lord Crighton's property,' replied our host, sitting up and stretching her neck to gain a better view. Holmes acquiesced and put forward his theory.

'Suppose, for argument's sake, the caravans were towed away hurriedly under cover of darkness. There is a rough farm track composed of crushed brick and loose stones, covered in wheel ruts and a multiplicity of footprints. I should say they went that way!'

'Across the open fields.'

'Precisely, for that is where the farm track leads.'

'In plain words, in the same direction where the burning smoke is coming from.'

'My dear Watson, your astonishment is justified.'

'But you mentioned earlier a violence had taken place. The Romany men are a tough breed, well able to look after themselves, and raise their fists in anger. Oh dear, are you seriously contemplating abduction, a mass of tinker folk forcibly restrained, taken somewhere against their will, along with their horses and live-stock?'

'I am, Lady Penworthy. I propose a large number of persons were most likely herded together, forcibly restrained by an armed gang using threats of violence to assert their will. You are completely correct. Under normal circumstances the gypsies are more than a match for anybody, but if we're talking about being overwhelmed, weaponry must have been employed in profusion, nail studded clubs and shotguns, I refer to.'

'How ghastly! What are we to do?' our dear lady friend remarked.

'Hup, hup, we are to pay an impromptu visit to Lord Crighton's country seat, put caution to the wind, a good sustained gallop, if you please, groom. Time is of the essence. Our aliases shall on this occasion be Mr Fairfield and Doctor McCann.'

★　★　★

Peabody Hall was a long, low house of mellowed brick, much added to over the years. Set in a large garden that ran round three sides of an ornamental pond, there were rose covered terraces and a smooth silky lawn surrounded by beech, elm and laburnum.

The owner of some four hundred and fifty acres of arable and grazing land happily met us in the sunny drawing room of his house, which was tastefully furnished, gilt mirrors and old oils depicting hunting scenes upon the walls.

Hurrying over from the mantelpiece, considering two of our company were complete strangers, he was most generous and shook us each in turn warmly by the hand, kissing her Ladyship on both cheeks.

Lord Crighton appeared at first sight a dashing country gentleman, ruggedly handsome of feature, greying hair combed back. I should say aged eight and fifty with a swarthy trim figure, he was elegantly turned out in jacket and plus fours, yellow waistcoat and open-neck shirt with a cravat. Bright kindly eyes revealed a keen intelligence and love of hospitality, an aura, charisma, whatever, he possessed it in spades and in his presence the sun seemed to shine the brighter. His abounding energy and obvious enjoyment of life was infectious.

'Why, how do you do? You are most

welcome to my home, Lady Penworthy. I am once again delighted to make your acquaintance. We see so little of each other these days, and in future we must remedy that. You have re-decorated, I hear.'

'I am slowly but surely getting there with the assistance of my builder and decorator, Mr Ranscombe. The sitting room and dining room are more in the Georgian taste, pastel shades, pale green damask silk. William Morris print designs for curtaining and seat covers. I've tried to purge the house of that awful gloomy atmosphere, the heavy velvet drapes, dark oak panelling and leather club chairs. You must come and visit, your Lordship.'

'I should be honoured. I last visited a year or so ago when your husband was I believe away exploring Africa. And these gentlemen are . . . ?'

'Mr Fairfield and Doctor McCann, two dear friends of mine from town, down from London for a holiday. We were driving in my carriage and on a whim decided to give you a call. Your hedges are the envy of the county. All those royal red roses, jasmine and deep cupped convolvulus. How lovely your park and garden is in bloom.

'Most complimentary. Take a seat on the ottoman, gentlemen. Iced glasses of lemonade shall arrive shortly. Are you enjoying your sojourn in our county, Mr Fairfield?'

'Very much. The weather has been outstanding, our stay all too short, for I and my friend must depart for the smoky metropolis this evening. May I perchance enquire about that squat wooden tower on wheels we saw coming up the drive to the house?'

'Well, let me explain. I am presently involved in supervising the installation of a large silo on my land. Those dratted carpenters and workmen have been hammering and sawing away for weeks. Such a nuisance, banging in nails, and the cart loads of timber, the lumber required, I ask you, but thank goodness the silo is now completed and I can get some peace and quiet at last.'

'The squat triangular base and sloping sides and all those steps leading up to the hopper certainly must have taken some time to build,' said I.

'The silo, Doctor McCann, is able to store a massive tonnage of grain.'

'The flight of steps leading to the top are presumably so men bearing sacks of corn upon their backs can attain the dispersal point. If so, it's a jolly steep climb.'

'A mechanical cog-driven winch and steel cable powered by a separate steam traction engine have yet to be installed. Difficult to envisage at present, but when it's all up and running I shall be the proud owner of one of the most advanced silo storage facilities in the country.'

'Your own design?'

'Good lord, no! Messrs Middleton and Updyke of the firm Prestwicks in the town must take credit for that.'

'You know,' guffawed Lady Penworthy in a delightfully girlish, uninhibited way, accepting a glass of lemonade from a servant in attendance, 'folk will be able to view your tower from miles around. I believe you have unwittingly created an immense folly to rival the pyramid tomb of the Georgian squire 'Mad Jack' Fuller of Brightling, your lordship. My husband adores such things.'

'Aha, I think you may have a valid point there, my dear. Drink up, Mr Fairfield and you too, Doctor McCann, plenty more lemonade in the jug. Fred, when is lunch?' he called out to his butler.

'Ten minutes, your grace.'

'And the fire burning on your land is connected in some way to the building of the silo, I take it?'

'Farmworkers are presently incinerating rubbish. The smoke is a bind, but it is only once a year. I'm not expecting too many complaints from the natives.'

'Natives?'

'The villagers hereabouts, Mr Fairfield.'

'Of course.'

So genial and sociable was our host that he insisted we stay for lunch. There were never any airs or graces about the man. Etiquette was kept to a minimum and after being shown round his immense library, which was indeed impressive, for he was a noted antiquarian and collected many rare and valuable volumes, we were presented with a fine meal of roast beef and blackcurrant pudding and later left Peabody Hall in fine fettle after being so well fed and watered.

'By the by, did either of you happen to observe those tiny perforations upon the earlobes, nostrils and fleshy bottom lip of his lordship?'

'Well, I know for a fact, Mr Holmes, Romany menfolk are very partial to gold earrings, but I grant you piercings are not very becoming for an English country gentleman of Lord Crighton's standing,' remarked her ladyship, concerning herself more with the passing scene as our carriage drew away from Peabody Hall, the horses gathering pace, kicking up the dust.

★ ★ ★

That same afternoon, with the sun beating down upon our brows, we were far from idle. At Holmes's insistence the groom reigned in the horses, parking her ladyship's open carriage on the outskirts of the village. Across the lane was a little cob cottage designated as a police house. Roses and ivy clung in profusion to the frontage while heavy clumps of jasmine covered one wall where peonies grew amongst currant bushes.

We slipped under a rustic porch and were met by the gruff village policeman who inhabited the place. However, he seemed at first disinclined to let us in. It was only when he caught sight of Lady Penworthy hurrying up the path from the gate in her striking blue silk dress and shawl, that he instantly began buttoning his tunic collar and looking officious and attentive.

'Afternoon, ma'am. I did trouble earlier to cycle over to Langly on account of the Romanies but was able to glean no further information.'

'Constable Pickles, might we come in? We have just visited Peabody Hall.'

At once we were led into the cool stone-flagged parlour with its cottage dresser displaying china knickknacks and neatly swept hearth. A black cat lay sound asleep upon the sunny sill.

'Lord Crighton's place. Was 'e well?'

enquired Pickles, putting aside his enamel mug of tea and rolling himself a cigarette, paper and strands of tobacco deftly held betwixt fingers and thumb.

'His lordship was in fine form and gave us a jolly nice lunch, but there are certain issues pertaining to him we need to discuss.'

'What issues be they?'

'Burning vital evidence,' interrupted my colleague bluntly, sitting down in the constable's armchair and crossing his long legs, puffing on his pipe while a hazy whirl of tobacco smoke floated in a bar of sunlight, striking the fireplace.

'Burning evidence? Whatever do you infer?'

'Lord Crighton is in very deep concerning the gypsy encampment and old Tom Yearling. I believe he is keeping them prisoner against their will.'

The local officer grew visibly annoyed, his eyes glowed with indignation and he lost no time in dismissing the allegations.

'Lord Crighton is beyond reproach. I'll hear no slander directed towards that gentleman. What he does on his land is his own business. It's barely credible, the daftest, most rotten speculation I've heard in a month of Sundays. My old cat could come up with a better line of enquiry. All on account of incinerating some rubbish, I ask you!'

'If you'll just hear me out, Pickles, you might learn something. By the snapped twigs, broken branches and torn shreds of clothing I surmise there was a scuffle. The farm tracks leading off the heath were where those caravans were towed, and the Romany folk forcibly marched along in single file. The ground is parched and dry but the dust was imprinted with mingled footprints and wheel ruts.'

'Leading where?'

'To the barns and outbuildings on Lord Crighton's estate. I know I have as yet no proof, but it is a plausible theory. Would not it be possible to imprison the Romany travellers in one of those barns, while burning up their possessions and caravans?'

'But to what purpose? What you'rn suggestin', Mr 'Olmes — and I 'ope it ain't — is that muggins here goes off on my bicycle, knocks at Peabody Hall demanding admittance and enquires, ever so 'umbly, whether 'is lordship is 'iding a smelly old tramp and a rabble of good-for-nothing tinkers on 'is farm. I'd be laughed out of the force, I would.'

'A brief search of the stockyard and cursory examination of the fire pit is all that is required to put our minds at rest. Surely you would not wish to cause Lady Penworthy still further anxiety?'

'T'aint nothing to do with what I wishes or not. You'rn meddling, Mr 'Olmes, in country affairs that you and Doctor Watson, both townies, have no understanding of. There is an ordained hierarchy out here in the provinces; can't thee give this matter a rest, the problem's bound to solve itself. Lor', those blinkin' tinkers is dishonest and unreliable anyhow. Ain't worth the bother.'

'An abduction of innocent women and children and their menfolk on my land,' remarked Lady Penworthy. 'An armed assault against a group of Romanies camped on the heath because I gave my authority? I simply cannot allow this matter to go either unpunished or uninvestigated, Pickles. I can tell you, your superiors shall come down very hard on you if you neglect your duties. It is your job to cooperate with Mr Holmes, and furthermore, as a policeman paid for by the county, to make enquiries and sanction an arrest if necessary.'

'Suppose so,' he admitted grudgingly. 'But as the village constable, your Ladyship, I must also be impartial. I am indeed empowered by the county to serve both the constituents and yourself and Lord Crighton. I must be fair and even-handed. I don't want to ruffle no feathers unnecessarily. Well, let me hear your proposal.' Pickles lit his hand-manufactured cigarette and settled back to listen.

'Bravo!' exclaimed my colleague, relighting his pipe and slinging the spent match into the empty grate. 'Tonight after dark we shall make a little excursion following the trail of the abducted Romanies across the arable fields in the direction of that bonfire. I assure you, constable, we shall not commit trespass upon his lordship's property for more than fifteen minutes.'

'The remains of the trash will be smouldering by then, the fire died down,' said I.

'Precisely, Watson. Mr dear Pickles, what have you possibly got to complain about now? If we do it this way, no feathers are ruffled, your relations with Lord Crighton remain on a good footing and at the same time you have honoured your obligations as a policeman to Lady Penworthy.'

★ ★ ★

We met when the sun had gone down. Pickles parked his bicycle against a fence post on the heath and without further ado we set off on foot across the fields. The rough track was bordered by tall hedgerow and made up of crushed bricks and bare rocks, loose stones flung on regardless, making for an uneven, rutted surface and most irksome to walk on.

Even with the light from our bull's eyes

requisitioned from the police house, the way remained dark and ponderous. Her ladyship clung onto my arm like grim death for fear of tripping over or twisting her ankle. The vigilant policeman trudged on ahead. On one occasion I recall upon the bank we saw the bright gleam of green eyes reflected in the beam from our lamp; a fox and her cubs peeping inquisitively from a warren partly concealed by nettles.

'Half a mile or so that way be Peabody Hall,' said Pickles, pausing to take stock. 'Now, for the yard and farm buildings we follows that hedge around the perimeter of the field. Mind your'n step, there be a mangled old plough abandoned in the ditch amongst the brambles, your ladyship.'

'You will observe,' said my companion, leaning over and jabbing at the ground with his cane, 'how the course of the wheel ruts departs away from the rutted track, curving off towards that five-barred gate over there!'

'Aye, that way across the field will eventually lead to the same place we be heading only we're taking a short cut along a narrow bridle bath on the other side of the stile.'

'Capital, Officer Pickles. We have thus established with a fair degree of certainty the route employed by the armed gang. Hallo, what's this? Watson, shine your lamp over here by this tree, there's a good fellow.'

Adjusting the beam, I hastened across and we joined Holmes, gathering round the gnarled trunk of a venerable old beech. Highlighted in the glow from the lamp it was plain enough to see someone had shoved a rolled-up scrap of paper into a woodpecker's nest, a pecked-out hole roughly seven or so feet from the ground.

Sherlock Holmes, being the tallest amongst us, stretched his arm all the way up and just about managed to extract the roll of paper, which was brittle from long exposure to the sun and crawling with ants. Flattening it out, we studied the hastily scrawled message with interest.

'*Please help us*
Thems with shotguns came in the

night when weez sleepin. dunno where they be tekking us.
Romany Sal.'

'Well, I must say, this note puts a rather predatory and sinister light on proceedings,' said Holmes cheerfully.

'I'd agree, 'less someone's pullin' our leg, of course. You'd better 'and me that slip of paper, Mr 'Olmes, and I'll put it in my pocket book, official like, for later.'

'So it's true, those poor Romanies were deliberately rounded up, but for what purpose? The reason entirely eludes me,' admitted our lady friend. 'I cannot fathom such wickedness.'

'Forced labour,' said I, putting forward my own view. 'Like the southern states of America where once slavery abounded. Does Lord Crighton intend to expand his workforce using unpaid labour, I wonder?'

'The Romany travellers do 'ave skills, Doctor Watson, particularly breakin' in 'orses and rearing bloodstock, but workin' the land from morn till dusk wouldn't appeal to them free roamin' types. I doubt if they'd be much enamoured to digging and ploughing all day long — or very proficient at it.'

'Fruit picking or flower gathering more in their line, you mean constable?'

'Poachin' I refer to, ma'am, on other people's property.'

Proceeding east we traipsed around the edge of the aforementioned field, wading through tufts of wheat and wild grasses until we found ourselves facing a timber stile. Beyond could be clearly seen the shadowy outline of a group of farm buildings and away on the horizon the dark silhouette of the silo hugging the night sky. We had at last attained our goal and quite possibly established, the where-abouts of the gypsies and Tom Yearling, the dosser from Steeple Magna work-house, also.

'The lurchers is my worst worry,' said the constable, taking out a silver-plated timepiece and most astutely checking and recording the time in his pocket book with a pencil stub. 'Any blessed yapping or growling of dogs would be an absolute pain, although from a previous visit when I was called out by 'is lordship to attend to poachers, I 'ad no real bother. Let's 'ope they've been well fed. His lordship's greyhounds is kep' in a separate kennel up by the house, and domesticated and gentle animals.'

'As previously agreed,' said Holmes, throwing his scarf over his shoulder, 'we will not trespass for longer than is absolutely necessary. Pickles and your Ladyship, if you can make a swift assessment of the fire pit — any evidence pertaining to burnt out caravans — and keep your eyes peeled for detritus such as assorted ironwork, coiled springs, melted household trinkets, that sort of thing. Watson and I shall investigate the yard and outbuildings. We meet back over by that fence post in, say, fifteen minutes.'

'We had better not underestimate Lord Crighton. He is an Oxford-educated man, Mr Holmes, a noted antiquarian, a world traveller, far too wily and clever a personage to simply lock away the Romanies in a barn without arousing suspicion. Surely one should be able to hear cries for help, murmurings, rustling about in the straw because of the rickety

183

nature of a barn's construction, the wooden slats and so forth.'

'Agreed, but I think it prudent to check. The rubbish fire I concur may provide a windfall of damning evidence. Anything amongst the clinker that we can link to the gypsy encampment upon the heath means they must be close by, perhaps being kept prisoner up at the hall. As for Lord Crighton's intellect, one only has to visit his vast and sprawling library, as Watson and I did before luncheon, to know we are undoubtedly dealing with a personage of considerable culture and taste, and doubly dangerous because of it.'

* * *

The fire pit was still far too hot to make any useful deductions. The temperature of the incineration at its height must have been extraordinary, well able to consume and melt iron and glass but fundamentally, because of the intense heat and flaring gases being emitted, none of us could get near enough to rake through the smouldering clinker in search of viable evidence.

We had arrived back at Figglesbury Manor that night worn out and deflated and in a state of ill humour. No sign whatsoever of any persons being kept captive in the outhouses on the farm, the only things alive and kicking in those thatched barns being rats and dormice.

I confess morale was low and it appeared, apart from Romany Sal's note which on its own would not suffice, for as the constable pointed out, it could have been planted or written as some part of a childish prank, we were no nearer to discovering the truth. My own pet theory concerning slave labour still had no takers and after a last pipe and cup of tea I was off to bed, leaving Holmes fretful and pacing up and down in front of the sitting room hearth, being consoled by Lady Penworthy who, like her husband, remained always cheerful and positive when beset by trials.

A couple of hours later I was enjoying a deep and dreamless slumber when I was annoyingly woken up by Holmes repeatedly shaking me by the shoulder, and turfed out of bed. It was already getting light and a dawn chorus of birdsong in progress!

'Watson, I have it at last, old fellow! But we may be too late.'

'Too late for what? What are you blasted well driving at?' said I, fumbling with my trousers and tucking my shirt in like someone half dead.

'To save lives. Hurry, we are on an emergency footing. Lady Penworthy sent Mr Grieves pedalling off to the police house to alert Pickles of my intentions. We shall pick up the constable on our way to the furthermost field on Lord Crighton's land and I shall impart directions to an assistant police officer who is meeting us at the cottage. Davis the groom harnessed the carriage a few minutes ago and is bringing it round the front as we speak. Certain Indians of the South Americas favour piercing in their nostrils and bottom lip, but the display of gold ornamentation and exotic feathers surely so out of character for an Englishman.

Damn and blast, what a fool I've been, Watson, concentrating too much brain energy on the gypsy conundrum and far too little on the lifestyle and achievements of Lord Crighton himself. I missed the entire crux of the affair by a mile. His vast learning, his travels, his farming interests — the Romanies must have been kept prisoner inside that dratted silo, isolated far away on the other side of the estate!'

'The Trojan Horse principle,' I remarked.

'Quite so, that's it. Pipe, matches, wallet — now let's get downstairs, Watson. The sun has already been up for a whole ten minutes. Oh, it is too late, even now it is far too late . . . ' he muttered under his breath incomprehensively.

★　★　★

The sight that awaited us in a country field upon a calm and beautiful morning in June, the sun blazing in the sky, spreading warmth and brightness about the land, defied belief. For here in a quiet

187

corner of rural England, the culture of the pre-Christian and ancient Aztec and Inca empires of the South Americas steeped in superstition and fear was encroaching upon our own age.

At the base of the steps leading up the sloping front of the so-called silo, the wooden tower being in effect a flat-topped pyramid, were already heaped the tangled remains of three persons, a fourth who I believe was poor Tom Yearling I saw tossed down the steep flight of steps, dismissed like so much India rubber, the slashed-open body rolling over and over, tumbling the whole way to the bottom of the structure, leaving a trail of viscous gore in its wake.

While still alive, his heart had been cut out for the fearsome priest wearing a toga and gaudy golden headdress of colourful feathers, his bare arms decorated with gold and bead bracelets, his pierced nose and bottom lip adorned with gold ornaments and still more feathers, stood brazenly at the top of the tower before a kind of chamber with an arched entrance, its true purpose more of a temple of sacrifice rather than the dispersal point for pouring loose grain into a hopper we had been led to believe.

Accompanied by the swirling discordant music of reed flutes and conch shells, the similarly attired crowd below roared their approval, and the high priest raised a dish up to the sun containing the dripping, fleshy organ, the bloody heart of Tom Yearling.

Their god shone benignly in a clear blue summer sky. Tom and the Romanies were being systematically slaughtered so that a fulsome harvest might be assured, the grain crops in Southern England flourish, the wheat, the barley and the flax yields that year to attain the highest prices at market.

'Prosper and fill your baskets with gold,' the crowd chanted, lifting their bronzed and feathered faces towards the sun, preparing for still more appeasement, an insurance against a repeat of last summer's rain, floods and unseasonal storms.

Yet another poor wretch, this time a

Romany girl, was led up the blood-saturated steps to the summit, her arms pinioned behind, no doubt given some potion to dull her senses but nonetheless keenly aware of her status and the terrible fate awaiting her upon the altar under the priest's eager blade.

I confess we were for a time paralysed with horror, stunned witless, our conscious mind, the very fibre of our being, taken back to another long distant age of bloodletting and human sacrifice.

Sherlock Holmes alone managed to remain passably functioning. He had brought along with him from the gun room at Figglesbury Manor a large, shabby brown leather case. Showing great presence of mind he calmly undid the brass clasps and prised open the lid, reaching inside for a bolt action Webley rifle. My colleague slowly and deliberately raised the stock so that his sharp eyes were level with the gun sight.

In an ecstasy of blood lust as the crowd once more bellowed, 'Prosper and fill your baskets with gold,' I heard a loud report as the rifle bucked and a smell of cordite filled the air.

Lord Crighton, self-appointed high priest, who had wallowed in a lake of blood, upon impact dropped the bejewelled dish through his fingers and, still mesmerised by the sun, a surprised look on his face, pitched forwards, a tiny hole drilled into his broad, bronzed forehead by my colleague who had evidently fired his cartridge shell with deadly accuracy.

His lordship's shoulders hunched and this time it was he, the harvester of bloody hearts, who toppled in an undignified mass of tangled limbs down the many steps to the bottom.

The foul, but mesmerising spectacle had reached its zenith. Those gentlemen farmers and agricultural workers, who had gathered from many counties, knowingly embracing the cult of Mayan sun worship, were to rue the day they first learned of Lord Crighton's radical scheme of ensuring fine weather and abundant crops.

The sound of galloping horses, police whistles, and a wall of dust rising from the ground over by the tree line was our first indication that an operation of containment and arrest was currently underway. For by this time a company of mounted police officers was charging across the field.

It must be reported the village constable was much relieved that Holmes's last minute strategy of sending his young assistant officer off to the town's police headquarters to warn the force at large, utilising the early morning milk train stopping along the branch, gained fruition and had thus saved many lives that day.

6

The Brighton Aquarium Mystery

Braving the dust kicked up by horses, the incessant lines of omnibus, hansoms and delivery carts converging upon the junction at Old Steine, Marine Parade and Madeira Drive, cross over the main thoroughfare from the aquarium and due east, beside the beach, one finds a convenient little chalet-styled ticket office with a tiled roof presiding over a platform. The Volks Electrical Seaside Railway operates from here, although I believe an extension is up and running from Banjo Groyne to Rottingdean, a terribly fangled double-decker contraption supported on long wheeled stilts that run along the seabed. We shall not concern ourselves with that.

In this narrative I intend to refer only to the Volks electric rail cars that, with great regularity, trundle back and forth along the seafront. The line passes beneath the land end of the suspension chain pier further up where the steam packets depart and follows along beside Madeira Drive.

I well recall it was the height of summer, very warm and sunny in Brighton. Holmes and I were staying at the Grand in Kings Road facing the sea, near the West Pier. That very evening to attend a popular touring play, *Riches to Rags — a Life of Profligacy* at the Theatre Royal put on by the impresario Langton Lovell and his business partner, the distinguished actor Charles Lemon, who were dear friends of ours and ran the Wimborne Theatre in Drury Lane for a number of years.

On that particular morning, a little before eleven, we ventured forth from the entrance hall foyer beneath the ornate glass and iron hotel porch when a chubby, most distinguished-looking fellow with a flowing white beard came dashing after us, grabbing Mr Sherlock Holmes's sleeve most fervently.

'Gracious heavens,' he puffed, trying to

compose himself. 'One thousand guineas, name your fee, sir — a calamity, an infamy. My name, sir, is Mr Wilfred Nathaniel Watters. I am chairman of the well-established jewellers C.W. Clarke and Co. You may be aware sir, our branches are all over the county.'

'Mr dear Mr Watters, calm yourself,' insisted my companion with a good deal of tact and sympathy. 'Let us adjourn back into the foyer out of this boiling sun. Your fee is really quite substantial but I'm afraid you have the advantage of me. If you just take this lounge sofa over here — that's it. Watson, fetch our friend a glass of iced cordial.'

'Dear me Mr Holmes,' he sighed, dabbing his brow with a handkerchief, all the while appearing considerably per-plexed. 'This calamity would happen today of all days. I am meant to attend my niece's wedding in Old Town at three o'clock this afternoon and it is to be such a jolly occasion, and now this wretched intrusion into my personal life — a robbery!'

'Ah, I at last comprehend,' answered

my colleague, settling himself beside the elderly gentleman and lighting a cigarette procured from his silver gilt case. 'One of your multitude of county shops has been burgled, I take it. If so, I really think the official force, the Brighton police, is your best course.'

'A smash and grab — really, Mr Holmes, this is a serious issue. A Mr Wilkes of our Lewes branch, an emissary of my most distinguished firm, was visiting Brighton this morning to meet up with one of our most valued clients, Lady Bradley, at her late Regency sea-front villa further up. Being inclined to a little sea air and exercise he decides to take a brisk stroll from the station along the seafront, pausing at an Esplanade café for a cup of tea and bun by way of refreshment. He remembers little save waking up upon a Volks railway car at Aquarium Halt, groggy and much confused as to why he should be there. Fortunately he was, before being taken to the general hospital for a checkup, able to furnish a police constable and an attending doctor with his impeccable business credentials, his purpose for being in Brighton, and the outrageous fact that a leather pouch previously safely confined to the inner pocket of his summer blazer was now unaccountably missing. The pouch, Mr Holmes, contained an enormous and valuable African diamond. It was only twenty minutes ago I was notified by the police. How fortuitous I count myself to be staying at the Grand when you yourself are, according to my morning newspaper, in town to attend tonight's performance of *Riches to Rags*, starring Charles Lemon at the Theatre Royal. For that I can at least be thankful.'

'Watson, gather your straw boater and cane,' said he getting up to leave. 'We must henceforth venture along the front to the Volks railway. Mr Watters, I suggest you return to your suite and make due preparations for your niece's wedding. I shall meanwhile look into this pressing matter for you and report back presently. Your generous fee is accepted, by the way.'

★　★　★

'Mrs Luff, I apologise profusely for intruding upon your ticket duties. Might I trouble you for your recollections, to clarify your initial impressions when Mr Wilkes and the other excursionists arrived back here at Aquarium Halt?'

'Well, sir, like I says to the constable, I was alerted by the driver of the incoming rail car, Mr Radcliffe, and a concerned family of five, that a certain gentleman had failed to get up from his seat. Suspecting an inebriated sot, I left my post in the capable hands of my junior ticket clerk Miss Carmody and hurried onto the platform. Boarding the car, it soon became evident that an individual with a pipe stuck in his mouth, whom I recognised from earlier, far from being drunk looked decidedly poorly — exasperated — because the man lost consciousness and was unable to respond to our entreaties and people were waiting to board the rail car. What more could us staff do than alert the police and summon a doctor?'

'With a positive outcome?'

'Certainly, for they managed to bring

him round and he explained his sorry predicament.'

'Now, if we might focus upon the gentleman's arrival at the Volks station earlier — he was alone or accompanied by others? Mrs Luff, this represents the most important part of my enquiry.'

'I recall a disabled man approaching the station halt in a wheeled chair. He was accompanied by two women and did appear somewhat 'gaga', a bit confused, not quite aware of what he was about, but like I says, many disabled folk come to our resort and at the time I saw nothing unusual or remarkable about a person in a wheeled chair.'

'And the women?'

'Eastenders without a doubt. Cockneys, the older woman, apparently his wife, proved most chatty, a fun sort of person, while the younger — Kitty was her name — remained smiling and fussing over, I supposed, her father's rug. Mrs Parker was very pleased to be holidaying in Brighton with her family and they were going on to the pub after. Well, the disabled gent attracted a good deal of sympathy and in no time other passengers managed to help him out of his wheelchair onto the platform and seated him very comfy alongside his adoring wife and daughter. But you will understand, gentlemen, I had no idea what was about to unfold.'

'Quite so, for a precious diamond was stolen, madam,' said Holmes gravely, 'and most audaciously.'

'Truth be told, I don't give a fig for that jewel,' exclaimed Mrs Luff heatedly, 'for it now appears, sir, that them brazen hussies scarpered, left him sat there like a dummy with a pipe thrust in his mouth for effect. Them so-called Parkers, the wife and daughter, were a complete pretence — bloomin' shameful, that's what I calls it!'

'That aside, were you aware of any distinguishing marks upon the two women? Crooked, uneven teeth, a scar, a mole, a squint, say, or a certain way of walking?'

'They both wore large floppy beach hats, sir, the wide brims drawn low over their eyes. But I'll vouch the younger of the pair had a large squarish chin with a dimple, a deep cleft. Heavy set, if you get my meaning.'

'You have been most edifying, Mrs Luff. From your ticket office window, did you perchance notice where these holiday tourists were headed, after disembarking, I mean?'

'A group of 'em crossed the road to visit the Aquarium, some headed up Old Steine to the Royal Pavilion.'

★ ★ ★

'Well,' said I, as we stood upon the Esplanade facing the road, breathing in the heady odour of fried onions and candy floss whilst the sun beat relentlessly down upon our brows; it was now barely noon and even this close to the beach, very hot indeed. 'What are we to make of this case of theft so far — apart from the fact two very clever and daring women are involved?'

'My dear Watson, we can safely deduce that our Mr Wilkes was closely followed from the station down Queens Road, past the clock-tower into West Street. He thereafter strides briskly along the prom and disappears into a café.'

'The ladies were aware of his identity all along?'

'Without a doubt. These women knew his face and were privy to the reason he was visiting Brighton in the first place.'

'Are we dealing with an organised criminal body? Who was it, I wonder, provided the necessary details concerning the delivery of the jewel?'

'I should personally ascribe to Wilkes's wife. Oh, don't look so flabbergasted; you know how women will gossip and share confidences with each other. I suspect, quite unawares she let slip to a close friend or neighbour her husband's important commission. We can of course discount Lady Bradley, what with her impeccable linage. Being a dowager duchess, she should be surrounded by a retinue of loyal and trusted servants who should never dream of divulging details of her personal life. Likewise, I consider it highly unlikely an informant exists within the jewellery firm of C.W. Clarke & Co.

No, Watson, I'd personally plumb for the wife — she is at the centre of this mischief, I'll warrant.'

'Unknowingly.'

'Quite, although, dear boy, one must always keep an open mind on such indiscretions.'

By diligent enquiry amongst waitresses and counter staff along the seafront, it took us less than ten minutes to locate the café Holmes suspected poor Mr Wilkes was abducted over a pot of tea and a bun.

'A pot of your strongest, and a round of crab and mayonnaise sandwiches for two, my good man,' said Holmes, leaning over the counter with a certain vulgar familiarity when placing our order. The owner, with his pugilist's nose and ears, warmed to my companion's effete manner, appearing not to notice he was about to be plied for information. 'You know, I had a dear old chum of mine come in here earlier. Striped blazer, prone to fits, epilepsy. I wonder if you recall whether he was with his wife?'

'Now you comes to mention it, sir, couple of cockney ladies wearin' big floppy sun 'ats so I couldn't really get a good look at their faces, come in 'ere earlier. I'se distinctly recall that gent you talk of h'occupying that table over by the winda. 'Where's that 'usband of mine, Alf Parker — gord it's so 'to ain't it,' the elder one remarked, sitting down beside 'im with a plonk, while the younger steps over 'ere sharpish and orders a pot of tea, like. 'Daddy gets ever so flustered,' she says giving me a wink, nodding in the direction of that same chap who had arrived on his tod and I'm pretty certain didn't know 'em from Adam. 'Bloomin' heat makes Pa come all over queer, don't mind if he gets a bit wobbly, we'll look after 'im.'

'And presumably they did just that?'

'Well, sir, brought a wheeled chair round the front h'an I even helps carry the poor fella outside 'an sticks 'im in it. Just like she says, 'ad a convulsive fit or similar. The wife pushed 'im along the esplanade quite brisk like. 'Appy as larks, them eastenders, ain't they. Stepney, I think she said they come from.'

'Well, Holmes, I admire their sheer

gall,' said I, polishing off the last sandwich and pouring us both another cup of Liptons strong, rusty, brown brew. 'To have managed to discreetly lace his tea with powders, to poison his system, incapacitate him was first-rate.'

'Well, old chap, the café, even at that hour of the day, would have been crowded with holidaymakers nattering away. No one should have noticed anything the least untoward.' Holmes puffed on his old briar-root pipe thoughtfully.

'So we have our café, powders administered surreptitiously, the brisk push in the wheelchair to Aquarium Halt and the consequent removal of that pouch during the journey up the beach and back.'

'Bravo, Watson!' said he, knocking out his pipe on his heel. 'Now I fear we are left with little to go on save the fact that some of the tourists, upon leaving the Volks station after disembarking, headed across the road to visit the Brighton Aquarium while others headed up Old Steine towards the Royal Pavilion.'

★　★　★

The main hall of the Aquarium is a most convivial public space lined with tanks housed beneath a splendidly vaulted ceiling. Above the front entrance is a large, distinctive clock adorned by a copper steeple, turned a greenish hue from long exposure to salty sea air.

Preceded by a group of punters, we paid our coin and entered the spacious hall to begin our tour of the aquatic tanks. The first time visitor marvels at the sheer variety of sea creatures on display. However, not all the myriad species of fish and marine life were of an exotic tropical turn; some came from our own coastal waters, lakes and rivers and appeared equally colourful and attractively scaled and finned.

Further along, we were alerted by a sudden skirmish of attendants busily consulting amongst themselves, due to what turned out to be something of an event, for a terribly big carp, a true giant, presently lay flat on its side, perfectly still and dead on the shingly bottom of a freshwater tank. As a backdrop, under water the waving pond weed, shoals of bream and sticklebacks, rocky outcrops strewn with many varieties of anemone, a Chinese bridge, groups of colourful, ornamental glass stones and King Neptune himself, a stream of bubbles issuing from his crowned head, his three-pronged trident held haughtily aloft, so placed to enrich our experience.

By now, a fair crowd had gathered to view the expired carp.

'Poor old Peter, one of our most venerable and aged fish. He had a good innings at any rate,' the tallest and most vocal of the attendants informed us.

'He really is a big fellow,' agreed a top-hatted gentleman stood just behind me, leaning on his cane. 'Have to stuff him and put him in a display case. I'm a keen angler and envy the chap who netted him. What I would give to catch a similar — a firm rod, sliding float, lug and rag-worm bait for that beauty.'

We all laughed heartily but the attendants remained serious and furrow-browed. 'Our scientific department shall dissect the carp, carry out various tests, all data painstakingly graphed and mathematically assessed.'

'A damnably famous blighter then!' said I.

The aquarium attendants proceeded to direct us swiftly to a sea-life tank across the way.

'Now, ladies and gentlemen, can I recommend a visit to view our Pholis Gunellus and Callionymus Lyra?'

★　★　★

Time was getting on and Holmes thought it prudent to return to the Grand and make known to the chairman Mr Watters our findings and suppositions. It would be a disservice if prior to his three o'clock appointment at his niece's wedding in Old Town we could not have the courtesy of calling on him.

Back at reception they informed us a Mr Wilkes had apparently been released from hospital and already gone up to the chairman's suite. Thus it was Holmes took me aside and gave me instructions for he wished the conversation to be steered onto a certain topic swiftly. I of course agreed to follow his cue and no sooner were we shown by the house-boy onto the cool and sunny hotel veranda where Mr Wilfred Nathaniel Watters and young Wilkes, a pensive chap, bronzed of feature and wearing a pair of round spectacles sat on lounge chairs drinking coffee than I exclaimed in a loud, trashy way, flinging my straw boater over the side of the veranda with a flourish for good measure, 'Women, you know I have seldom encountered so many beautiful ladies as upon the Brighton Esplanade. I am quite fallen in love with six beauties already today!'

'Ha ha,' my colleague tittered caustically as pre-arranged downstairs in the lobby. 'We have our chinless wonders of course, but you know I do so loathe those ladies with big chins, like Mr Punch. Do you not agree, Mr Wilkes, a large dimpled chin on a woman is particularly ugly?'

'Damn your impertinence,' he thundered, rising up from his seat to strike my companion. 'You disgust me, Holmes. Women are the most wise and gentlest of creatures. A large chin is no distraction. By your crass, insensitive remarks I assume you are a woman hater, sir.'

'Stay your hand,' said I, darting forward, seizing the rightly irate young jeweller firmly by the shoulder before settling him down once more into his lounger.

'Holmes only meant to reach the crux of this damnably impressive jewel robbery in as short a time as possible. No offence intended.'

'Now, Wilkes,' continued my colleague, his relentless questioning, his search for the truth undiminished. 'Who is she, who is this lady whose honour you defend so admirably, so loyally? Is it your wife? If so, I must be brutally frank. My opinion is that in a moment of indiscretion it was she who spilled the beans about your Brighton trip, providing others with the wherewithal to launch a spectacular robbery.'

'Not my wife, Mr Holmes, rather the daughters of her best friend Mrs Dent. Although I know them only from afar, I can verify Amelia and Connie Dent share this characteristic of the large cleft chin you allude to. My wife mentioned Connie now lives in Kemptown above an antiques shop.'

'Connie — is she a student? Does she work in Brighton?'

'She is certainly bright and, I am told by my wife, has taken a temporary summer job as an attendant at the Brighton Aquarium, hoping to learn about marine life and go on to university to study.'

'By Jove, we have it, Watson. What confounded nerve.'

'I fear you find me out of my depth, Mr Holmes,' chuckled the elderly chairman, aware of his maritime pun, placing down his coffee cup and getting up to leave. 'But I am damned impressed, sir, by your evident grasp upon the matter. Wilkes will tell you, I had a Brighton policeman up here earlier, an Inspector Gibbs, a slow witted and slouchy fellow who did not exactly fill me with confidence regarding the successful retrieval of my African jewel. I trust there is now a line of enquiry open to you and your colleague

Doctor Watson here. Well, I must be off to my niece's wedding in Old Town.'

* * *

The conclusion to our quest might appear at first oddly understated. I, Holmes and young Mr Wilkes took refuge in an omnibus shelter along Old Steine with a good view of the Aquarium. At a quarter past six, a young lady emerged pulling behind her a wickerwork shopping basket upon wheels possessing India rubber tyres. Wilkes quickly confirmed this was indeed Connie Dent, her chin being, it is true, pronounced and dimpled although I hasten to add she was exceedingly pretty in appearance, blonde and wearing a fashionable ostrich plumed hat, bodice and long, flouncy skirt.

Coming along Old Steine in the opposite direction were observed two very determined and equally pretty women who strode purposefully, the elder looking very satisfied and content with life. Crossing the road, they waved gaily at Connie, who waved enthusiastically back, a wide grin of recognition on her face.

'Why, gracious, it's Mrs Dent and Amelia!' ejaculated our young companion, about to wave and call out. 'How surprising. I must go and say hello. Allow me to introduce the ladies to you, Mr Holmes, Doctor Watson.'

'Not for the present. Have a care, if you please, Mr Wilkes,' begged my companion, insisting on no account should we draw attention to ourselves.

'Do you wish to press charges, else involve your firm in a court case, by the way?' he added as an afterthought, his wan, hawk-like features alive both with expectancy and some amusement.

'What on earth are you implying? Press charges, you say — against whom?'

'To have the regular police become involved — quickly man, your lady friends shall each most assuredly receive lengthy prison sentences. The trio will, I'll wager, spend many a long year oakum picking. The decision entirely rests with you. We shall have the African diamond safely in our possession presently. Thereafter I strongly advise you to continue your brisk walk along the Brighton front and pay a belated call on Lady Bradley, who shall be livid by now.'

'Mrs Dent, you infer, talking with my wife happened quite by chance to learn of my visit to Brighton and its purpose, thereafter planning with her daughters to abduct me from the Esplanade Café, steal the diamond and make money from the venture.'

'Wearing disguises, adopting a cockney accent and chirpy mannerisms, Mrs Dent and Amelia conspired to drug your tea. On the plus side one really must applaud such cleverness and daring, but on the other hand you, Mr Wilkes, were I fear severely incommoded and risked a damning reprimand from your chairman — even losing your position.'

'Drat and blast,' said he, considering his scanty options. 'Is there a way forward Holmes, avoiding Mrs Dent and her daughters' embarrassment and criminal prosecution? And my darling wife — I'd hate 'Beany' to be caught up in any of this.'

'Indeed, but upon your shoulders be it.

I propose our artifice is to make you out to be the forgetful sort, a simple matter of temporarily misplacing the pouch. It turns out you had the dratted diamond in your trouser pocket all along. I had demanded this afternoon a thorough search of your clothing and we found the blessed thing in amongst your loose change, a risible enough explanation that a child of ten could see through, but it will suffice to appease your chairman for now. Leave myself and Doctor Watson to apply ourselves to the hasty retrieval of your diamond. You meanwhile, Wilkes, head for that Corner Hotel and stay put until we arrive. There's a dining area, I believe. No word about the truth of this matter must ever emerge. When next you encounter Mrs Dent, or her pretty daughters, you must behave as naturally as possible and watch your temper. No inkling of your knowledge of their involvement in this morning's robbery must be allowed to surface.'

'I understand, Mr Holmes. I shall be more careful in future not to discuss the firm's business with my wife. I should not, however, wish Mrs Dent or Amelia and Connie to go to prison for a long stretch.'

'Most commendable, but the ladies are about to get their knuckles firmly rapped. Now, Watson, are you game to implement my little pre-arranged scheme without further delay?'

'Ready and willing, old chap,' said I.

'By the by, keep an eye out for constables. Excellent, I see they have paused before an omnibus stop. Our chance has arrived. No policemen in sight.'

We rapidly gained on Mrs Dent and her daughters and my colleague, using all his considerable dexterity and dancing footwork inherited from his time spent in the ring, managed not only to bump into Connie, but toppled over her wheeled shopping basket as well, causing it to spill out a large fairly bulky bundle onto the sunny pavement, whereupon I managed, without fumbling, to seize the newspaper-wrapped parcel — sloppy to the touch and fairly leaking, which being surprisingly weighty I was careful to hold securely with both hands.

So we were away, leaving Mrs Dent and her daughters stood staring at the now empty, overturned basket trolley, no doubt presuming us to be a couple of dandified petty thieves after their shopping.

The simple strategy worked! Thus, losing no time, we took advantage of a convenient alley that led us out onto Poole Valley, where were Brill's Bathhouse and a most prestigious bun shop, but more importantly a convenient bolthole, a tradesmen's entrance round the side of the Corner Hotel.

We hastened through swing doors to the dining restaurant and kitchens where the culinary chef was summoned and appeared delighted when we produced a very large and appetising freshwater carp.

The enormous fish was laid flat upon the kitchen slab and knives sharpened. Alphonso, the head chef, expertly gutted the fish, making short work of its immense expanse of flesh.

'The fillets of freshwater carp are of course your province, my dear chef, to no doubt delight the palates of diners on this evening's menu. However, I insist upon staking my claim to this most excellent sparkler nestled in its gullet. Watson, be a good fellow and dab it clean with that napkin, would you? Ah, Mr Wilkes, I believe this to be your firm's property. Off you go; Lady Bradley shall be expecting you, no doubt.'

★ ★ ★

The play at the Theatre Royal proved most enjoyable. Charles Lemon, taking the part of the bounder Sir Christopher Grimes, had him to a tee. His fall from grace eventually leading to a life of vagrancy until he meets Ida, a one-time maid of his, and they marry and prosper, portrayed magnificently and to great acclaim from the audience.

The following morning found us comfortably seated in the compartment of a fast passenger train shunting out of Brighton station beneath the sooty iron and glass canopy before heading along the main line to London Victoria, our tobacco pouches and bundle of newspapers to hand and Holmes in fine fettle, able to elaborate on certain highlights of our Brighton adventure, helping me to comprehend more clearly the various clues and circumstances that had led him to intercept that fine carp and complete the case in record time.

'You know, Watson,' said he, rhythmically knocking the stem of his old briar pipe on his knee as our train gathered pace, 'that deuced expired carp played upon my reasoning faculties no end. You might have observed a heap of pretty glass chunks upon the bed of the freshwater tank in the Aquarium hall, a decorative touch along with old Neptune bubbling away, the perfect hiding place to secrete a valuable gemstone. Working as an attendant presented the perfect opportunity for Connie Dent to receive the stolen goods from her mother and sister, and dispose of them for a day or two, allowing her kin to walk about Brighton, free in the knowledge that if a policeman happened to stop them for whatever reason they should not have the stolen

African jewel in their possession.

'By means of one of those long-handled grab-claw devices the attendants use, she was able to plant the diamond amongst that heap of ornamentation. By Jove, the gem when perceived underwater would appear just like any other piece of glass.'

'A clever means of concealment,' I agreed, lighting my pipe and settling back upon the cloth-covered seat. 'However, Peter the giant carp upset the applecart somewhat.'

'Oh indeed he did, dear fellow,' Holmes chuckled, filling up his old briar-root pipe, 'for working in close proximity to the tanks, behind the scenes, as it were, we must suppose it did not take Connie long to realise that her precious diamond had vanished from the pile of colourful glass chunks. She would have suspected some wretched fish of gobbling it up — but which one? Well, it soon became evident through its sudden demise: the giant carp who swam about in that same tank was where it now resided.'

'In the fish's gullet.'

'Just so, Watson, and no doubt a hasty

meeting was arranged and, over an ice cream cornet Mrs Dent decided upon a slightly more desperate tack.'

'Your determined if somewhat insensitive reference to big chins paid off handsomely. I confess quite honestly Holmes, I should never have considered a lady's chin of the slightest importance to the case.'

'By Jove, it's Mrs Luff at the Volks Railway ticket office we have to thank for offering us that smidgeon of leeway, allowing me to pursue the big chin issue. Now, Watson, I should prefer an hour or so to consult my *Times* and *Telegraph*, and catch up with all the London news. Pass me those Vestas, could you, old man, and then I shall light my pipe.'

7

The Church Conundrum

In the summer of '84, Holmes and I decided to visit the Kentish harbour town of Whitstable for the day, known for its distinctive weather-boarded houses and shingle beach. We took the train down that morning.

I recall vividly we had been in the town but a few hours and had searched out a café, chairs and wrought-iron round tables grouped outside, when a tall and most dapper gentleman possessing a sharp, angular face dressed in spats, frock coat and top hat asked in a clipped and courteous way if he might join us. We assented, and he forthwith ordered a tray of elevenses. His name, it turned out, was Mr Huntley and he was married and lived locally and the previous evening had of all things encountered a ghost, a singing nun at that, for, believe it or not, the third time!

'I admire your choice of gaspers, Mr Huntley. Might I trouble you for one of those untipped Capstans?

'Help yourself, dear boy, and you too, Doctor er . . . I didn't quite catch the name.'

'Watson,' said I leaning forward, dipping into the cigarette tin before pouring us another cup of tea.

'I regret despite my wife Helen's disapproval I continue to smoke some sixty cigarettes a day. Dear me, my tin appears rather depleted. I shall venture to my tobacconist shortly, but as I was saying, Mr Holmes, her madrigal sounds so heartfelt, so full of pathos one is almost moved to tears.'

'A soprano Italiano?'

'A contralto, actually. Now you, sir, strike me as musical. Do you sing or play the piano?'

'I play violin.'

'Oh, how charming. My little nephew is starting out. He attempts to play the violin, but Johnny will attack the strings as if he were sandpapering. More cream eclairs if you please, Irene,' he called out, waving at the chirpy waitress to gain her attention. 'Yes, as I was saying, my nephew will scrape away making such a confounded din.'

'So, we have our singing ghost, and she is a nun. Pray, I cannot bear the suspense, Huntley. How and where did you first encounter her? You've seen her three times, by Jove, that's surely something of a record!'

'My house is next door to the church, an old rectory in fact, and looks directly onto the tidy churchyard. It is my routine of a warm summer's evening, as near as dammit at quarter past eight, to fling open my French windows, play my musical box upon the sideboard, and thence take a turn around my garden to enjoy the call of eventide birdsong, the church clock striking the quarter and like as not admire the lovely flowers planted out by myself and Helen.'

'And your wife no doubt accompanies you on these walks?'

'Helen it so happens is away, staying

with our daughter for a fortnight in Beckenham.'

'Might I suggest the close proximity of the churchyard leaves one surely open to fleeting impressions, for example the shadows of birds flying across the lawn as the sun goes down? Might that be misappropriated for a spectre?'

'You, Mr Holmes, are most astute, and I'm pretty sure you are right. However, my singing nun, whom you will recall I have seen on three occasions in the last week and a half, is a most composed vision of loveliness. I see her, I grant you, only fleetingly.

'Where does her ghost supposedly appear?'

'Upon the churchyard path, used invariably as a short cut, very close to a tomb, the last resting place of Sir Thomas Cavendish. There one moment, gone the next as ghosts are supposed to do.'

'At eventide?'

'Just so, the light beginning to fade. Her exquisite singing begins but a short time later. You can hear it from the direction of the stained glass window.'

'Whereabouts inside the church, I wonder?'

'The choir stalls, the sacristy, hard to say. It seems to me one instant she is a ghost upon the path, the next a disembodied voice.'

'Dear me. Excuse my prying, but for how long do you usually take a stroll?'

'Maybe five, sometimes ten minutes. It varies. But now I insist on referring you to a tatty little two-penny pamphlet I purchased some time ago from a second-hand book emporium in Margate, Church & Parish, by A. W. Fleming, M.A. Oxon. I have it here upon my person — 'A Short History of Whitstable.'

'Bravo! Might I relieve you of that last cigarette, Huntley? I'm absolutely riveted by your story so far. Have you a housekeeper, by the way?'

'Minnie does for us, cooks and cleans and so forth, but as I was saying, I have before me a very interesting chapter relating to the history of the church, and I must read it to you, or at least give you a flavour. We must go back to medieval England, follow?'

'I do.'

'Well, it appears of all the coincidences, our parish church is built upon an ancient Kentish priory of St Celia of Avignon, an order if you will and, by Henry, here I see spelled out before my very eyes as clear as day upon page thirty-one —

'*Abess bricked up behind convent wall on account of carrying on with a certain suspected warlock, Sir Thomas Cavendish, outside convent when the moon was full.*

'What it also states here on page thirty-two which ties in wonderfully with my recent experience is that, '*her angelic voice could be heard singing sweetly madrigals of the romantic variety for at least three days and nights till she was no more.*''

'Mr Huntley, I must warn you in the plainest terms, it is my view, and I have had much experience in these matters, being a consulting detective by profession, that you are to be shortly burgled.'

'Burgled? You have the advantage of me, sir. I am no city banker or financial speculator. I worked for a number of years as a family solicitor in Whitstable and put a bit by. But robbery? Rob me of what?'

'Be that as it may, I cannot but perceive you have become infatuated by your singing nun — fallen in love with her voice. Perfectly harmless in ordinary circumstances but, Mr Huntley, I say very dire if a criminal interest lies at the heart of this charade when your attention is deliberately diverted and your house left unattended.'

* * *

While we drank the remainder of our tea at the Harbour Street Café, Mr Huntley proposed, considering my colleague's obvious concern, we return to his house, an old eighteenth-century rectory in Whitstable that he leased from the Church of England Diocese.

'My housekeeper Minnie shall be more than happy to lay out another couple of places for lunch.'

That afternoon I confess was spent primarily trying to wrack our host's brains as to whether he actually possessed anything, anything at all of great monetary value in the house. But no, he explained succinctly, there was no safe, no old master in oils hanging up in one of the rooms, no bounty of silver plate displayed in a glass case — not even a stash of banknotes hidden under the mattress.

'Helen has a little jewellery kept in a box on her dressing table — earrings and brooches and various necklaces but more of a sentimental value than worth,' he mentioned by way of passing. 'Much of it paste, which in some cases she prefers.'

'Legal papers,' suggested my colleague, believing he had hit on something. 'Do you possess any incriminating legal document of value to some long ago dodgy client on your roster?'

'I dealt mainly in matters pertaining to deeds, bills of sale and wills, Mr Holmes, very little criminal court work. Anyhow, all my paraphernalia was passed onto the new firm when they purchased my old solicitor's practice — nothing of a legal nature is stored here.'

'Your housekeeper's hours are what, exactly?'

'Well, Minnie works from 7am to 7pm generally.'

'And you inform us your wife is at present staying with your daughter in Beckenham, therefore we can conjecture because you remain in the house alone more often than not of an evening, this makes your home more susceptible to burglary.'

'Well, Helen shall be returning on Sunday.'

'So our robbery, if it is to take place, will be planned for the next few days.'

'Although flattered by your evident concern for my homely possessions, Mr Holmes, this so-called burglary remains somewhat speculative, a fiction in my mind at least. I cannot work up any enthusiasm for it. More whisky, gentlemen?'

Accompanied by the clock ticking upon the mantel shelf, we sat snugly before the homely hearth in the sunny drawing room. Mr Huntley, as open and friendly as could be, informed us of his long and happy marriage to Helen, and spoke further of his varied social life.

'For many years now my wife Helen and I have been fond of acting in amateur theatricals. There is a crowd of us in Whitstable. We've put on a fair number of productions, comedy, farces mostly. I mean, the critics are so-so, but we do try to entertain. It's more of a winter thing, really.'

'Treading the boards must be most rewarding,' said I, knocking my pipe upon the brass fender, whilst glancing at the rectory garden as seen from the French windows, the colourful flowers, the well weathered clay brick wall bordering the churchyard supporting climbing roses and a variety of fruit saplings, a neatly mowed and rollered lawn drenched in the warmth of a perfect summer's afternoon.

'You meet here at your house — here at the rectory?' enquired Holmes, puffing on his briar-root pipe, avidly searching through a vast pile of old hoarded newspapers, the Kentish Times and the Whitstable Echo amongst them, making notes with his propelling pencil.

'Yes, quite. We meet round each other's houses as a rule and enjoy ourselves immensely reading through lines, developing our parts. I am the official treasurer, Mr Ferris and his wife are at the helm, Philip and Constance are first-rate directors and producers. Tilly, Debs, Mrs Parks and Sid Hurst are regulars. Helen generally prefers parts like aunts and irascible old biddies, Mr Doughty and his wife Madgela do the sets, painting the backdrop and getting hold of props while their daughter is our prompt. Henry Chantry's our best leading man — for romantic roles, I mean.'

'When did you players last meet?'

'At my house, you mean? Oh, last March I think it was.'

'Mr Huntley, I know this may sound presumptuous, but would you do something for me?'

'Of course.'

'This evening, take your stroll around the garden as usual, fling wide the French windows, play that music box of yours, act at all times perfectly normal. Doctor Watson and I meanwhile will remain concealed. By the by, have you perchance that violin, your nephew's chosen instrument of torture? I'd very much like to tune the pegs and try it out.'

'My dear sir, please, I beg of you, produce a snatch of Beethoven's Violin Concerto. There, I have put in my request to the maestro. We can sing some snatches of Gilbert & Sullivan after. It so happens my nephew, when last visiting, left behind his violin case accidentally on purpose upstairs in one of the spare rooms. I shall fetch it at once.'

Later that day, as evening encroached, Mr Huntley in customary fashion flung wide the French windows and strode boldly out into the garden, the quietude of eventide broken only by the piercing notes of a songbird, the striking of the church clock.

The present church had stood on this site for nigh on eight hundred years, the nave being thirteenth-century built of flint from the local beach.

Holmes and I kept a vigilant watch

from the drawing room, that ancient tomb, the last resting place of Sir Thomas Cavendish of special focus.

The light had begun to fade, and remarkably we were witness to a figure that appeared to rise eerily from behind the ivy festooned tomb. I saw Mr Huntley, like us, suddenly aware of this devout nun quietly at prayer, dart across the lawn, leaning over the garden wall. Alas, by then she had vanished. However, in the meantime we were both wary of another person shifting perceptively from behind an immense profusion of bushes growing quite near to the house, before ducking back into the shadows. I should judge our intruder to be a tall, fairly well-built man intent upon keeping the rectory under close scrutiny.

'The idea being, Watson, that while Mr Huntley's attention is occupied, he creeps inside the house and steals whatever it is he's after before disappearing out the front door. Simple as could be if he can pull it off. But observe, our intruder hesitates,' whispered my friend from behind the curtain.

'But how on earth did she disappear? How did she do it, Holmes?' said I at a complete loss.

We were in for a further surprise, for presently the most beautiful voice, a contralto of immense power and diction, began to sing her lovelorn interpretation of a medieval madrigal. Holmes snatched the violin and instantly began to accompany her.

'Now I shall really put the cat amongst the pigeons, Watson,' he laughed, sweeping his bow across the fretboard and producing stirring melancholy notes as expertly as any professional. Hearing herself being accompanied on the violin caused our not too ghostly nun's voice to waver. I detected a hesitation, which of course was exactly what my friend intended. The singing abruptly curtailed, Holmes accordingly ceased his playing of the violin and we waited for Mr Huntley to return to the drawing room. Our host stepped back through the French windows.

'Not a ghost after all,' said I.

'Perhaps not; but Mr Holmes, your violin accompaniment was very listenable.'

'But the spectre,' I reiterated.

'You know, Doctor, Helen and I regularly travel up to London to attend concerts and recitals and I distinctly heard her voice waver — obviously the woman masquerading as our singing nun was surprised when the violin started up — most humanly, incidentally. Your method of unmasking the pretence was very clever.'

'My dear Huntley, if I am not much mistaken, Doctor Watson and I shall presently have the pleasure of meeting your contralto face to face and gain you her autograph. Now, we must make great haste along the main road that takes us round the other side of the church, which of course remains hitherto concealed from this vantage.'

'There is a timber lychgate and the beginnings of the path.'

'Just so, as you earlier inferred, which Mr Huntley used as a short cut. I must, I fear, strongly advise you to lock all windows and doors and await our return. Keep a firm lookout for an intruder we saw earlier lurking behind the bushes. You may yet catch a glimpse of him. Our contralto meanwhile should have had a chance to remove her makeup and don a change of clothing. I look forward very much to meeting her.'

Some five minutes forward, our brisk walk along the pavement took us beneath the timber lychgate and up the path towards the church. Coming directly towards us was a very pretty young lady, slim and petite, wheeling her bicycle, its sulphur headlamp aglow.

'Good evening,' she said gaily, giving her shiny bicycle bell a sharp 'ping-ping' and pausing for a chat. 'The church looks so lovely at this time of day, don't you agree?'

'I am told the interior, the sacristy, is of particular interest,' replied my colleague, raising his cloth cap before dashing across and undoing the straps of a canvas cycle pannier.

'So nosy of me. May I unstrap this flap and peer inside?'

'What do you think you are doing?' She sounded miffed.

'Ah, just as I thought,' Holmes replied shortly. 'A nun's habit neatly folded, even a box of theatrical greasepaint to hand. You know, Mr Huntley who lives at the old rectory is become most enamoured by a singing nun who purportedly haunts the church path at eventide and has a first-rate singing voice. Miss Felicity Lessing, both I and my colleague Doctor Watson are honoured to make the acquaintance of such a talented artiste. It was I who accompanied you on the violin earlier.'

'You know my name.'

'Why, certainly. The *Whitstable Herald* was full of that article announcing your recent engagement to the antiques dealer Henry Chantry. Fortunately Mr Huntley hoards his dailies in the coal scuttle, allowing me to catch up on Kentish news. Your professional career as a soloist caught my eye, as did the photograph illustrating the feature. My name, by the way, is Sherlock Holmes. I am a consulting detective from London. We are friends of Mr Huntley.'

'It was a protest,' she exclaimed, looking very demure but rather concerned all the same, gripping her handlebars tightly.

'Very well, a protest is as good an excuse as any — protesting against what, exactly?'

'The very real neglect by the council,' she pouted very prettily, even when frowning, 'to officially commemorate Sister Agnes and the medieval convent of St. Celia of Avignon, most deserving of a more prominent place in both the local history of the town of Whitstable and Kent in general. No plaque, not even a simple etched flower urn in church — disgraceful!'

'But a protest — surely that is a bit forthright,' I interrupted.

'All the bother of writing umpteen letters complaining to the Town Hall, visiting the council offices, all to no avail. So now I have decided upon a very personal statement. If not a protest exactly, more of a homage perhaps.'

'You are to marry Henry Chantry, I

take it — congratulations.' My companion smiled warmly, eager to change the nature of the conversation.

'Next July,' she beamed. Obviously we had hit upon a topic that pleased her more than prying into her ghostly antics.

'Might I and my companion trouble you for an autograph, Miss Lessing? I have my pocket book at the ready.'

'You are too kind. Your violin playing was really quite good,' she laughed. 'It was my idea to dress up as a nun — to reverently pray at the tomb of Sir Thomas Cavendish before passing into the church to sing a madrigal. I am very partial to early music. You may have learnt of the abbess's shocking fate.'

'To be bricked up alive, yes, one sympathises — the madrigal singing of course. Goodnight, Miss Lessing; we mustn't keep you any longer. I'm sure you want to get home. It's been a pleasure to have met you.'

'Goodnight gentlemen,' she called out, running along before mounting her bicycle.

Holmes seemed ebullient as we strode

briskly back along the main road to the rectory.

'Haha, by Jove, Watson, that's a cool and calculating young madam if ever there was one. She managed to worm her way out of betraying the slightest hint of her involvement in this scurrilous enterprise. But I'll warrant that's the last we ever see or hear of our singing nun. My unsubtle mention of the words 'consulting detective' have put paid to any further burglary attempts, I think. Oh, and that fellow we saw skulking round by the bushes — Henry Chantry shall likewise be cautioned.'

'That leading actor is involved?' said I incredulously. 'One of the Whitstable players?'

'The same. An antiques dealer, Watson, who runs a harbour shop in Whitstable. He is the centre of this web of deception and even purloined the services of his fiancee very usefully to act and sing. He must have spied something at one of the players' meetings held at the house.'

'But surely this object, presumably a rare antique, must be of extraordinary value to merit such careful planning?'

'If only, my dear Watson, we had an inkling of what the dratted thing actually is, I'd be happier. But so far, I am at a total loss.'

★   ★   ★

Early the next morning, the sun high in the clearest blue sky and a beautiful day in prospect, the Kentish town of Whitstable would profit by the fine spell of hot, sunny weather, the harbour side no doubt that morning crowded with fishing boats bobbing on the sheen of twinkling, sunlit water, having earlier landed their sacks full of oysters harvested since Roman times.

Striking a match to his pipe after an excellent breakfast, Holmes directed that we venture next door to the churchyard and examine the aforementioned venerable old table top tomb whence Miss Lessing made her remarkable appearance and even more astonishing vanishing act the previous evening.

'I shall not offer too tedious an

explanation,' said my colleague, puffing on his short pipe, tearing up the path dressed in his long grey travelling cloak and cloth cap. 'Safe to say the Kent coast is, and was, notorious for smuggling; and as I was to discover when I went out for a stroll at daybreak, our church across the way once proved a useful place for storing contraband, the parson no doubt more than happy to accept his quota of excise free brandy and tobacco as generous payment for his allowing an ingenious network of tunnels to be excavated, the tunnels eventually converging beneath the church aisle, a unique trap door incorporated, and as we shall see, Watson, a very cleverly conceived one at that!'

Not long after, removing a precisely chiselled-out slab from the side of the Cavendish tomb, for the most part concealed by encroaching clumps of ivy, there was just enough room for us to crawl inside, and thereafter we found ourselves in a very narrow vault with stone steps leading down to a tunnel entrance hewn into the flint rock. No aged coffins or skeletal remains did I see

— plenty of spiders and cobwebs though. Lighting a stub of candle, Holmes led the way; and although stooping very low, moving forward in a very confined space, we eventually reached the end of the gloomy passage carved into chalk, and I observed a set of steps leading steeply upwards.

'My dear Watson, and you too, Huntley, as you will no doubt be aware, we find ourselves standing beneath the church aisle. Up there you can see a finely chiselled crack running round a hexagonal piece of masonry. From what I deduced earlier, beyond this point the burrowed tunnel divides and in olden times would have led eventually to a concealed opening somewhere along the beach, but that does not concern us for now.'

'Good gracious, Holmes, I see a glimmer of light round the edges of that slab,' I exclaimed, gazing up, much impressed with our underground tour so far.

'That is the smugglers' exit from the tunnel. I shall just remove these stout timber supports. That's it, Watson, shove with all your might, push hard with your hands and up'll go that dashed ingenious trap-door.'

Amazingly we were soon able to poke our heads out from the gap, to see the church interior and the encaustic tiles leading up the centre aisle, stretching along by the pews toward the dark oak carved rood screen, the choir stalls and the altar, above which was a magnificent arched window. Bars of sunlight streamed through the leaded and stained glass panels. The smugglers' most clever effect, however, was undoubtedly to have made use of their trapdoor created from a carved and incised horizontal monument placed along the aisle and walked over by countless parishioners over the years.

'Remarkable,' said I, full of admiration for my colleague's line of reasoning. 'That certainly helps explain how our singing nun, Miss Lessing, was able to disappear so quickly and start singing in church.'

'And, you know, I picked this up from the floor of the tunnel earlier, my dear Watson.'

'Why, it's a child's toy, a spinning top.'

'Thus we can easily surmise that children knew of the secret tunnels and often played games down here. Might one of those children have been a little girl, later to become Miss Lessing, our talented contralto? Hence her knowledge of how to gain entrance to Sir Thomas Cavendish's old tomb and down into this, I am certain, one of the most splendid examples of smugglers' tunnels in Kent.'

★　★　★

Upon returning to Mr Huntley's house, Holmes brushed his shoes on the hall mat and, about to casually sling his silver-topped cane in amongst a crowd of umbrellas and stout walking sticks jammed into a bulbous, knee-high, rather cracked and dirty-looking vase, hesitated.

'Why are you stooding there like a blessed statue, glaring at that old vase?' I asked, removing my tweed cloth cap and hanging it up.

'One of a pair; the other vase is used to catch rainwater. We have a leak in the attic, you know,' Mr Huntley remarked.

'Good gracious!' my colleague exclaimed, kneeling reverently before the undistinguished cheap replica pottery, caressing the lacquer finish with long, bony outstretched fingers.

'I must have seen literally hundreds of those things, mass produced tat, bearing Chinese brush-style transfers,' said I.

'That dish — the one your housekeeper uses to feed the cat placed on a sheet of newspaper in the kitchen, similar decorative style, wouldn't you agree, Huntley?'

'I suppose the style is similar, my dear Holmes. Funnily enough, Chantry of all people enquired after them, offered me ten shillings for the pair but we stood firm and despite an increased offer of four pounds would not part with the cat dish or the old vases for the world, for they belonged to Helen's grandmother. Stick your cane inside the dratted thing and have done.'

'Mr Huntley, prepare yourself for a shock, for this vase, one of a pair, and that cat dish you erroneously take to be cheap and cheerful china, may indeed be genuine Ming — very rare and priceless porcelain! You must contact a representative of Sotheby's at once, my dear fellow.'

'Helen will be pleased,' the old chap expostulated with a grin. Thereafter we all trooped into the sunny drawing room to enjoy a glass of sherry before sitting and relaxing in the garden, for we had an hour or so to spare before we caught our passenger train from Whitstable Town station thence to Canterbury on the South Eastern railway and back to London that morning.

I can report the 'old Chinese tat' was indeed the genuine article from the Ming Dynasty and, I believe, Helen Huntley gave most of the substantial proceeds from the record sale at Sotheby's away to her favourite charities, including giving a donation to next door's restoration fund, so the vicar could at long last re-lead and fix that leaky roof.

8

The Gordon Square Case

The first week in December, Mrs Lodesley, who lived over by Regents Park, came dashing into our rooms in some state of agitation. A harsh and persistent frost had settled overnight and when I awoke my bedroom was chilly with a layer of ice crystals formed upon the window. Seeking warmth and thinking only of an appetising breakfast, I hastened to our front sitting room in my dressing gown, only to find Mr Sherlock Holmes, already dressed and immaculately groomed, deep in dispute with that same lady whose late husband had been a considerable force in City banking and Holmes had assisted in some fraud case. She lived at that most prestigious terraced address at the southern end of Regents Park.

'Your dog is really not within my province, Mrs Lodesley. A local policeman or else a park attendant is your best shot to trace the whereabouts of your missing pet. I have only limited time and resources.'

'I tried, I tried! I tell you Mr Holmes, I've tried everything. I was taking my Scotch terrier for her usual walk in the park when she slipped her lead.'

'Understood,' sighed my colleague, giving me a withering glance before settling back in his armchair to smoke and read the newspaper.

Warming my hands before the blaze in the hearth, I felt mounting annoyance with his indifferent attitude. Where was the sense of urgency? How could anyone not feel sympathetic towards this poor lady, her whole world just now shaken to the core? I believe at that instant she would have offered Holmes half a million in sterling to get her dog back. I exaggerate, of course, but it was piteous to witness her plight and not be able to offer much save kindly platitudes.

'I shall walk back with you, Mrs Lodesley. We can retrace your route across the park. Maybe someone will remember seeing your Scotch terrier in the gardens. Have you some important case then to attend to this morning, Holmes?' said I, rather tartly.

'I tried, Doctor Watson, I really tried,' Mrs Lodesley again insisted before bursting into tears. I did my best to console the woman, settling her down upon the basket chair closest to the fire, serving her a cup of coffee and plumping the cushions.

'Mrs Lodesley,' asked my friend from behind his *Daily Telegraph*, 'if I may be so bold, what was that piece of paper you were clutching so fervently when you entered the room?'

'Oh, I forgot.' She dabbed her swollen eyes with my proffered hanky. 'Mrs Merrit wrote me a message, my next-door neighbour, you know. How fast she attains her handwriting, scribbling loops, abstract jottings on a pad with her pencil that eventually turn into a fairly readable script. I was desperate, you see, anxious to find out where my dog has got to so sought 'their' help.'

'By 'their' I presume you refer to dead

people?' said my companion, puffing on his pipe with total disinterest.

'Enlightened angels, high begotten guides I refer to sir, not re-animated corpses,' she answered, a trifle hotly, misunderstanding my friend's comments to be a criticism. She hastily passed across her note so that Holmes could better peruse its contents.

'Well, it appears plain enough. What do you make of these Egyptian hieroglyphics, Watson? I confess I am unable to translate, however.'

'Just that,' said I, getting up and passing the single sheet of paper back to Mrs Lodesley, careful not to be insensitive and unwittingly cast some off-the-cuff disparaging remark about mediums or spirits. 'Egyptian hieroglyphics? Did Mrs Merrit offer any clue to its meaning?' I asked guardedly, helping myself to more ham and egg, glancing out of the window at the frosty slate roofs and smoking chimney pots of the houses opposite. 'Presumably she possesses a gift for spirit writing, an ability to convene with the dead.'

'This ancient language of the Nile was entirely new to her, Doctor. Mrs Merrit confessed she had never encountered such picture symbols before in her long mediumship.'

'A pity. What can one do when faced with such an unsurpassable barrier? Now, if the message were written in plain English, we might be able to proceed.'

'Well, we could venture to the British Museum,' I suggested, by now bordering on becoming infuriated. 'They have a Department of Egyptology, I believe. Are you really so busy and occupied at present on a case, Holmes, not to spare a morning or so to help Mrs Lodesley out?'

'Oh, very well.' My companion, chucking his newspaper aside, leaned over and replaced his long cherry wood pipe back in the rack. 'Professor Neal is the head of department and I have not spoken to him in quite a while. Our baffling little line of Egyptian hieroglyphics shall brook some amusement anyhow. Now Mrs Lodesley, you and your absentee Scotch terrier have our full and undivided attention for the morning.'

Thus it was upon that bright, crisp morning, not yet ten of the clock, a static chilliness resilient in the air, we summoned a four-wheeler and, bound for the British Museum with Mrs Lodesley, huddled anxiously in her furs, we quietly pondered the mystery of Mrs Merrit's spirit writing.

Just after the crossroads to Bloomsbury Street, we paid our cabman his fare and made straight away up the steps of the museum, heading for the Department of Egyptology.

Professor Neal, in charge of the wealth of Egyptian artefacts and sarcophagi in Rooms 62-3 upon the upper floor, was delighted to see Holmes, who at this juncture of his career was regarded as something of a celebrity in certain intimate circles of London academia, and directed us into his office, alive with all the clutter of a head of department. My colleague was not long in getting to the crux of the matter, showing Neal the scrap of paper. I confess quite candidly I was amazed when we actually got a serious measured response and were not laughed out of the premises.

'The line of hieroglyphics is genuine and refers to the joys of owning pets, in this case a dog, and the masters wish the dog should be embalmed and join him in the afterlife — not uncommon. King Sett's tomb at Abydos springs to mind. His favourite hound being regarded as sacred and mystical was, after being poisoned, embalmed and wrapped in linen before being placed at the feet of the king inside the coffin.'

'Have you an example of these pet burials we could look at?' asked Holmes.

'We do, but the rooms are at present closed for renovation. Old Griffin has a very splendid mummy case at his house containing the wrapped, embalmed remains of a pet dog and its owner, a wealthy cloth merchant called Elsaff.'

'Sir Alexander Griffin, the respected Egyptologist and archaeologist so acclaimed for his digs at the Naquada sites of Qau El-Kebir and Matmar, that hoard of bracelets, beads of gold, carved hounds and lapis lazuli was surely worth a fortune, much of the treasure now on display here at the museum,' remarked Holmes.

'Yes, we were very fortunate — old Griffin's proved a great ally. The days of his great pioneering digs are over of course, but at eighty-six he's as mentally astute as ever, very friendly and always approachable, even though I hear he's in poor health. He made a great study of mummified pets and has even written a book on the subject. You'd best pop round and see him, Holmes, and show him this scrap of paper. He will be able to decipher and offer a better translation. Gordon Square, I've got his address somewhere.'

★　★　★

One block north of Russell Square, once in Bloomsbury, under lowering dark grey skies that threatened sleet or snow, our cab trotted to a standstill outside a very handsome Georgian residence and we lost no time in raising the servants. The bell-pull clanged and not long after we were met upon the step by the senior housekeeper who was wringing her hands and appeared most distressed upon some matter.

'Is Professor Griffin at home, perchance?' enquired my companion civilly. 'We have come quite informally on a matter pertaining to his mummy case.'

'I'm afraid Professor Griffin has passed away sir; we have yet even to inform the undertaker, let alone his many friends and colleagues.'

'I am a doctor,' said I. 'Would you like me to verify the cause of death? I can at least put your household at rest concerning certain medical aspects.'

'His own personal physician from Harley Street shall be calling presently, but what harm can there be in an impromptu specialist opinion? I myself suspect old age alone was responsible for my dear master's demise. Perhaps you will confirm that, Doctor? Professor Griffin, although mentally alert at eighty-six, was in failing health since suffering his stroke last month. He could speak in barely a whisper but his words were jumbled and his eyesight deteriorating. Do come in out of the cold, all of you. Please take a seat in the hall, madam. Gentlemen, step this way, he is in here.'

In that darkened, comfortably furnished room, curtains drawn out of respect, the cowering corpse sat stiff and dead before the fireplace, the deceased, pasty-skinned and fragile wearing a quilted smoking jacket and matching tasselled cap stared ahead with mouth agape, surprised beyond measure his life's work should be curtailed so abruptly, so finally, so irrefutably.

I carried out an examination of the old gentleman, but Holmes chose not to stay in the sitting room and retreated back into the hall to join Mrs Lodesley. I was of course attended at all times by the rather formidable black-clad housekeeper Mrs Ellingham — she that hovered behind me, and watched my every move. After giving my prognosis that in every way agreed with her own — natural death caused from heart failure — I was surprised to discover upon quitting the

Gordon Square mansion and heading back out into the wintry cold that in a very short space of time Holmes had managed to establish many discrepancies which he conveyed with great glee and enthusiasm to Mrs Lodesley and me as we rattled along in our four-wheeler, journeying our way back to regents Park to search for that same lady's missing dog.

'You naturally observed the chair, Watson; that is of the most critical importance.'

'What chair?'

'The chair old Griffin was sitting on, of course!'

'Well, it was of carved oak.'

'And . . . '

'Ran on casters.'

'Bravo! I shall provide a more succinct and detailed analysis. The chair in fact, Mrs Lodesley, was a swivel chair of the type that normally sits behind a study desk. You will note a sturdy oak piece with a revolving hub, carved arm rests and leather studded back — office furniture. You were also I trust aware of the deceased Egyptologist's posture, dear boy? The right hand in particular.'

'The arm was stretched out, certainly,' I admitted, remembering the gnarled, stiffened hand clutching out at something.

'You will therefore recall the ink smudged third finger?'

'You infer Professor Griffin was holding a quill pen engaged in work of some kind — writing notes for example. I've no argument with that, Holmes, although he was not sat at his study desk, was he!'

'He most certainly was, Watson, that is prior to him being wheeled hastily across the hall into the sitting room by a very worried second party hoping to revive the old gentleman by placing him better before the more lively fire of the sitting room than the practically extinct coals in the hearth of the study.'

'So he was working.'

'He was at the time scribbling this most excellent jumble of nonsense, Watson. The hour was late, the servants and that housekeeper, Miss Ellingham, abed. I conjecture old Griffin had agreed to meet with an American, most likely — who, I have no idea, and was engaged in communicating something of importance when he quite abruptly conked out. The resident mummy case by the way had, I observed, been opened and the bound relics of the mummified dog and owner tampered with, shifted roughly about.'

'An American? How on earth do you deduce that, Holmes?' I asked with a frown.

'Two concise pieces of evidence emerged. I noticed for instance upon the corner of the study desk someone had knocked out the ashes from their pipe. A very distinct make — a corn cob, I might add, with a small, well-burnt bowl, an array of corn husk fibres mingled with the pile of ash. The coarse, rich mixture of tobacco smoke, the aroma of which still clung about the room, was clearly 'Olde Mayflower', a brand uncommon to Britain's tobacconists. Another clue — a very valuable Egyptian dish had, despite its rarity and great age, been rather thoughtlessly used as a spittoon.'

'But you were only in that room for a

few minutes,' enjoined Mrs Lodesley, full of admiration for my companion's flare and audacity.

'Enough time to glean much useful data. While you, Doctor, were busy prodding and probing the corpse and that hawk-eyed housekeeper's attention occupied, I had meanwhile nipped across the hall and made a brief examination of the study. Sure enough I did come across this scrap of nonsensical directions upon the desk atop of the blotter. Make of it what you will. Mrs Lodesley, let's hear your pennyworth. It'll take your mind off your dog.

'Well, Mr Holmes, written in a shaky hand it says simply *'the B.W.S. is by my oath hidden in th* — .' The writing abruptly veers off and we have blotches of ink. 'B.W.S.' What in heaven's name does that refer to?'

'The quill pen had been dropped on the floor, I saw it for myself. Ah, here we are at the park. We shall leave our little puzzling 'B.W.S.' note for another time. Watson, Mrs Lodesley's dog must be our foremost concern for now.'

I can report that during our extensive walk around the park, even taking in the edge of the zoo and the canal, Holmes remarked that the matter of dead Egyptian pets placed in sarcophagi might be worth developing. Was, he proposed to Mrs Lodesley, her beloved dog in fact trapped inside some park hut or beneath the bandstand? The bandstand proved a dud, but taking yet another stroll around Queen Mary's Gardens, we spied in the distance on the grass a typical tea and ices open-fronted refreshment hut on wheels, left out of season during the winter with the metal shutter closed down and padlocked.

On closer inspection, hopes were raised for it appeared the severe ground frost had caused the planking, which was so thick the dog's barking would be muffled, to expand, thus the kiosk door was wedged tight. Holmes and myself managed to wrench it open and there inside we found the little terrier whining and scratching away with its paws.

What joy, what a wonderful reunion. I shall never forget dear Mrs Lodesley's cooings and endearments as she held her yapping pet once more in her arms. My colleague quickly deduced the dog must have got in through the partly open door when a passing well-meaning grounds man or park attendant closed it tight, not realising the errant animal was within.

But to return to the main feature of this adventure we must go back to our familiar lodgings whence the following week, the first snow of the year having fallen and settled leaving an inch or so speckled upon roof tops and pavements along Baker Street, we received a surprise visit one afternoon from a tall, strikingly handsome and cultured American, a gentleman of middle years staying in London for a period of time.

'Mr Holmes, my name is Brad Griffin. I'm a lawyer from New York. Although long estranged from my father, the much respected Egyptologist, I received a letter from him asking me to come over to England at once, for he had suffered a stroke and was in poor health. Our meeting was to be kept entirely secret, and no wonder — back in those days of glorious plunder for the empire when as an ambitious archaeologist he was still making a name for himself, he and his cronies robbed a royal grave. The stolen find being no less than Princess Aesculapius's necklet of precious stones presented to her by King Solomon on her marrying one of his sons. Priceless Mycenean and dug up in Nauplia. It should never have left the country and would be regarded as a national exhibit to be properly displayed in a museum. I think the old man felt guilty about his hoarding such a valuable relic, keeping it for himself to gloat over all these years.'

'You will not be aware of this, Mr Griffin, but Doctor Watson and I accompanied by a Mrs Lodesley called in to see your father informally on quite an unrelated matter upon the morning of his death. Neal of the British Museum was patently unaware of the serious nature of his illness and recommended him to us. Interestingly, I was drawn to form certain tantalising conclusions. Pray continue.'

'There was a scrap of paper; I've lost the confounded thing or a maid threw it out. I was staying at the Langham at the time and after wheeling my father into the sitting room, hoping to revive him and making a brief search of the downstairs rooms, I retired for the night back to my hotel.'

'And presumably that same note left on the study desk which I have here secreted in my pocket book had not the professor died would have revealed the precious necklet's whereabouts.'

'Hell, you're quick off the mark, but you're correct, and then allowed me to proceed with negotiations for its swift return to the rightful country of origin. What a damn shame the poor old guy died at the very moment he was about to write me where the necklet was hidden in the house. The stroke left my father unable to speak coherently, or in more than a jumbled fashion. However, he was just about able to put pen to paper. 'B.T.W.' incidentally refers to Blackthorn Walking Stick, the silver engraved handle unscrews with a neat compartment inside for the necklace to be placed for safekeeping. That much I do know.'

'Remarkable,' said I. 'That clever handled walking stick is a prize worth finding.'

'If only I knew where to find it! That's why I've come to see you Mr Holmes. I'm damned if I haven't looked close on everywhere in that Gordon Square house at Bloomsbury short of actually tearing up the floorboards. That night of the meeting I even opened up the mummy case and had a rummage round inside but discovered not a dime's worth. Now I'm officially staying at my pater's house in Gordon Square for the funeral and the will to be read, but despite offering a ten pound incentive to the servants and roping in Mrs Ellingham for a household search we found nothing.'

My companion stretched his long legs on the hearth rug and, refilling his old black clay with tobacco, offered the Persian slipper to our guest who instantly retrieved a well-appreciated if battered corncob pipe from his coat pocket and took advantage.

'Very well, Mr Griffin,' said he, lighting his own pipe with considerable panache, 'I and my colleague Doctor Watson should be willing to accompany you back to Gordon Square. Let us search out this Princess Aesculapius's necklet. Ha! If we managed to trace Mrs Lodesley's dog in the whole of Regents Park I see no reason why a valuable artefact should prove that elusive. Perhaps you would be good enough to write a list of the places already searched and a rough map of the downstairs rooms.'

'Very well, Mr Holmes. Say, I'm real honoured to be associated with London's foremost consulting detective. Just wait till I get back to the States and tell the fellows at my club.'

★   ★   ★

Our New York lawyer's unequivocal adulation of Holmes, although pleasing to behold, was a trifle premature. Brad Griffin was no doubt aware of my colleague's considerable fame both here and abroad through reading the various published accounts of his cases, but dare I say this, he had yet, unlike for example Inspector Lestrade or young Hopkins of the Yard, to actually encounter his radical and controversial methods first hand. That morning I well concur both he and the retinue of servants' wits were sorely tested. After a long and intensive interview of each member of staff in the kitchen, which seemed to drag on for hours, Sherlock Holmes began a slow and methodical search of the lower rooms; some time later he exclaimed to all and sundry towing along in his wake, 'I shall require a shotgun.' He lit his briar-root pipe and began pacing back and forth scowling at the walls and ceiling of the drawing room. 'Ladies, cotton wool to be placed in your ears thus,' he directed the servants.

'Do you intend to cause damage, placing the structure of this Georgian town house in peril, Mr Holmes?' enquired a horrified Mrs Ellingham, doubting his very sanity.

'I do. The recovery of the blackthorn walking stick is paramount. All costs including my expenses will be met. Ah, Mr Griffin, you have found a suitable weapon — voila! Be good enough to draw back both hammers, old chap. Mrs Ellingham, you are clearly certain the painters and decoraters were last here in August?'

'I have already gone over this with you umpteen times, sir. You interrogated us in the kitchen. I reiterate, the walls in the drawing room were re-papered, the ceiling and surrounds attended to by painters and plasterers. Professor Griffin oversaw the work.'

'Just so. Now close the door and stand outside, all of you ladies. Watson, and you too Mr Griffin, remain. Somewhere in this new decoration lies a weakness, a flaw. Let us lose no time in finding it!'

Holmes aimed the shotgun ceiling-wards and fired. Such was the loudness of the explosive blast in that enclosed space of the drawing room that one of the windows blew out — and the trembling cut-glass chandelier clinked and chimed for a long time after. The shock wave, the intense reverberation shaking the room, proved highly effective in loosening a section of cornice along one edge of the ceiling, a hail of plaster and dust and fragments of mock Georgian moulded grapes entwined with oak leaves showering onto the carpet.

But there was something else which came crashing down — a walking stick with a silver unscrewable handle that had been cleverly concealed in the hollow of the length of cornice running round the top of the far wall.

Brad rushed across the room, kicking aside loose shards of fallen plaster before seizing the blackthorn walking stick in both hands and shaking it vigorously about. Gracious, one could hear stones rattling, clinking against each other inside the hollowed-out handle.

'Unscrew it — unscrew it!' Holmes exclaimed.

Sure enough, once the silver engraved handle was twisted anti-clockwise, inside was found the most exquisite piece of ancient Mycenaean jewellery to rival any on display at the British Museum. Princess Aesculapius's necklet was gloriously found.

9

A Woman Scorned

While I write at my desk, the year being 1897, curtains drawn, globe lamps brightly alight for it is winter, and dark and crisp and frosty outside, a fire crackling in the grate to provide us with a good deal of warmth and cheeriness, I have a mind to recount a little adventure, a rather intriguing one at that, but it begins plainly enough. I well recall upon a dismal night at around ten of the clock, Inspector Bradstreet came calling. He retrieved from a leather Gladstone bag a group of trinkets, which he laid carefully upon a small polished table beside Holmes's armchair. There was a ladies' wristwatch with leather strap, a lock of hair, grey and silvery, and a pair of innocuous round spectacles.

'Well, Mr Holmes, I should value your assessment of these pieces. They were sent in a package by normal post office channels to a Mr Daly of The Cedars in Henfield, and his sister Elma brought them in to a local police station claiming certain startling allegations. But before I elaborate further, let us hear what you have to say . . . '

My colleague, drawing out his magnifying lens from his dressing gown pocket, leaned over and minutely examined each item separately.

'By Jove, Bradstreet, I'm intrigued. The fact you have taken the trouble to visit our Baker Street digs upon such an inclement October evening — and at this hour besides — bodes well for my consulting practice indeed.'

'Firstly, our ladies' watch; you will observe, my dear Watson, the silver plate is much tarnished and worn away. Oxidation, this greenish deposit, indicates moisture, as does the state of the calf-leather watchstrap. Behind the misted watch face we have both rusted hour and second hands, the winding mechanism obviously seized.'

'Moisture, you say. Go on.'

'I shall stick my neck out, Inspector. Upon first impressions I judge the wristwatch to have simply been exposed to the elements for some time, dropped somewhere, on a pavement, in a garden, mislaid if you will. But taking these items as a whole . . . a very singular and separate possibility emerges.'

'Indeed, what the devil is that?' said I, sipping my whisky, aware of the wind and rain hammering against the window.

'Taken together, this braided lock of hair, the ladies' wristwatch and the spectacles, the wire frames showing every sign of corrosion, are to my mind the sort of personal effects one might expect to find inside a coffin, valued in life, placed there for sentimental reasons by the deceased's relatives, husband and so forth prior to the lid being sealed and screwed down, of course. I therefore surmise that for some unaccountable reason this group of inanimate objects that should by rights be buried six foot under, now find themselves in the land of the living once more. I rest my case.'

'A remarkable deduction,' blustered

Inspector Bradstreet, gulping down his whisky before lighting a proffered cigar. 'And very pertinent. I put it to you, gentlemen, that Elsa Daly, a considerable personage much respected for her charitable works and being a board member of Daly & Dukes India Rubber Moulding Company, a family concern, informed a desk duty sergeant at the police station that the wristwatch was responsible for her brother's sudden death, and she blames whoever posted these items as responsible for his utter fatal collapse at the breakfast table of the home shared by them in Henfield, for she is adamant that when her brother gazed upon the wristwatch for the first time he suffered a heart seizure.'

'And we can thus infer this lady, who is obviously highly intelligent and far from 'a hysteric', regards the sender as malicious, culpable of no less a crime than murder! Capital, capital! What a devious and subtle method if we could only but prove it. Not just a case of coincidence, else imagined infamy.'

'There was neither note nor letter of

explanation offered for the contents of the package. However, the post mark reveals it was sent from nearby Hurstpierpoint.'

'That is surely evidence of a criminal mind at work? We are obviously dealing with a burial of the last few months, Inspector. A decent interval is standard procedure before a grave is headstoned or turfed, else marble adornments added.'

'Thus, to dig down and achieve access to the coffin and replace soil just as before without alerting suspicion, less arduous.'

'Precisely.'

'But a single person?'

'With physically strong accomplices, not inconceivable.'

'But, Mr Holmes, I ask you, who in heavens name would go to all the bother of opening up a coffin just to retrieve a few trinkets, unless they were . . . '

'Insane! Not to the way of thinking of the person who devised this scheme and wished to cause Mr Daly harm. They see themselves as purposeful and wonderfully employed upon a righteous quest, but we have as yet no clue as to whom these grave items belonged.'

'I'm afraid that is the case, Mr Holmes, and I might add, to blame a ladies' wristwatch and braided lock of hair for causing a fellow's death is unheard of and as a deliberate means of murder. I'd think that would be very difficult, nigh on impossible to prove in a court of law.'

'Just so; nonetheless, like you, Bradstreet, I am dashed curious to discover whether there is indeed a sinister motive behind all this. We must interview Miss Daly further.'

'You and Doctor Watson will accompany me back to Henfield tomorrow morning then, Mr Holmes?'

'Certainly.'

'I see from our copy of Bradshaw's,' said I, pondering beneath the globe lamp our well-thumbed bible of train timetables and railway information, 'it indicates here we must first change at Horsham and thereafter take the Steyning line branch, Henfield being the next stop after Partridge Green.'

* * *

Our country route by train crossing the rivers, fields and meadow plains of the Adur valley, passing many little villages and hamlets besides, each with individual church and spire, brought us to the town of Henfield settled fairly close to Devils Dyke. From the station we firstly booked rooms at the nearby Railway Hotel and after dropping off our bags made haste upon a rainy, drizzly mid-morning towards The Cedars, a mock Tudor property, the house set back from the lane, enclosed by fine foliage and fruits, and we were invited in by Crawley, a maid-of-all-work who politely showed us into the comfy, low-beamed sitting room, a warming blaze crackling in the grate, both the comfortable furnishings and decor pleasing to behold.

Miss Daly got up and greeted us out of the cold and wet, briefly calling back Crawley to take some letters to the post box before settling us all down to sherry. Dressed conservatively, I should judge aged around two and forty, Miss Daly possessed a sharp nose and somewhat elfin features, both delicate and appealing. Her air of refinement and confidence no doubt through being a successful board member and at the helm of a large family concern fairly shone through. What with her gathered shock of blonde hair and brightly sparkling, intelligent eyes I felt instinctively there must be something genuine in what she had feared about her brother's death, and that such a formidable woman as this would never dream of wasting police time, or anyone else's for that matter.

'According to your medical practitioner Doctor Simms, whose surgery is in Little Dole, your brother suffered from a pulmonary disorder, a malady affecting the left ventricular chamber.'

'I am fully aware of that, Inspector, but our doctor was always confident that regular daily exercise, bicycling, walking and cutting down on his smoking would suffice to keep the worst symptoms at bay. Oh, what am I to make of it, gentlemen? My dear hardworking brother about to marmalade his toast, the rack and jar close to hand, we were I recall discussing over breakfast a play we had so much enjoyed at the Theatre Royal, and then Crawley our maid brings along a fresh pot of coffee and as usual places the morning post beside his plate, and within a couple of minutes he's lying expired on the carpet.'

'And you maintain, Miss Daly, that the ladies' wristwatch was directly responsible for his suffering a fatal seizure?'

'Laughton ripped open the brown paper package, assuming it was some gentlemen's scent he had ordered from Harrods. I know, because I saw him do it. Suddenly his whole body tensed, a look of what I can only describe as abject terror crossed his features; he snatched the watch, gazed at it incredulously for a moment and fell down dead. All of us in the house tried to revive him, Doctor Simms was summoned and arrived by horse and trap, but by that stage there was nothing any of us could do. I believed, and still do, that the items in that brown paper gentleman's package were deliberately sent through the post by a person who knew of his heart condition.'

'I do not wish to intrude further upon your grief,' said my colleague in a kindly way, 'but nevertheless I must relate my own findings.'

'Please do go on, Mr Holmes. Here, let me refill your sherry glass.'

'The lock of braided hair, the watch and the spectacles contained in the package were in all probability stolen from a coffin, and belonged to a deceased woman with whom your brother was romantically involved. The watch may even have been a gift from he to she and thus of great sentimental worth.'

'That is truly despicable — I had no idea. A coffin! Was it dug up?'

'The grave would have been excavated, certainly.'

'I should explain, Miss Daly,' said Inspector Bradstreet with a grimace, 'that that is the reason I have requested the services of Mr Sherlock Holmes, who is a consulting detective and may be able to help us at the Yard unravel your claim to find out whether a serious crime has in fact been committed. Did you perchance do as I requested and search your brother's personal effects for any photographs, notes, postcards else personal letters?'

'I have arranged a bundle here. I trust my late brother's correspondence shall be of some use.'

'Tell me, Miss Daly, was your brother ever married else involved in a long term relationship?' Holmes asked.

'Laughton was a lifelong bachelor and never married. He was from the age of fourteen principally committed to our family firm in Greater Dole and the overseeing of plantations abroad. Of course, since papa's death, as managing director he took the business to ever greater manufacturing output and profitability. Although dour and taciturn I suppose, being smart, well off and a handsome sort of chap he, inevitably formed relationships. I hasten to add, I was never privy to his personal love life and certainly he never brought his lady friends here to our home in Henfield. He was in possession of a London flat in Victoria, anyhow.'

'You have been most helpful, Miss Daly,' said Inspector Bradstreet, gathering his hat and getting up to leave. 'I repeat that I take this matter very seriously and you have my full assurance that we at the Yard shall do our utmost to seek out any wrongdoing, but I must emphasise that as yet we have no real evidence to set before a court and that the case rests on very slim pickings.'

'You and your colleagues, Inspector Bradstreet, have my fullest confidence. My brother's funeral is on Wednesday, and it will certainly be of great solace to know that his surprising death at the breakfast table, which in my view was deliberately provoked, will not be unquestioned.'

★ ★ ★

I should perhaps add that Inspector Bradstreet found himself very much out on a limb and so far as senior officials at the Yard were concerned, even when dealing with a lady of Miss Daly's obvious business pedigree and wealth, due to the level of supposition and lack of hard evidence, they were unwilling to devote much time nor resources to the death of Laughton Daly, a Henfield man, although of course we, that is Sherlock Holmes and myself, most certainly were! Indeed, my companion was convinced there was a case to be had.

Back at the Railway Hotel we had lunch and, fortified somewhat by an excellent bottle of French wine, went up to our rooms and began sifting through the bundle of correspondence Bradstreet had entrusted to our keeping. He himself had been called back to London upon some police matter.

It so happened quite early on we came across a sepia print photograph recently dated in printed ink upon the back in the form of a mark, an oval stamp bearing the name of the Henfield photographic shop — Quentin's. The posed portrait consisted of a backdrop of ferns and drapery with a pretty, bespectacled lady fashionably attired, smiling wistfully at the camera. Under strong magnification, just below her flounced cuff could be seen a slim wristwatch identical to the one in our possession at the hotel. The wire-framed spectacles also matched.

Without delay we visited the High Street and a Morris Quentin, being proprietor of the shop, furbished us with certain data pertaining to the photo-graphic plate and thus in no time we were able to locate without much difficulty the name and address of the lady in the picture, a local woman, Miss Joan Lupton of Number Four Church Lane. Flourish-ing a Bradleys cigarette while we walked briskly along the rainy high street towards the bakers on the corner, Holmes appeared elated.

Number 4 turned out to be a detached square, white three-storey house set on a leafy rise, with a good view of the parish church with its clock tower and distinc-tive rows of clipped yew hedge. A little town cemetery approached by spiked gates, well weathered and bleached grey, was just across the road from the church. Alas, we were to discover the house was deserted of occupancy. A 'For Sale' board was staked into the front lawn.

Peering in at any number of unwashed ground floor windows one was only able to glimpse empty, vacated rooms, bare boards, blank wallpaper, nail and screw marks, blanched areas from picture hangings, gas fitments removed, no furniture, the mantelpiece empty of homely adornments; nobody home.

We loitered about for a bit until fortunately a lady from next door wearing a long pleated black skirt and starched white blouse and jacket, slim and attractive with ginger hair flecked with grey gathered in a bun came to our rescue. Striding briskly up the paved path, she smiled sweetly.

'I am Miss Thornton, the housekeeper from next door. Are you interested in the property? I can give you directions if it's the agent you're after.'

'Most kind; tell me, ma'am, I wonder does a Miss Lupton live hereabouts?'

'This was her home until her death last year. It is up for sale, as you can see.'

'Dear me, she died?'

'After a short illness; my mistress was well acquainted with her, they often took tea together. Such sadness, but these things cannot be helped.'

'Did she perchance have a gentleman friend — Bailey, Daly, some such name?'

'From the window I could not help noticing them holding hands in the garden, visiting the summer house to read and relax. They looked a very handsome couple, but discreet always along Henfield High Street. Mr Daly lives up the road, I believe?'

'Quite. Well, thank you for your time Miss Thornton. I think I shall apply about this property. Where is that agent again?'

'Bristow & Kean, number forty two High Street, just past the ironmonger's and provision merchants on the left next to the pharmacy.'

Holmes, wishing to replenish his dwindling supply of tobacco, suggested we headed back to the High Street and, making casual conversation with a Mr Coombes the proprietor whilst he sorted out jars of graded tobacco mixtures, my colleague casually mentioned a Miss Joan Lupton. We were duly informed that same lady had passed away. 'A very nice hearse and procession, and good turn-out for the wake. Shame she died so sudden like,' he remarked, folding a paper bag.

'We met with a housekeeper from next door,' said I.

Genial and rotund, Mr Coombes with his walrus moustache and beady shrewd eyes, evidently a very knowledgeable local, wiped his hand on the front of his apron and frowned.

'Housekeeper? To whom do you refer, sir?'

'Why, a Miss Thornton with reddish hair, a lady wearing a black skirt, tall of stature, elegant, charming to talk to,' I emphasised.

'Tall and skinny redhead? That would be Mrs Pickering. She lives alone at present with her cats. Her husband Mortimer, a very pleasant sort, smoked I recall St. Bruno. A good darts player, went off to India doing a stint as a colonial policeman, so she said. Oh, must have been quite a while back. There's definitely no housekeeper, she does her own gardening, and my wife goes in to clean and cook from time to time. Mrs

Pickering prefers it that way. Has two devoted boys — twins, carrot tops — Fred and George. Great strapping lads over six foot three and strong as oxen. You see them occasionally mooching along the High Street, thick as thieves — when they are allowed out, that is, to visit their ma.'

'From school — are they educated far afield?' I enquired, making a purchase of a tin of cigarettes, putting some coins on the counter.

'From the asylum, sir — breech birth the pair of 'em, mental incompetents, live happily on the ward. It's called Cane Wood. Not dangerous, mark you. I mentioned the asylum but I do not mean the kind of violent lunatics that we hear about kept under lock and key, but patients cared for by orderlies, allowed free run of the grounds, very friendly and approachable.'

Holmes seized my arm in astonishment. Here then was an interesting line of enquiry: was Mrs Pickering in fact a 'scorned woman', the malicious sender of that package and quite possibly responsible for Miss Lupton's untimely, as described, 'sudden death'? Surely, having two physically strong sons who could have easily provided the necessary strength to excavate and rob Miss Lupton's grave implemented her in this affair!

The possibilities were not lost on either of us, so thanking Mr Coombes for his highly enlightening comments we hurried back along the High street and made haste to Church Lane.

We knocked repeatedly but could get no answer, thus seeking the side gate to Mrs Pickering's house we unlatched it and proceeded round the back. The place appeared locked up and no one about, but down the end of the long stretch of garden leading to a wooded clearing was a summer house. This took Holmes's interest and we trudged up the path to investigate. The rain had stopped and everywhere was lush and gleaming.

An old abandoned black pram had been left close to the steps and we were curious to peep inside. Amongst the waterlogged clutter were bobbins of cotton, bunched sprigs of, by now, mouldy heather wrapped in waxy paper and various samples of coloured twine and reels of ribbon, long faded and rotten.

'Now Holmes,' said I with a chuckle, 'this pram I perceive, using your methods, what with its seized-up tasselled hood and buckled wheels is, I'll wager, the property of a lucky heather lady, a gypsy who camped hereabouts in summer and I deduce upped and left, leaving her tinker wares for the magpies. Am I up to the mark?'

'Completely so. 'Old Gypsy Meg' it is then. Let's take a look inside the summer house, Watson, although I suspect with all this autumnal wind and rain of late hardly the place to linger very long.'

We ambled up the steps, our footsteps clumping on the boards, and entered the shelter. The gloom encroached upon us and it felt damp and unused. About to settle on the dovetailed bench and gaze out at the garden, it soon became abundantly clear we were not alone, and had a companion of sorts sat slap alongside us.

The owner of the black pram, in fact the gypsy woman, appeared to be somewhat skeletal and decomposed, smothered from head to foot in a gossamer shroud of cobwebs. Her calcified bones were home to scurrying spiders, busily checking their larder stash, finely spun cocoons trapping myriad insect life for future and present delectation.

Parting the cobwebs, upon closer inspection the skeletal remains were clothed in a black serge skirt and tough old buttoned moleskin jacket made threadbare and decayed from having sat there for so long. Over where the shoulders would have been was a moth-eaten and mildewed lacy shawl. The woman had been knitting at the time of her death for clutched between bony knuckle joints were a pair of needles enjoined to a rotted square of woollen knitting.

'Significant,' my colleague remarked, leaning across and plucking a gold-banded ring from one of the skeletal fingers.

'A death — even from natural causes,

must surely be counted as significant,' said I, eyeing Holmes curiously. 'As a matter of fact,' I emphasised, 'the death of anyone without friends or family to grieve, who dies alone and unnoticed, is certainly significant.'

'My dear chap, I refer to this gold ring, not the manner of death,' my colleague reprimanded me. 'Now pray let us consider the ring. What do you deduce?'

I snatched the gold band and examined it further over by the steps leading down to the garden where the light was better.

'I am surprised,' I remarked. 'This ring, Holmes, is both chunky and predominantly masculine, a male signet ring, and there is clearly etched by the jeweller into the agate stone the letters 'E.H.P'. Good Lord, Pickering?'

'This is surely the skeleton of her husband, dear boy. Not gone off to India but gone off to the hereafter, prompted no doubt by a liberal dose of arsenic or strychnine in his tea.'

'How deviously clever — leaving him to rot down like this, dressing him up as an old gypsy woman doing a spot of knitting.

The local police if notified about the death, decomposition being so far advanced, would see absolutely nothing suspicious and the body should be taken away and buried in an unmarked grave as a pauper.'

'Thus, we deduce Mrs Pickering wanted her husband out of the way so she could further nurture an affair and eventually marry Laughton Daly. However, her next door neighbour, the equally attractive and persistent Joan Lupton, caught his eye and the next thing, she's jilted, and her poor old husband murdered for nothing.'

'Bradstreet must be called upon to set about gaining the necessary Home Office permissions for an exhumation. Joan Lupton is most likely buried at that little town cemetery across the road, else at the old church graveyard.'

'You know, Watson, I am perfectly confident an autopsy on Miss Lupton's body shall reveal either arsenic or strychnine as the poisoning agent that did for her. Our skeletal friend here, alas I'm afraid only fit for anatomy classes . . . By

Jove, by Harry, I've a good idea where Mrs Pickering may have got to! Watson, have you your pocket edition of Bradshaw's handy — what the deuce is the time of the next train for London, I wonder!'

I frantically searched through my pockets, found the railway timetable book and thumbed through its pages. 'A good half hour, passenger service comes up from Steyning,' said I. 'Change at Horsham.'

'The woman must have panicked, lost her nerve. If we're not quick she'll escape the gallows, Watson.'

'London's where she's headed, anonymity amongst the masses. Great Scott! Once it is discovered her husband is no more in India than Timbuktu, unlike poor Joan Lupton murdered not for spite but as a mere convenience, it's the Old Bailey alright.'

'And to think Miss Lupton was wholly responsible for spoiling her plans of ensnaring Laughton Daly. Just as Mrs Pickering gets her claws into our hard-working wealthy businessman, why of all people her next-door neighbour Joan Lupton makes unforeseen advances and succeeds in usurping her romantic intentions.'

We approached the country station, quite near to our hotel in fact, and were greeted by a porter bearing a wicker cat basket in each hand, ashen-faced and evidently ordered to close the ticket hall and make the platforms out of bounds to those wishing to travel either to Horsham or Steyning.

'Station closed until further notice, gentlemen,' he said emphatically. 'Woman thrown herself on the line, in front of a passing goods train. I'm afraid you'll have to catch the omnibus along the High Street. We'll be shut for the foreseeable future.'

'Was she red-haired, a tall woman?'

'So sad, sir. It's Mrs Pickering. Why on earth she did it, I can't say. Wait, she dropped this . . .'

The fellow put down the cat baskets, the poor little furry black mites restless inside, and fumbled in his pocket, producing from his waistcoat a chain-linked gold locket inscribed on the reverse '*To Pixie from Laughton.*' Unclipping the cover, one could see a portrait of them taken together. 'Do you know — is that her husband, sir?'

'Most certainly not,' said I gruffly. 'You know, Holmes, perhaps it was for the best.' We strolled back across the road to the Railway Hotel.

'You're right, of course, my dear Watson,' said my companion, gazing up at the sky as rain began to pelt down, and we started to run for the shelter of the lobby.

'Later we can sift through that bundle of letters; there might be correspondence between Laughton Daly and Mrs Pickering useful as evidence.'

'Doubtful. Daly was very, very canny, discreet regarding his women friends. Remember, Watson, he never once introduced them to this sister, which I grant you is eccentric, although not entirely without precedence. By Jove, amatory passion, rivalry, jealousy, the three barbed prongs of the devil's trident — well I'm absolutely famished. Is that the dinner gong I hear?'

10

A View From Pinckney Street

The year that my colleague Mr Sherlock Holmes received his honorary degree from Harvard University bestowed by Harvard President Merle James Conant at the Tercentenary Theatre, found us across the Atlantic bearing up to an incredibly cold New England winter in Boston. I recall we had already visited Cambridge (Massachusetts) and taken a tour guided by Doctor Elliot Perkins, Master of Lowell House, seeing for ourselves the pines of Harvard Yard, Wadsworth House, University Hall, the Lamont Library, Blaschkas, the glass flowers and plants in the Agassiz Museum and many striking educational buildings besides.

In the meantime, back at our hotel, the city of Boston came calling in the form of Moreton T. Rockford, the Chairman of the immensely prestigious banking firm Rockford Associates, who for an unprecedented fee, after settling us beside a smart little red brick town house up Beacon Hill where in no time we were installed at No. 64 Pinckney Street, the Charles River flowing close to the lower end, requested Holmes spend some time investigating a fraud, most of which involved sifting through a stash of confidential papers and a box file of accounts invoices entrusted to him and did not require his presence on a daily basis at the bank. Identifying a forged document served at least to occupy his clever brain and stave off black moods and with a New England winter in progress we were housebound, for the most part anyhow.

Lounging in my rocking chair, a cleverly knocked together piece of Shaker furniture, I was in two minds about whether to pour myself a second mug of coffee from the enamel pot resting on the wood burner. My friend, I observed, entirely engrossed, puffing on his briar-root pipe, was stooped resolutely over a sheaf of papers with his magnifying lens, spreading out the documents that lent meaning to this bank fraud business upon the smooth top of the antique French polished table.

I gazed out of the purple glazed window, seeing the occasional muffled up pedestrian clinging to the rail, making their way precariously down the snowy hill. A very sleek and nifty looking sleigh tinkling bells, a 'cutter' I believe they are called locally in New England, whooshed past. Taking in this wintry scene, I was moreover intrigued to observe a brightly faced, rosy-cheeked young lad towing a small timber toboggan upon which were placed a neat stack of books. He appeared to be heading directly for our house, thus I hastened along the hall and upon opening the front door, took a deep draught of Boston's wintry, freezing cold air. It had snowed earlier and a white drift piled high on the step.

'You them Londoners from Baker Street?' The boy spoke with a youthful gaiety.

'We are,' I answered.

'Mister Sherwood Holmes lives 'ere, don't 'ee?'

'Sherlock, sonny, Sherlock Holmes, but indeed he does. No. 64.'

'You Mister Shylock?'

'No, but I'll willingly pass on a message.'

The boy pushed some gummy substance he was chewing to one side of his cheek before answering.

'Say, Mister — tell him an old guy called Hedonist Carr bin asking for him down at the Athenaeum Library Wants to see 'im, says it's real important — values your time an' all.'

'The 'Master of the Macabre' — *that* Hedonist Carr?' said I incredulously, my chest bursting with a rush of excitement at the mere mention of the author's name.

'Yep, the same. Why, you read his books? I like 'em lots, but Ma detests every word. She'd ban 'em, says reading the likes of Poe and Carr'll turn me into an axe murderer 'fore time I git to thirteen. Says I'll carve up my own grandmother an' bury her beneath the stoop.'

301

'I'm sure she's being playfully facetious,' I laughed, 'exaggerating somewhat.' Ruffling his hair, I pressed a shiny new dime into the palm of his woollen mitten. 'We'll get down to the Athenaeum right away.'

'Library looks onto the granary burying ground — can't miss it.'

'And grand good luck with your reading endeavours,' I called out after him as the boy, looking very pleased with himself, went on his way, dragging that toboggan of his with its runners scraping along the walkway.

The New England author Hedonist Carr, I should explain, at that time outsold Poe, Harriet Beecher Stowe, Mark Twain, Nathaniel Hawthorne and Melville by many millions with what critics on both sides of the Atlantic were wont to describe variously as novels of 'execrable garbage', 'macabre to the extreme', 'horribly good' and 'blood-soaked and grisly enough for the charnel house', which goaded the general public, myself included, to go out and purchase his books that I personally found always first-rate and entertaining. It turned out he resided in Louisburg Square where there is an oval-shaped iron fenced little garden bearing a stone carved figure of Columbus in its midst, although I only found this out later. But I digress.

At first, loath to quit his, I am certain, very able and exhaustive search for a forged document, my companion I suspect welcoming a less arduous diversion, at length gathered his stout fur-collared coat, deerstalker, galoshes and silver-topped cane and together we set off downhill.

★   ★   ★

We took the trolley-car to the front of Park Street Church and walked briskly from there, fresh flurries of snow and a sharp wind making it feel all the colder.

Darting through the doors of the Athenaeum Library, we made our tentative approach to the curved rosewood desk behind which presided a formidable, bespectacled lady librarian, no doubt an academic, wearing formal grey skirt and starched white blouse, eyeing us with the proper invested authority of a privately run institution founded by a number of subscribers in 1807. She bade us come hither.

'Can I help, gentlemen? Which floor do you require? The George Washington Exhibition is in the Trustees Room on the fourth. Were you specially invited by Doctor Willard Cogswell? A number of guests have already gone up,' said she politely.

'No,' I whispered in respectful tones, informing the librarian that a certain local New England author had requested our presence for an interview. She indicated, beyond the panelled reading room with its well-ordered books, spotless chairs and desks, long tables and marble busts displayed in wall niches, to a cosy nook where before a cheery coal fire we caught our first glimpse of a very plump and friendly-looking gentleman with long silvery hair, dressed from head to foot in black, who upon seeing us, walked us over, settling us in a pair of most excellent leather club chairs beside the fire.

'Be seated,' said he, his chubby face aglow with good cheer. 'I have an entire collection of your case accounts from *Lippincott's* monthly magazine bound in brocaded green vellum, and I am honoured to make the acquaintance of London's famous consulting detective and his no less worthy biographer.'

'It's a pleasure,' I answered, gripping the venerable scribe's outstretched lardy hand in mine, close to tears for in truth I had over the years devoured his many novels of horror and indeed possessed, under my bed, a tatty suitcase stuffed with many worn and much read yellow-back editions.

'You are familiar I take it with 'Old Ed', he enquired, relighting his corn-cobber with enthusiasm.

'Certainly,' Holmes replied with sombre reflection, retrieving his briar-root pipe and sealskin pouch from his coat pocket. 'Edgar Allan Poe, you refer to of course. I've read many of his works. *The Narrative of Arthur Gordon Pym of Nantucket*, his short novella. I found wanting and patchy, but his shorter fiction shows promise. *August Dupin* has some merit, I suppose.'

'Merit! Why, that little guy Poe practically invented the fictional detective. I knew him of course. A hopeless sot — any time I saw him in New York he was invariably drunk. Poe was a ferocious critic, you know, and never possessed a kindly or helpful word for any of my early novels. But his genius will one day be recognised, although he earnt little money from his writing when alive, and me a mere scribbler gets by very nicely.'

'You have the popular touch, Mr Carr,' said I. 'that's a rare enough gift in itself.'

I was, I recall at the time, grinning like a besotted puppy dog.

Over a lifetime's career, Carr must have become almost blasé about receiving similar praise and adulation for in no time he seemed distracted and even while I was eagerly waxing lyrical about his books was looking straight past me. In any event, I twisted round and there was a dormer window with a view into the main square. I observed a glass-sided hearse trotting through the churned-up snow while in the other direction on more compounded substance, a convoy of sleighs drawn by single nags swished across the square, bells jangling.

'Seems to me,' the writer muttered, peering inquisitively over my shoulder, 'that damn undertaker Kraal is our hometown Rasputin. How the women flock round him, charisma, charm, whatever you label such manly effervescence, he sure possesses that quality — an' him with that city funeral parlour and handling corpses day 'n night!'

'Quite,' said Holmes firmly, 'Mr Carr might I interpose as to why exactly you wished to . . .'

Barely were these words spoken by my companion than the old fellow's jowls quivered and a quantity of pipe ash spilled down his black waistcoat. Carr, with a look of admonition, stumped his ivory handled cane thrice upon the bare varnished floorboards and boomed in a loud, commanding voice, 'Say, call me Hedonist — all my friends do, please, gentlemen. You English are too damned formal. Let's cut Her Majesty the Queen

Vic's airs and graces for now, shall we?'

'Very well,' answered Holmes good-naturedly. 'Hedonist, why did you request this interview, given that Watson here is an enthusiastic consumer of those shilling shocker novels of yours back home and will shortly demand an autograph?'

'Most kind. Well, Sherlock, and you too, doc — I guess I should strike to the quick. Truth is I could use some of your expertise, your overview if you will. There's a new book I'm planning, non-fiction, an expose of sorts. Mark you, I've had my suspicions for a long while, oh yes, and I'll not be intimidated, nor side-lined. So help me, I'll make sure justice is done. It's all here in my head, see, clear as day, nothing committed to paper as yet, you understand — safer that way. I'll get to the finer details presently, but for now . . . '

Striking a match and lighting his pipe, Holmes became visibly agitated. 'I must caution such labours for they often have a habit of backfiring. For instance, if you be proved mistaken you open yourself to lengthy and painful litigation. If you slander someone, Mr Carr, you can be sued in a court of law for every cent you possess. Your reputation, your comfortable author's existence here in Boston, all threatened, your fortune much diminished by fearsome legal expenses. Is it, I put to you at your time of life, this noble quest to accomplish a somewhat precarious literary endeavour more often as not fuelled by some petty grudge, envy else a misguided sense of moral purpose, really worth it!'

'Most ably put, Sherlock, and I thank you for your considered apprehensions. However, I did not embark upon this mission of expose lightly. I have a top publisher's legal team in New York whose job is to keep me out of trouble and my long time agent Owen Mallet is the best. I say to you gentlemen yet again that despite risk, pecuniary or otherwise, justice will be done. My one aim all along has been to bring this sonofabitch to . . . '

At the time concerning myself filling my pipe with 'Auld Mayflower' tobacco, whilst simultaneously listening to Carr's pleasantly spoken New England burr, I was all of a sudden aware of a long drawn out sigh — a wheezing expulsion of air from the lung sacs, and glancing up was in time to witness the elderly shocker writer topple forward in his chair.

By his collapsed condition and the lack of response when my colleague Mr Sherlock Holmes shook the old fellow firmly by the shoulders, shouting for a nearby attendant to fetch a glass of brandy that instant, I was in no hesitation judging him to have breathed his last.

If readers imagine that this sudden death of a notable writer was deemed to be in any way remotely suspicious, they will alas, like Sherlock Holmes himself, be bitterly disappointed.

As a retired physician, I was first to examine the author's motionless figure slumped before the library fire and can vouch a deceased heart and the ravages of old age responsible for his death — simple as that — and this prognosis was backed up by the medical examiner Hank Streeter, who later informed us that Hedonist Carr had for some time been suffering from a faulty heart valve.

However, the timing of the death was, for us at least, frustrating, for I and my illustrious colleague were left with no clue as to whom exactly the writer intended to expose, nor, either, the nature of criminal intent involved. Being but visitors to Boston and knowing few people in the capital was not exactly helpful either.

★　★　★

We attended the author's funeral some days later and whilst the glass-sided hearse slowly proceeded from snow-bound Louisburg Square, followed by a sedate line of mourning coaches, pausing at the steepled church and universalist meeting house before heading up the hill to the cemetery, it was obvious that Hedonist Carr 'the Master of the Macabre' was held in great esteem by members of the public for the route was lined by a fair number of mourners.

Thus on that exposed hill awaiting its next assiduous topping of snow, we observed whilst Thomas Kraal stood proud as Attica overseeing the removal of the large hefty coffin from the rear of the hearse by his assistants, a late carriage draw up at the gates. It came to a halt and remained poised as it were, but no one stepped down nor could any hint of a visage be seen at the window, so it seemed to me this particularly reticent mourner chose to witness the internment discreetly from a distance, having no desire to join the rest of us crowding round the graveside.

But to elaborate, let me recall a queer incident that occurred halfway through prayers. We mourners stood huddled together shivering as a group, whereupon a tall, elegantly turned-out lady, her face concealed by a veil, rushed amongst us and attempted to ferociously seize the arm of the undertaker Thomas Kraal, who quickly stood back, avoiding her grasping hand.

'My fault, all my fault,' she cried at him bitterly. 'But you, you in whom I put my whole faith, you, sir, have left me misguided, piteously adrift. Oh, what have I done but got what I deserved — this terror unending!'

Alas, the sloping, uneven ground caused one of the heels of her dainty calfskin boots to skew awkwardly, as with arms flailing she nearly ended up toppling into the yawning mouth of the recently excavated grave, but was prevented from so doing by a rush of gallants, that is quick witted gentlemen, Nathaniel Hawthorne's grown son Julian amongst them, who I had been informed travelled down from Concord to attend, and it was they who managed to subdue this poor, distressed creature hurrying her away across the white carpeted landscape of partly sunken and crookedly angled headstones to that same mysterious carriage we noted earlier, waiting further down.

Holmes and myself, I hasten to add, were none the wiser as we first headed back down the hill as to the identity of the veiled lady, and it must be said the undertaker Thomas Kraal managed admirably to keep his composure for the remainder of the burial ceremony, apparently unruffled and maintaining outwardly at least an appearance of calm and affability.

Then came some enlightenment from the officiating minister, the Reverend Hartford, who sat in the same carriage as we, although rather pasty faced and sickly looking, a most affable and talkative individual.

'You know, gentlemen,' he remarked, taking a generous pinch of snuff, 'I've seen over the past month the emergence of an increasing number of veiled ladies who attend church just for the Sunday and say nothing to anyone, nor mix with my flock after service. I'd dread to think we have a secret mediumistic society in our midst. I mean, London's got the bug ain't it — levitation, table rapping, the planchette, all the rage I guess; but here in Boston, I pray not.'

'You were chatting with Hawthorne's son earlier. His father, Nathaniel, I recall wrote a novel entitled *The Blithedale Romance* which made much mention of a veiled lady,' said I.

'I never read it myself, Doctor Watson,' remarked the minister languidly, peering out of the carriage window. 'He tended to rather play up his Salem ancestry and makes much mention of witchcraft in his novels and shorter works, of which I disapprove.'

'By the by,' asked my colleague, pulling a rug further over his long legs, 'the veiled lady back at the cemetery, the one who tried to accost Thomas Kraal — any idea who she is?'

The minister stroked his cleft chin thoughtfully. 'Nancy Vandergaard, a wealthy Bostonian heiress.'

'Resident in a sanatorium, perhaps?'

'Great heavens, I should hope not! Her summer residence is one of the most exclusive mansions in Bellvue Avenue, Newport, and she keeps a house in Boston of course — and a host of secretaries and servants besides.'

'Do you perchance have any inkling as to the reason for her nervous rage?'

'My guess is as good as your, Mr Holmes — a rival for her misplaced affections, a falling-out, some silly carrying-on — women do get so intense, so passionate over a man they wish to ensnare, to possess utterly. I thank the

Lord I am a committed bachelor.'

My colleague laughed but his beady eyes either side of that great beaky nose were sly and calculating.

'Given that Thomas Kraal has a reputation as a lothario, something of a ladies' man, yet I cannot countenance a well-heeled Bostonian heiress involved in a tawdry affair with the owner of a funeral parlour. Although feasible, an assignation seems to me unlikely,' he sighed. 'I'd wager the cause of her passionate outburst was entirely unrelated. I think we can discount any romantic entanglement but she had it in for him alright, that much was clear!'

* * *

At half past six of the following evening, beneath the steady glow emitted from the ornate lantern bracketed outside our little red brick abode, a cutter sleigh drew up at Pinckney Street and I beheld from the front window a tall, exquisitely attired lady drop aside her whip, stepping nimbly down into the crisp snow and after

316

patting the pony, reassuring the beast, made haste across the walkway to our front door.

She wore a fashionable and very exclusive white mink coat and fur hat and, despite her veil, strode with considerable confidence, whereupon I opened the door to our surprise visitor.

'Mr Sherlock Holmes, the London consulting detective?'

'I am Doctor Watson, but pray allow me to take your winter furs, my dear. Step this way. Holmes is presently wracking his brains concerning a banking scam and will I am sure welcome lighter diversion.'

I confess quite candidly that I myself much welcomed this feminine diversion also. Her perfume, a divine fragrance, wafted in her wake about the front hall and, despite the covering veil I sensed a warm and charming personality lay concealed beneath, being thus doubly rewarded when once ensconced in our cosily lamp-lit parlour with its contrasting mix of Shaker and eighteenth-century French antique furnishings. She gracefully removed her veil and we were privileged to gaze upon her strikingly handsome features. My heart raced contemplating this blonde Bostonian beauty, and as I showed her to the cushioned divan she offered me a considered look, an earnest appraisal as to whether perhaps I could be entirely trusted.

'Miss Vandergaard, welcome,' said Holmes kindly. 'A glass of sherry, although I hear you eminently fashionable young ladies of Boston and Rhode Island prefer a 'gin sling', else bourbon on the rocks.'

'Nothing for me, thank you, Mr Holmes. Myself, I prefer not to touch the stuff.'

'Your wearing the veil adds a touch of flair — you become a woman of mystery.'

Miss Vandergaard gave a timid smile.

'I wear this veil out of respect for the late and much lamented writer Hedonist Carr; a personage, I confess, who loyally and in confidence tendered me advice some time past which I alas failed abysmally to heed and have as a consequence lived to pay a large price. It was his funeral only recently after all, a decent period of mourning is surely in order — where is the mystery in that?'

'Forgive me; I shall proceed to lighten our discourse somewhat by begging you a trifling favour.'

'Go ahead,' she laughed, sensing my companion's good humour.

'Those wonderfully beguiling ruby earrings you wear, might I closer inspect them? The settings appear very 'Regency' and stately.'

'The earrings were bequeathed me by my late mother. They are my favourites. Old English Cheapside silver and gem-stones, to be sure.'

My companion gently settled himself down on the divan beside Miss Vandergaard, allowing for her to tuck strands of blonde hair behind one ear. She was flattered, pleased with the attention. Pleased, that is, until her womanly intuition became suddenly aware that her entire face was being meticulously appraised, which naturally unsettled her.

Sensing he had been over intrusive,

Holmes took out his silver case and offered round cigarettes. I lit hers with a Vesta.

'Might I enquire the actual reason you chose to visit us this evening, Miss Vandergaard? As a consulting detective, if it is in my power to assist you in any way I will do so. My talents are at your disposal. Your impromptu visit concerns Thomas Kraal, I take it.'

The woman's eyes appeared bewildered, pleading. She shuddered.

'Him, yes, no. Oh, I meant to have such a heart to heart with you. I'd planned such a pow-wow in my head, you see, gentlemen, but now I'm actually here I would fain tell you the truth but cannot.'

'You argued, or at least you appeared to wish to confront the undertaker about some galling issue. Does it concern payment of large sums of money? Are you, perchance, being blackmailed? For that is I confess my own assumption. Miss Vandergaard, it is requisite that you give me some indication of your part in the affair.'

'Him, yes, yes — but no, not blackmail,

nothing like that. Pardon me, Mr Holmes, but I have to leave. I came here honestly hoping to enlighten you as to my predicament but it's no use, I must go at once. Forgive me — my fault, all my wretched fault.'

She wrung her hands. So pitiful to behold this attractive Bostonian heiress seize her veil and replace it, her countenance ravaged by some inner turmoil of conscience.

I did my utmost to pacify our visitor but to no avail. She allowed me at least to enfold her in voluptuous white furs and, thanking me profusely, Miss Vandergaard rushed into wintry Pinckney Street to board her waiting sleigh. I and my companion could hear the harness bells jangling way down the hill.

'Well,' said I, slumping in my rocker, nursing a stiff whisky. 'That's about as useless a half hour as we've ever spent, old man. If only she'd confided in us more, trusted us.'

'On the contrary; Miss Vandergaard, quite unwittingly it so happens, provided me with a host of excellent data. But firstly Watson, consider this old copy of the Atlantic Monthly. Let's see what you make of the picture spread. I ringed a particular photograph in red ink.'

Leaning forward I snatched the publication and gave it the greatest scrutiny. The article in question was self-explanatory, due to the pictures and captions. *'Miss Nancy Vandergaard, along with her pug dogs Winnie, Bess and Jerome, is seen showing the palatial interior of her mansion at 243 Bellevue Avenue in Newport, designed by architect Standford White.'*

'Look here, Holmes,' said I. 'There has clearly been an editorial error. The woman shown in this photograph is surely the mother. Our pretty visitor tonight is, I should say, six and twenty. The lady shown here, although similar of feature, must be five and forty.'

'My dear Watson,' said my erstwhile colleague, lighting a cigarette with the benevolent air of a patient teacher persevering with a rather dim-witted pupil. 'Do you recall my examining those earrings of hers rather closely?'

'I do. Your remarkable if uncharacteristic intimacy, the nearness of your face to hers, caused her certain consternation, her breathing quickened, I noticed that.'

'Excellent! Your observation does you great credit, although you saw none of the faint scarring I take it. Of course you didn't.'

'What I saw, my dear Holmes, and who amongst us men could forget, was a very pretty face.'

'Did it not strike you that her lips, particularly the lower, protruded somewhat, appeared over-inflated?'

'Sensuous and pouting is the more proper description,' I laughed. 'Why do you analyse so?'

'The loose folds of skin about the throat had been diminished. Did that allure you also?'

'What on earth are you driving at?'

Leaning back in his chair, Holmes appeared very grave and thoughtful. Staring a while at the rumbling wood-stove, he lit yet another cigarette.

'So, it has come to this,' he reflected dolefully. 'Now it appears they can actually embalm one before you're even dead. At least the Egyptians allowed a decent interval. I can hardly credit such audacity.'

'I'm not quite with you, old chap.'

'Let us return to the earrings,' said he seriously. 'Under close scrutiny it became clear to me that the frontal part of her head, that is from forehead to chin, had been subtly restructured. Just above the hairline I was astounded to see the skin stretched upward to allow for a smoother, younger appearance, reducing the lines of natural aging. I observed very faint, barely discernible scars where stitching had been applied. For instance, beneath the chin and pertaining to the throat, the pouches beneath her eyes so evident, so normal at her time of life somehow lessened. My dear boy, you only have to consult the periodical to witness the ordinary aging process to which we are all incidentally beholden. The actual age of Nancy Vandergaard, the lady we saw here tonight, is indeed five and forty if a day.'

'But that set-to on the hill at the funeral,' said I. 'I mean, from what you infer, I abhor the undertaker's back-room practice, yet clearly she has nothing to complain about, her countenance is duly enhanced. She looks younger than her years.' I gulped the remainder of my whisky. 'All this self-loathing, wringing of hands; what in the Lord's name has got into her?'

'By Jove, Watson, it's a case of crushed vanity, dear boy; dashed hopes. One can but conjecture that she learnt fairly recently from another wiser, more perceptive party that her new enhanced looks are but medically flawed and fast waning, which had never been the initial idea. This is what causes the turmoil, this dichotomy to rage within her breast, and yet she cannot adequately find it within herself to condemn the deceitful perpetrator, the one who promised a safe and sure procedure. That is why of course she visited us this evening, I'll warrant. Has the penny not dropped yet, Watson? That wise informant I mention is Hedonist Carr. The villain of the piece he wished to expose in his proposed book being none other save Thomas Kraal for malpractice.

The decent thing for us to do now is to the best of our ability finish off, to conclude that which the shocker and latter day writer of conscience actually intended. Thus tonight, under cover of darkness, we perform a necessary break-in. Pour us another glass of that first-rate Bourbon, dear boy, and pass over that pouch of 'Auld Mayflower' tobacco you've been hogging.'

★ ★ ★

Later that night, wrapped up fitfully but by no means impervious to dipping temperatures, Holmes and I set out on our quest. Beside the houses was an iron railing, useful for us inhabitants to hold onto when going up or down the hill in slippery conditions, employed also for tethering horses, and we clung to this like grim death. It was an icy night and we eventually crossed to the edge of the embankment at the bottom of the hill, upon the other side of which the Charles River flowed. The main road was deserted; no one was abroad, neither Hackney coach, sleighs or trolley-car in evidence, and we headed more stealthily into the city without meeting a soul. A Boston pictorial guide offered adequate directions, but it was still an hour or so before we reached the funeral parlour premises belonging to Thomas Kraal.

I checked my silver pocket watch. Here we were, about to perform a break-in. My nerves were on edge, Holmes employing his tried and trusted formula for springing the most stubborn lock — the humble yet wholly effective pipe-knife. Bent low to the keyhole, twisting and poking about until the mechanism gave a resounding click, the door creaked open and we crept inside.

By choosing the side entrance round by the stable block we avoided the reception rooms and coffin showroom, preferring to take our chances with the rooms at the back. Presumably coffins were conveyed through this door and slid on rollers into the back of the hearse for funerals.

Cautiously lighting a shaded oil lamp, we moved almost it felt like inch by inch between a group of coffins perched on trestles.

'This is the chapel of rest, Watson. Our nocturnal quest takes us, however, toward that thick velvet plush curtain on the far side with the boldly inscribed notice 'PRIVATE — MORTUARY DEPT' above. Be a good fellow and open my cigarette case, will you. Help yourself, yes. Let's light up, it's as damnably chilly in here as outside I fear.'

The curtain was deftly drawn aside; my friend shone the lamp beam about the tiled room. Glinting in the shadowy glow from the light reflected on the shiny surfaces were shelves of stoppered glass medical jars, with which as a doctor and one time student at Barts, I was well familiar. I confess the first occasion both of us took fright in that home for the dead was the instant we spied what floated inside these receptacles, for we were confronted by row upon row of pickled, cut away faces suspended in varying strengths of murky preservative solution. Women, men both old and young, and children thereby whose facial features resembled at best deflated India rubber masks, void of eyeballs and teeth.

'Well, don't look so perplexed, dear boy,' said Holmes, doing his best to compose himself after the initial shock. 'One must expect Kraal learned his craft by initial experimentation. Why, it appears even our writer friend Hedonist Carr failed to escape being facially scalped. See here the fleshy distinctive features reside in jar No. 32 where I'm pointing with my cane.'

'These insipid masks,' said I, 'heretofore severed by his, the mortician's, artful fingers from tissue, means many a body was committed for burial up at the cemetery not whole or entire — a despicable business.'

'I concur, and, my dear Watson, we can therefore take immense satisfaction in burning down the premises forthwith. Once we have removed the horses from the stable, that is, and settled them in the far field.'

'Burn the place down, Holmes! Are you mad?'

'I have an urgent requirement to see

Police Chief Gordon and the District Attorney. What quicker way to bring this business off than a town fire?'

'You'll not burn anything!' answered an angry voice from beyond the velvet plush curtain. 'This be my property, raised on my land. You'll be civil enough to move out of my embalming room to where I can see you better, gentlemen.'

'The facial remains in the jars accuse you,' said I haughtily.

'The faces in the jars greatly helped me learn my trade. As a trespasser, your moral rectitude does you credit, sir, but it struck me early on that my particular funerary line of trade left me uniquely placed to broaden my business interests. I am also aware of the little vanities women be so susceptible to. What harm can there be cutting about stiffs bound to rot under six feet of clay anyhow? However, movin' on — 'why am I here?' you fellas may well ask. Well, not to tend to the stiffs, that's for sure. I'm here on account of Hal Morgan 'cross the way who, bein' a goodly neighbour of mine saw a queer light movin' about and sent his son to alert me of criminal mischief. Lucky for some, but not you English, I guess.'

'Recalling no doubt this great capital's patriotic fervour during the Boston Tea Party, we need to talk, Mr Kraal.'

'No time. Why, I've got a pair of cheapskate pine caskets I'd be glad to part with fer free, and once I've shot you both dead that's where ya'll be layin' fer a long while, fellas.'

But while Thomas Kraal concerned himself with our imminent execution, totally distracted, five veiled shapes by means of the conveniently open side door entered the gloomy precincts of the Chapel of Rest, gliding amongst the gloating array of trestle coffins with barely a rustle, forming a committed procession. It appeared under the preternatural ambience of the moon; mayhap a visitation of shades from the hilltop were emboldened to create night time mischief.

Dainty on her feet and purposeful, the first, the leader, a very tall and lithe figure crept up behind the boorish undertaker.

'You are most kind to offer us one of

your cheap coffins, Mr Kraal, but I think a trifle prematurely. I should prefer to wait awhile. I'd rather fancy a lead-lined . . . '

My companion Mr Sherlock Holmes kept up a mildly sarcastic banter. Barely had Kraal raised his Colt revolver, about to squeeze the trigger and aiming at my chest, I being nearest, my heart counting the seconds I had left to live, when a finely bladed scalpel lashed through the darkness striking our Mr Kraal above the collar, at his fleshy, exposed neck. The blood spurts following reminded one of a bull ring in Malaga, but here at the downtown funeral home more than one conquistador was vying to weaken and subjugate the bull.

The broad shouldered, squat under-taker had barely a chance to fend off a second vicious assault delivered by another participant, this time from the front. A long-bladed scalpel was thrust through the gelatine-like substance of his left eye, causing Kraal to fall to his knees in an ever-widening pool of blood. Moaning and clutching his face, still more blows reigned down until he lay quite dead, sprawled out amongst the coffins he was so famous for supplying.

Thus the five veiled ladies hastily departed, their long skirts and winter fur coats rustling across the floor as they each headed for the stable yard.

Barely had the mysterious ladies left when Holmes thrust a carboy of formaldehyde spirit into my hands and together we began sprinkling preservative all about the place. Whilst I hurried to the stables and proceeded to lead the horses away to the safety of the field, my companion meanwhile struck a match and thereby began a chemical blaze of considerable force that quickly took hold. In fact, I recall by the time we arrived back at our little red brick house in Pinckney Street after walking up the hill, dawn was breaking and morning boating activities beginning on the Charles River.

While I lay comfortably abed in my upstairs room, still I heard quite distinctly the jangling bells of steam fire pumps, no doubt tearing across the city joining other machines converging else present at the scene of the by then, surely, utterly destroyed and smouldering remains of the funeral parlour.

★ ★ ★

The following morning we awoke later than planned and were eager to discuss the implications of the night before. Outside, it was a sunny blue sky and the snowy outlook reflected whiter than before.

'The affair, I grant you, is a complicated one,' admitted Holmes, settling down before the wood stove after he had consumed a hearty breakfast of steak and eggs and about to smoke the first pipe of the day.

I might add, a crucial letter had arrived that same morning from a Professor T.W. McCord, a lecturer at Harvard Medical School who had diligently answered a number of points put forward by Holmes in writing regarding radical surgery to the face. I shall not bore the reader here with medical jargon else long drawn out anatomical details, but, I hasten to add, it made disturbing reading.

In his view, and Professor McCord had extensive and first-hand experience of battlefield injury, making incisions, stretching facial skin into shape thus reducing aging lines posed something of a dilemma. Temporarily the initial surgery would perhaps hold up well, but in this age at least be only sustainable for six months or so whereupon the fleshy matter should collapse leaving the face terribly mutilated and deformed. He warned Holmes against any such procedure and thus was plainly spelt out the awful fate awaiting Nancy Vandergaard, of which she must surely have been made aware, and the other wealthy Rhode Island ladies foolhardy enough to place their looks and wellbeing in the hands of that unscrupulous undertaker Thomas Kraal.

My colleague, over a pipe full of 'Auld Mayflower' coarse tobacco, which had quite taken our fancy over the past fortnight while staying in Boston, surmised thus: 'My dear Watson, it is of course most likely these chastened women shall flee to Europe and thus live out their lives cloistered in a sympathetic convent far away from the public gaze.'

I objected, finding this stark prediction too depressing. I offered my own more optimistic alternative: 'Is it not more likely, Holmes, these New England ladies shall form a commune and buy up an attractive villa in Italy, else a sunny French chateau isolated by an immense tract of land and live secluded in the relative luxury surrounded by devoted servants?'

We agreed to differ and thereby was brought a fitting conclusion our efforts to validate the late shocker writer Hedonist Carr's worthy efforts to stamp out this folly of woman's vanity.

Perhaps in any case pursuing Thomas Kraal was a trifle more energetic than the rather low-key Boston banking scam, for which a line of altered accounts and a falsified signature were eventually discovered by my dear friend's skilled use of the magnifying lens searching amongst minutiae.

11

The Call of Rowland Shalford

After a fortnight of sustained activity
— much of the time disguised with his
usual brilliant artistry as an irascible old
dame lunching at the Savoy and toddling
around Bond Street and Hatton Gardens
in clandestine pursuit of an adroit Italian
gem thief who would, as a consequence
of that persistently annoying martinet,
spend many years languishing in a prison
cell — my colleague Mr Sherlock
Holmes, having no major call on his
time, remained thankfully poised high,
steeped upon routine, bringing his card
index up to date and had thus barely
uttered a word for an hour at least. I
meanwhile threw myself into an armchair
beside the fire, smoking a pipe whilst
assessing the pros and cons of a radical
advance in ocular surgery then being
discussed in the *Lancet*.

Neither of us was really aware of the world, nor barely stirred until the arrival of two contrasting individuals: our energetic Scotch housekeeper, Mrs Hudson, busying herself with a tray of tea things, rattling and clinking the chinaware, and, following close on her heels, a slender, acne-pocked, rather reserved young fellow with a shock of curly ginger hair and attired in grubby work overalls. Gazing despairingly about our front sitting room, he was seemingly stumped, at a profound loss to communicate his exact reason for being there, but rescue was at hand.

'Young Master Rowland Shalford requires a word, Mr Holmes. I have laid out cups for three,' our housekeeper intimated, showing every sense of propriety and tact.

'Thank you, Mrs Hudson,' answered Holmes, gazing up for the first time from his open file drawer at our slow-witted, scabby visitor with his vivid crop of flaming red hair. I instantly beckoned the fellow to be seated in the wickerwork chair, whilst Mrs Hudson merrily set out cups and saucers and poured from the pot.

'By the notable array of sprockets and spanners poking from your overalls, you are evidently a fitter by trade. Are you laying on gas nearby?' asked my colleague.

'Well, sir,' he replied, showing a trifle more pluck, 'I am in fact an apprentice. I only starts work this morning for a Mister Murrow. Oh, my poor mother.' Shalford's mouth dropped and his forlorn face was a picture of despair. 'At breakfast she beheld such high hopes for her only son,' he sighed deeply, 'but now my prospects is done for, even before my first week's wage packet is paid. I'm as good as sacked and I've my boss to thank for casting me into a most 'orrid situation. Dear-oh-lor', if only I had settled to eat my mother's sandwich, apple and flask of chicken soup, none of this wretched business should 'ave occurred and I would be going homeward to Crystal Palace on the omnibus — proud of a day's work well done.'

'Well, well, I perceive you are somewhat

vexed, a little overwrought and perhaps prone to exaggerate the severity of your predicament. I'm sure there's a way forward and that your mother need have no reason to be disappointed in you.'

'If only that were the case, Mr Holmes. Anyhow, I'd best tell you how it was — and thank you, I will have one of those gaspers.'

Once the carrot-topped young man, the apprentice gas fitter, was settled before the hearth with a cup of tea and a cigarette, comforted no doubt by the cheery fire burning in the grate, we listened with great interest as he spoke of his woeful afternoon and the daunting consequences.

'It was my boss, Mr Murrow, see — slinging my dear mother's lunch knapsack in amongst our tool boxes, he insisted I accompany him to the public house. 'I ain't got much money for beer,' I says honestly, 'a shillin's what Ma gave me for a pack of Woodbines an' me bus fare 'ome.'

'You're working for me now son an' I'm more than 'appy to stand you the

340

price of a pint. Don't you worry, Rowland, me and Mister Chatfield here 'll see you alright. You can pay us back in kind when you start earning proper wages.'

'That's regular generous of you, Mr Murrow,' I says, and with it being half twelve, us gas fitters downed tools an' mosied across the road to The Grapes along with the plasterers and painters. Truthfully, I fancied a plate of sausage and mash for after my morning's work. I felt hungry, but the only sustenance I'd receive that long, extended lunch hour stretching interminably would be pint after pint of Bass served on an empty stomach.'

'And these colleagues of yours,' I laughed, 'well used to their drink, quaffing large quantities of beer at one sitting were somewhat ahead.'

'Drank me under the table,' Shalford admitted, 'and they seemed to get more and more amused the drunker I got, watching me slur my words and become ever more inebriated until when we finally quit the tap-room at half two I could barely stand up straight a' was seeing double.'

'You are the dupe, a sort of workman's initiation,' I pointed out. 'You're quite wrong to worry about your employment prospects. Mr Murrow won't care a jot if you were a bit tiddly. They were having a good deal of fun at your expense.'

'A bit tiddly.' The young lad seemed mortified. 'I was flat out! Returning across the road I entered the wrong house for starters, the one next door that's also being converted but nobody was working on that day. It 'ad no front door as such, just a bit of loose tarpaulin 'anging down, and finding one of the back rooms full of paint cans, ladders and rolls of wallpaper, I am ashamed to say I slept it off, only awoken much later by a frightful stench of smoke, which is the reason why I'm here, gents.'

'Very good, you have our undivided attention. Pray continue, Shalford. That's it, help yourself to another cigarette.' Holmes crossed his long legs and lit his pipe, glancing over at me with unalloyed delighted.

'See, there was a body I am certain weren't there before. A woman slumped beneath the freshly glossed and sashed window. She were partly rolled in a tatty bit of carpet that to my mind I considered had been soaked in paraffin and, gawd forbid, recently been set alight and a fire deliberately started. At first, I was still groggy, unsure of my surroundings, but the flames leapin' about, taking hold, and the inhaling of smoke, sobered me up wonderfully. The mains water was turned on so I rushed to the sink an', tearing at the tap, managed to fill a couple of paste buckets to the brim. By repeating this task several times I was thus able to quell the flames before the fire began to rage out of control. Apart from me, I judged the house to be deserted and the hour late, for it was pitch black outside and I could hear no workmen's banter or sound of tools banging next door.'

'By Jove, you acted commendably young Shalford. Many in your situation should not have coped half so well. The woman in the carpet was quite dead, you say?'

'Much of the upper body crisp and black. I did not linger long nor gaze upon that woman's hideously blistered flesh; rather, I sought immediately fresh air and the distraction of a bustling, crowded Baker Street, wandering along the pavement in a dreadful state, muttering out loud, 'What shall I do, what shall I tell Mother?'

'Stepping out of the barber's shop, a kindly, elderly gentleman noticing my obvious distress, seized my arm and guided me along. I confided to him in a sort of muddled way that I suspected a dire crime had been committed an' — what a bit of luck — for he explained I need not enquire of the police as such for a Mr Sherlock Holmes, a consulting detective, lived but a few doors down at 221B.'

My companion removed his pipe from his mouth, exclaiming, 'Capital! Your guiding light from the barber's shop must be congratulated. What you have related so far, Shalford, is of superlative forensic interest. Watson, be a good fellow and fetch a dark lantern, will you. By Jove, we must presently make haste along Baker Street, a crime of immense intrigue beckons, practically on our own doorstep, no less.'

'Those houses,' I exclaimed, getting up and slinging Holmes his hat, overcoat and stick, thereafter excitedly pulling a scarf round my neck, 'I have frequently walked by and seen the erected scaffolding and builders' vans parked outside. Shalford, are you quite certain the fire was wholly extinguished, that there is no risk to property?' I enquired, fetching the lamp, at once ready to leave.

'Like I says, I was able to douse the flames. Although pretty overcome by the fumes of that paraffin, I flung open that window allowing much of the vile smoke to disperse into the back yard. I emphasise, the workmen next door, including Mr Murrow, had by that time left, and I was quite alone.'

'My advice to you, dear boy, is to hasten back to your mother, whom we must on no account allow to become fretful. Board the bus for Crystal Palace forthwith. Be of good heart, but think of some notable excuse — 'I staggered off to Regents Park, collapsing on the bench' — to impart to Mr Murrow. Turn up for work on time and have not the slightest fear of employment catastrophe. The idea all along was to get you drunk as a lord on your first day at work. As Watson here explained, 'an apprentice's initiation'. No one shall care a fig, but on no account say that you stayed in the next door house long.'

'I cannot thank you enough, Mr Holmes. I have at least been spared a police interview and court appearances. I trust you can make something of this awful business. Goodnight, gentlemen.'

★ ★ ★

That fortuitous night we tore along Baker Street, hardly believing a possible murder may have been committed only across the road, barely five minutes' walk away. What could be easier? Holmes and myself simply attained entry to the aforementioned property by ducking beneath a branch of scaffolding, whereupon we simply drew aside a workman's draped sheet of stiff tarpaulin acting temporarily for the front door until such time as one was properly affixed, just as young Shalford had reported. In fact, certain of the window frames at the front of the house having yet to be secured in place, our footsteps echoed upon bare, sanded floorboards and lamplight darted about the raw plasterwork.

Holmes led the way along the darkened hall and the room downstairs with the body was soon located.

Under such safe concealment, my companion was thus able to move about and make valued deductions. Ignoring the waterlogged remains, and widely ranged scorch marks on the walls, Holmes prised open the lower frame of the sash-window and, snatching the lamp, climbed outside, making a brief reconnaissance of the paved and turfed area of the back yard, most of the available space being taken up with builders' materials. Five minutes later we began an examination of the incinerated body, the ragged, spoiled heap slumped beneath the window that had once been a living, breathing person.

'There is a faint possibility . . . ' said I, shining the lamp about the newly decorated back room, devoid of course of domestic furnishings, the odours of recently applied gloss and wallpaper paste diffused somewhat by the underlying stench of roasted flesh that now permeated much of the house.

'And what is that possibility?' asked my colleague, nimbly stepping round a lake of sooty water.

'Well, it is termed 'spontaneous combustion,' I replied, 'and there have been recorded cases over the years. A very rare occurrence, I grant you, but one perhaps worth considering, Holmes. Either that or else, as a class of vagrant, during her peregrinations she may have conceivably got into the room, lit a clay pipe between her lips and, having fallen asleep, hot tobacco ash set her alight.'

'That rabid bit of Axminster utilised as a blanket, presumably?'

'Why on earth not?' I confess to feeling a secret gratification that my proposals were not being dismissed offhand as invariably happened. 'It was dark, she clambers in, unaware of stupefied young Shalford lying over here by the stack of paint cans.'

'Both these theories, however unlikely, are, I suppose, feasible. But I must inform you, my dear Watson, by use of my magnifying glass earlier it was possible to detect imprints of tyre treads running in muddy trails across the paving to beneath the window. I conjecture, due to what appears to be the likelihood of a cumbersome, lopsided load, one could plainly observe marks where the wheels had gouged into the edge of the flower border. The courtyard incidentally communicates with a short alley. A notable fact: the width of the rubber tread is considerably wider upon the back set of wheels, while narrower upon the front pair. We can thus dispense with a bicycle or a workman's wheelbarrow.'

'A four-wheeled perambulator, you infer?'

'Or conceivably a bath chair. Whatever wheeled contraption, it was bearing a heavy, bulky load, certainly weightier than an infant. However, to reiterate, let us for the time being negate 'spontaneous combustion' and observe what, if anything, our carpet lady relates to us in actuality.'

My colleague, like myself, hardened to the ravages of bodily decay else appalling damaged flesh, sifted through the ashy remains. Part of the woman's delicate facial tissue disintegrated as he nudged the charred, blackened corpse a trifle too enthusiastically while poking with the ferrule of his silver-topped cane into one of the eye sockets.

'Ah, we make inroads at last,' he ejaculated, after kneeling down and tearing away a strip of sodden carpet which reeked strongly of paraffin though untouched by the flames. The gleeful expression upon his wan, hawk-like features was, I confess, glorious to behold. He deftly retrieved from the burnt dress pocket of the dead woman what turned out to be a sodden, leather ladies' manicure set, certain of the various grades of scissors and clippers having survived undamaged.

'Hallo, some good may yet come of this, dear boy. Watson, we'd best alert Scotland Yard by means of an anonymous telegraphed injunction and leave Lestrade, the official force that is, to make of this charred female what they will. Rowland Shalford need never be implicated; your 'vagrant' theory stands up passably well to their way of thinking and shall no doubt be their first line of enquiry. Naturally they will concur a pair of dossers worse for wear and due to the consumption of meths came in here to spend the night. One accidentally sets herself alight, the other succeeds in dousing the flames but, realising the severity, the hopelessness of the fatal injuries, the vagrant rushes off somewhere. Plausible, if in this case erroneous.'

Pausing awhile, Holmes retrieved his magnifying lens from the inner pocket of his coat and made a lengthy and meticulous study of the fabric remaining of the woman's scorched skirts. I kept my lamp beam steady, following his every inclination. Replacing the old carpet, the body looked pretty much as we had found it. The floorboards were soaked in places by puddles of water and I was frankly relieved to clear out, especially recalling that awful collapse of the woman's charcoal face when Holmes poked into her eye. I wanted to get back to our digs for a welcome cigar from the coal scuttle and a stiff whisky before the hearth. However, the carpet lady must by necessity remain uppermost in our thoughts.

★　★　★

That night, while a fog lay thick upon London, the globe lamps in our front sitting room remained aglow and hissing for many a long hour. While I remained content to scribble away with my pen, writing up an account of a back-dated case for publication, Sherlock Holmes chose to sit over by his chemistry table thumbing through the advertisement sections of a stack of newspapers — back issues kept carefully stored that he was apt to consult now and then in relation to his cases, his clever mind ever alive to the possibility of some clue emerging as to the identity of the carpet lady.

'Are you any clearer as to discovering the motive of crime, or else who this confounded woman may be?' I asked, downing the last dregs of my whisky, ready for bed.

Peering at me over that great beaky nose of his, my friend, scratching a Vesta, relit his briar-root pipe and despite the lateness of the hour remained ebullient. 'I have attained a glimpse,' he answered, blowing out a wreath of tobacco smoke, 'an elementary insight into her mode of employment. You are aware, no doubt, of ladies who can offer various medical and personal services without requirement of a physician's degree?'

'I am; therapeutic hypnotherapy, homeopathic treatments — go on.'

'I have located a particular advertisement in the *Gazette*. See what you make of it.'

Mrs Fenner, operator of corns etc., 24 Paddington Street, opposite the post office — corns, bunions, defective nails speedily cured without pain else inconvenience. Respectable widow, many references.

'Well, old chap,' said I, hardly impressed by such gleaned intelligence, 'surely there are many ladies self-employed as such?'

'Granted, Watson, but the word 'widow' causes one to become encouraged,' said he, endowed with irrepressible positivity. 'After all, you do recall the fabric, the cloth out of which the woman's skirts were fashioned?'

'Not particularly.' Stifling a yawn, I peered at Holmes with aching eyes, desperate to lay my head on a pillow and hit the sack.

'Black bombazine, my dear chap; by gad, the material corresponding exactly to widow's weeds.'

★　★　★

The following morning, upon our way to Paddington Street, we happened to stroll past the houses presently being converted and, peering inquisitively through a ground floor windowless gap from which issued raucous oaths and good-natured builders' banter, watched with enjoyment a whistling ginger-haired apprentice gas fitter hard at work attaching a length of rubber hose to a brass fitment. Lestrade, it turned out, was next door, a number of police constables milling half-heartedly outside. Holmes could not resist stepping across and popping his head round the tarpaulin curtain and, upon seeing the ratty faced official detective appear in the hallway, calling out sarcastically, 'Ah, Lestrade, you have work in progress I perceive. I trust you have reached something of an impasse. Might I be of assistance? You know we go back a long way. Has a quantity of builders' materials been pilfered, a sack or two of cement, a wheelbarrow maybe, a bag of nails?'

'Very wry, very droll, Mr Holmes. I should hardly be concerning myself with petty crime. No, your services upon this occasion shall not be required. A mere case of accidental death, a vagrant, you know, got inside at the back and burnt herself to death through careless use of matches, hot tobacco ash igniting flimsy material. I've frankly come across this sort of thing so many times in my career. Such a waste . . . of police resources, I infer.'

'Oh, I will not bother you then,' ejaculated Sherlock Holmes loftily. 'Good morning to you, Inspector.'

With a curt nod and mayhap an air of one whose precocious talents are sorely undervalued, my companion seized my arm and we continued our pedestrian enterprise up Baker Street, the recollection of Lestrade's pompous aspect leading us both to laugh heartily as we approached the Marylebone Road to hail a passing cab. Yet my friend unexpectedly delivered a serious aside, which brought me up sharply.

'So far as our murderer is concerned, my dear Watson, a more pleasing outcome could not be envisaged. The police remain entirely hoodwinked.'

The chiropodist Mrs Fenner occupied the second floor flat, being one of three tenants inhabiting a very presentable villa with a neat little privet hedge and wrought iron gate opposite the general post office. There was a man on the roof. By diligent enquiry, according to neighbours the house was owned by a very quiet and retiring couple, Mr and Mrs Brinkley, who lived with their daughter Betsy on the ground floor.

Holmes lost no time energetically ringing the bell pull. Not long after, the door was opened by a plump little lady; silver-haired and I judged to be five and forty. My companion was typically acute in his opening gambit.

'Are you gentlemen seeking accommodation, bed and board?' she asked politely.

'A good day to you, Mrs Brinkley.' My colleague raised his hat. 'I wonder if you have seen Mrs Fenner about? I have a request from a dear aunt of mine for her valuable services of chiropody.'

'I'm afraid not; she may be visiting a client in Crouch End. We keep separate apartments. I have not seen her this morning.'

'Perchance is that your husband on the roof? Builder, is he? Bricklayer, doing a spot of chimney grouting?'

'Bertie can put his hand to practically anything. In fact he's a skilled roofer, City & Guilds. He freelances and works at many sites.'

'You know, I'm desperate to get some tiles fixed. I have a dratted leak in my attic. I should be prepared to pay the going rate. I don't want the bother of tendering out, else going through the builders' directory. I need an assessment urgently, what with winter setting in.'

'You'd better come in then. Bertie!' she called out, leaning over the porch step and craning her neck. 'Chap to see you about a roofing job.'

'I'll be right down,' shouted a friendly voice from above.

We were shown into a very comfortable and airy ground floor flat and proceeded to the kitchen where Mrs Brinkley began boiling a kettle on the range and assembling cups and saucers for tea, while begging us to be seated at table for her husband would be with us shortly.

Whilst I took out my pipe and pouch of Arcadia mixture, a dumpy, slovenly young lady came wandering through, still wearing her nightdress, yawning hugely and clutching to her considerable bosom a china-headed doll, its flat, jointed, no doubt sawdust-stuffed body clothed in a rich arrangement of satin and lace.

My first overriding impression was that she was surely much too old to be concerned with dolls and I found it unsettling the way she pawed so covetously at its thick mass of hair.

'Go back to your room, Betsy. These gentlemen have come about building work — nothing to concern you.'

'I shan't. I want tea and iced buns,' she answered, all the while hugging that doll close to her, whispering, cooing childish endearments into its ear. 'Iced buns and raisin cake,' said she coyly. 'Plenty for us *both*.'

Holmes, intrigued by the eccentric relationship this grown girl undoubtedly shared with the toy, changed chairs to be nearer Mrs Brinkley's daughter and in a kindly way asked the doll's name. Betsy's answer proved both startling and chillingly profound.

'She is my sister Clementine, sir.'

'Hush, Betsy, don't talk so — behave,' hissed the mother, pouring scalding water into the flowery teapot, giving it a vigorous stir, a pained expression of wearisome endurance revealing itself upon the mother's normally pretty, open hearted countenance.

'Your sister, how extraordinary,' remarked my colleague affably. 'I am honoured to make her acquaintance, and yours also.' Leaning forward, gripping Betsy's willing fingers in his own, he shook her hand, patiently awaiting a response.

'Clemmie is my best friend ever,' she blurted out, flushed with an unnatural enthusiasm. 'She writes notes.'

'And as beloved sisters you share a common bond. You trust completely in each other, confide in one another. Might I see one of these notes? I'm sure they're wonderfully fun.'

'Put that doll down and go to your room this instant! Do as I say, girl,' her mother scolded, and then glancing at

Holmes she implored him not to encourage her daughter further.

'Please, sir, I know you mean well, but her 'make believe' is not merely a childish fancy, a passing phase, though with all my heart I wish it were so.'

Her fickle daughter, losing all interest in the present company and unheeding of her mother's lamentation, grabbed a cake and slunk off, departing the kitchen, taking that awful 'clingy' doll with her. Heavy footsteps in the passage meanwhile alerted us to a much more pleasant and good-humoured member of the family.

'Hello, gentlemen. Did I hear mention of a roofing job?' said a strapping big fellow with a cheerful disposition and honest, open features. Tanned and fit, he went to wash his hands under the tap with a large slab of coal tar soap. Wiping his hands on a towel, he gave his doting wife a peck on the cheek.

'I perceive you have seen duty in Iran, the 3rd Bombay Cavalry, I'll be bound. My colleague here was an army surgeon in Afghanistan, you know.'

'Zounds! That's a telling statement. I

did serve in the 3rd Bombay, under command of General Sir James Outram. We defeated the Persians and killed seven hundred of 'em with very modest losses. How on earth did you know?'

'Simple observations, Mr Brinkley. You possess a bold tattoo of the regimental insignia upon your left bicep and the date of that momentous, gallantly fought tussle — 1857 — self-scratched in mauve ink by a blunt needle on your wrist. I wonder if, like my ex-military colleague presently pouring us tea, you keep a service revolver else a musket round the house.'

'Why in heavens name do you care, why do you ask such a thing? I believed you to be concerned about roof tiles, not handguns. I left the army long ago.'

'I concur, you are by trade a professional roofer, weren't you, attaching Welsh slate to the roofs a fortnight back of a couple of house conversions in Baker Street — not far from where I share diggings. Having completed the job I presume you would be intimately aware of the layout of each room and the builder's schedule being adhered to.'

'Preposterous nonsense.'

'I must warn you, Mr Brinkley, in the strictest confidence. I have enough evidence at my disposal to see you hang — unless, that is, you choose to come clean, then perhaps we can alleviate this terrible predicament you and your dear wife find yourselves party to. Mrs Fenner was shot at close range through the right eye. Despite partial immolation, the greater part of her torso and face being consumed by flame, the revealed eye socket showed signs of a bullet's trajectory. A person of considerable physical prowess wheeled her carpeted body brazenly through the streets of Marylebone, no doubt by means of an old pram stacked high with roped sticks of furniture to enhance the impression of a rag and bone dealer, and thence discarded Mrs Fenner in a darkened, supposedly empty, back room before setting her alight, presuming police would mistake her for a dosser careless with candle or matches.'

'You leave my house at once, sir,' cried the wife, glancing anxiously at her husband. 'You heartless, cruel man.'

'Furthermore, I have an interesting theory I wish to propound. My name is Sherlock Holmes by the way, and I am a consulting detective with affiliations to many police forces in the country. I put it to you that your daughter shot Mrs Fenner in an uncontrolled fit of rage when the chiropodist, aware of the tenacious influence the doll held over Betsy's reason, took it upon herself to either hide else throw away the doll in the dustbin, believing wrongly the short sharp shock would bring your daughter to her senses and restore a healthy mental equilibrium. If only Mrs Fenner had consulted Monsieur Givrés' most excellent three-volume work *Case Studies Relating to Psychotic Derangement*, your tenant's life would have been spared and she would never have undertaken such a rash course. You are both of you in grave danger; a growing psychotic dependency poses a threat to you as parents. I recall such a similar case ascribed most eloquently by Monsieur Girvrés in Paris. The outcome was fatal to all parties. I do not for one instance believe either of you, one a heroic campaigner of the Persian war, the other a dedicated housewife and mother, deliberately set out to murder your second floor tenant. Nothing becomes sensible to logical reasoning; the whole idea is preposterous and nonsensical. However, to shield another, that is the crime here. Your daughter must be confined and taken into care, Mrs Brinkley. I insist upon it.'

'Oh, we cannot yield, we cannot,' she implored. 'She is mine, mine own kin. I could not bear for her to be imprisoned on a ward, to spend a lifetime incarcerated in an establishment for mental incompetents.'

'Hush, dearest,' spoke up the husband, at last humbled by Holmes's sound deductive reasoning. 'You speak sense, sir, Lord you do. I suppose I'd best explain the circumstances surrounding Mrs Fenner's demise. One afternoon my wife heard a loud gunshot upstairs. She went up to find to her horror Betsy staring into space, holding my old revolver, which I foolishly kept cocked and loaded in a cabinet in case of burglars. The body of Mrs Fenner lay sprawled across the sofa. She was quite dead. You see, to my obsessive daughter's warped way of thinking Clementine her sister, which you rightly identify as the doll having been thrown in the outside dustbin, wrote her a note (I can show you a box where Betsy keeps such correspondence) demanding the chiropodist be done away with. My daughter responded and duly went upstairs and shot her. An atrocious act she has now completely erased from her memory and, if questioned, is unaware of, her brain defective in certain past impressions. The rest by some profound insight you are aware of, Mr Holmes.'

'An asylum specialist must be immediately alerted, I and Doctor Watson shall remain on hand to assist and clear the way for your daughter's evacuation. Believe me, it is for the best. By the by, Mr Brinkley, that piece of old carpeting nailed to the roof of your garden shed, which I can see from the kitchen window, the Axminster weave, the garish pattern seems rather familiar to me.'

LONDON GAZETTE — MONDAY, AUGUST 3RD 1897
TRAGIC DEATH OF GIRL WHOSE SISTER WAS A DOLL

Betsy Brinkley, who readers will recall insisted vehemently that her sister was a doll called Clementine, was killed by a train yesterday on the Sunday afternoon of the Queen's Jubilee at Farringdon Tunnel. Celebrations became somewhat muted, passengers on the excursion service supporting the Mutual Aid & Widows and Orphans fund too distressed and much affected by this terrible instance of death on the line.

A tragic skating accident caused Betsy to suffer a personality disorder having, poor thing, struck her head on a fence post and injured the brain matter irrevocably when she slipped on ice during the winter freeze of 1874.

Thence after, Miss Brinkley

became more and more convinced the enamel doll in her possession was in fact her sister Clementine who could communicate either by pencil or pen and ink, writing messages whenever she chose.

The doll's hold on the girl's psyche became such that her loving parents deemed Betsy could no longer remain cared for at home, an instance a note fortuitously discovered, one of many purportedly written by Clementine directing Betsy to poison her own father at the breakfast table and scald her mother with boiling water from the kettle so that the sisters might share the house without dominating parents to concern themselves over.

This dangerous state of affairs could not be tolerated, and Miss Brinkley, along with her possessive doll which she refused for a moment to be parted from, were committed forthwith to an insane asylum for long-term observation and treatment, and it was from here Miss

Brinkley escaped on the Sunday. The doctors later discovered a handwritten note under her pillow, which we faithfully replicate here. It should also be noted by readers that her doll had been recently confiscated with tragic unforeseen results.

Dearest Betsy,

The Queen's Jubilee is upon us, such fun, and the weather is so bright and sunny this week, too nice to be confined to a ward. Darling sister, meet me at the southernmost end of Farringdon Tunnel. You know the footpath across the fields from here leads there. Promise me you will stand in the middle of the tracks where I can see you properly, at twelve noon on Sunday. Wait for me and we shall have such a jolly lark visiting the fair and sweetie shop.

Your loving sister, Clemmie.

12

Christmas On Dartmoor

Glancing at my notes, I find myself drawn to one case in particular, a memorable adventure, an ingenious criminal subterfuge hitherto unbeknown to the public at large who choose to read my published accounts detailing my colleague's illustrious career.

It will be remembered that Mr Sherlock Holmes upon rare occasions engaged a rabble of disparate youths termed 'The Baker Street Irregulars' to assist him in certain far-reaching and sometimes dangerous criminal investigations. What is far less known by the public is that Holmes in fact funded the education of a number of these boys out of his own pocket, and that one named Wiggins, I recall, adopted through my colleague's influence by a most eligible and respectable married couple then living in Marylebone, a clergyman and his wife, being privately tutored attained Wellington Public School and later by scholarship commenced officer training at Sandhurst, no mean feat for somebody who began life underprivileged as a hovel-born street urchin. However, I must report that amongst that old band of wastrels, the so-called Baker Street Irregulars were alas certain 'bad pennies', destined to embrace a life of crime, driven remorselessly by base appetites and disgraceful behaviour, one of these 'bad pennies' attaining the hangman's noose at the tender age of fifteen. But let us for now stay firmly rooted in the successful and the sunnier remembrance.

I recall it was my good fortune at the end of December, the culmination of an exacting, busy year, to accompany my friend and young Wiggins — then in his first year at Sandhurst — upon a sort of winter excursion a railway journey upon one of the remotest branch lines in England across a desolate tract of granite moorland — twenty miles long by twelve broad — to Princetown in Devon. We stayed one night at the Rowes Duchy Hotel, within distance of Dartmoor Convict Prison; that grim, granite edifice, the impregnable near circle within a circle that readers will vouch cannot exactly be claimed a holiday destination. It was here within its stout, imposing walls set in the bleak landscape of Dartmoor that young Barnaby Seward himself — once a member of the Baker Street Irregulars, a 'bad penny' as it were — was shortly to be released after five years' incarceration for robbery with violence, a sordid crime in which a poor householder in Putney was left permanently blinded in one eye.

Seward was fortunate; the judge showed leniency, believing he had been influenced and unduly goaded by older members of the gang, and they, it must be said, received far harsher sentencing.

My colleague had pledged his assistance, not only by agreeing to meet the ex-prisoner at the hotel on the day of his release but thereafter accompanying Barnaby down to London where he would stay with a family over Christmas. Also through the auspices of one of his grateful clients, a job had become available at the East India Docks as a warehouseman, which would suit Seward admirably.

Young Wiggins, the officer cadet, that shining star in the firmament, that example of what hard work and a sense of duty could achieve, at the last moment insisted on joining us, wishing to impart to his one-time fellow Baker Street Irregular that an alternative to crime was preferable to the gallows and certainly achievable. It was heart-breaking because Seward had been such a good-natured lad, an enthusiastic street urchin who put himself out in some very tricky situations to gain Holmes' valuable information for his consultancy work, hence my companion's concern.

★   ★   ★

At Paddington, upon a wintry, overcast morning of sleety rain, we boarded a West Country express and headed upon Great Western metals to firstly Bristol and Exeter, the capital of Devon, some 194 miles distant from London, and thence via Tavistock to Yelverton.

Alas, our connecting train for Princetown remained stationary on its sidings, to be eventually shunted into the station, thereafter taking us the ten and a half miles across the scraggy moors to our destination. Since arriving, we had yet to encounter a porter or single member of staff. The waiting rooms were locked, as was the buffet. To cap it all, the weather was freezing.

'The West Country has much to commend it, yet much to be deplored,' Holmes remarked. 'Do Devonian trains uniquely run once every fortnight, do the stations hereabouts not require staffing now the summer tourists have fled?'

Young Wiggins paused to glance at his pocket watch; aware we might be in for a delay.

After a half hour of waiting, a glimmer of hope, an elderly gentleman whom I presumed to be local, conceivably much greater informed than ourselves as to train times, wearing a buttoned-up, fur-collared winter overcoat and a country cloth cap, marched out of the ticket hall brandishing a rain cape and folded umbrella under his arm. He appeared to recognise my illustrious companion and, drawn by the lure of celebrity, stepped briskly down the wet platform eyeing him inquisitively.

'Are you perchance *the* Sherlock Holmes, the consulting detective in the *Strand* magazine?' he enquired, squinting over his gold-rimmed half-moon spectacles.

'I am, and this is my long-time companion and biographer Doctor Watson. Might I also introduce Mr Wiggins, who is at present in officer training at Sandhurst. And you are?'

'Oh, William Hawtry. I am a local historian, the curator of a small museum. I live at Naseby Cottage along the way. Travelling to Princetown, are we?'

'That is the idea, if the train ever arrives. I have a little business that needs tidying up. My, the weather in these primitive parts leaves much to be desired. Rather bleak, Mr Hawtry. I wonder if we're in for snow?'

'Most likely. Look here, I shall be more than honoured if I may share your compartment, for as an adopted local and with a certain knowledge of these wild parts I can point out various landmarks, features on the landscape, and show you a bit of Princetown. I take it you'll be staying at the Rowes Duchy?'

'We are.' Holmes' attention was distracted. 'Ah, a porter has at length abandoned the comfort of his pipe and fireside chair and decided at last to make an appearance. The engine is steaming up; we may have some movement at long last. These lonely, out of the way branch stations are quite a trial at this time of year for us Londoners used to a quick and efficient motive power.'

'Yes, you are I fear far, far away from the bustle of Paddington and Waterloo and the busy underground. I believe our little moorland railway to be one of the remotest in the country. It was opened in 1883, constructed on an old mineral tramway.'

'Yes, quite,' interrupted Holmes. 'For

myself, Hawtry, I'm desperate for a warm first-class smoker. I trust you are not averse to stringent tobacco fumes? I am, as Doctor Watson will confirm, a hopeless addict to shag and Bradley's ready-mades.'

'By no means,' the old fellow exclaimed. 'I am as fond of cigarettes as the next man.'

Sleet began to rain down onto the platform, causing us to open umbrellas. It appeared our rustic porter, now joined by another expectant of an incoming train, proceeded to heave crates of live chickens and huddle of milk churns closer to the platform's edge.

At last the passenger service pulled in, and our crowd headed straight for the second coach along of what was virtually empty carriage stock. Once inside the compartment, we slung our luggage and sticks on the rack and settled down to bask in the warmth of a heated carriage. In fact, it was a real boon that Mr Hawtry had decided to join us because it turned out he was himself staying at the hotel for a Christmas Eve assembly of his society, and over the next day or so I would be much entertained by his scholarly, erudite commentary upon the history of that region.

A whistle blew and the locomotive chuffed steadily past the junction signal box, rounding the embankment. Our first stop, at the base of the hilly moorland expanse, was Dousland and our local historian was quick to explain its significance.

'Now this station, gentlemen, is where the guards and prisoners assemble to catch the train. You see them now and again during the week. It's all very depressing, especially when one remembers where these people, some of them quite young, are headed and for how long.'

'However, their crimes must be taken into account,' I answered reflectively as our train pulled out, the engine encountering the gradient.

'Of course, but personally I should go quite mad if I were to be confined, my liberty constrained at that damp, isolated prison for a long stretch. Just think of it,

Doctor Watson, for as far as the eye can see a desolate, treeless wilderness of shifting, bubbling peat bogs, furze, old granite and the rugged peaks of tors.'

Following the contours of the hills, the stopping service climbed steadily, gaining height, encountering sharp curves as it progressed, the single track bordered by post and wire fence, dotted at regular intervals by telegraph poles.

I cast my mind back to that 'bad penny' Barnaby Seward, jailed in London for violent assault, and could not, despite Holmes' fine charitable sentiments, summon much sympathy for his five year sentence when I thought of Mr Lampton bludgeoned in the face with a jemmy and disfigured for life. He was very fortunate not to have swung, given the appalling injuries to the brave butler and his master who defended that house so admirably in Putney when Mrs Lampton's emeralds were stolen.

I was pondering this London burglary when Mr Hawtry tapped me on the knee and in a lively manner enthused about a pamphlet he was then preparing for publication, the subject of which was concerned with 'ghosts and hauntings' in the locality and which he would put on sale at his museum for a penny. 'That's a splendid idea, Mr Hawtry,' said I.

'I have been researching for some time now, and a number of peasants and gentlefolk came forward bearing witness to strange phenomena, both on Dartmoor and the bordering villages. Might I read you gentlemen an extract from this future publication?'

Sitting across from us, young Wiggins was busy stuffing tobacco into his pipe, a fairly serious, composed individual with his mind mostly turned to military matters I supposed, vaguely amused at the turn our conversation was taking. Sherlock Holmes, his gaunt, lean features compressed into a frown, was puffing on his pipe, gazing out of the compartment window, lost in thought.

'By 1816 it was recorded 1,748 deaths had occurred, the bodies of inmates disposed of in an altogether roughshod and unchristian manner.

We must now add to the folklore of this country 'The Lost Prisoners of Princetown'.'

Mr Hawtry read most succinctly from his written paper:

'First witnessed by a country parson riding upon his horse to Launceton was an 'quivering undulation' coming from the area of a foul, vaporous quagmire, long supposed to be an unmarked burial ground associated with the prison. Overcome by a feeling of apprehension, his horse whinnying and rearing up, the goodly parson swore to the fact he saw a number of tumescent, sack-like, peaty, hairy beings with silvery pupil-less eyes as though reborn, rising up from the mire, seeking to approach and drag him or any living person or beast down into the depths of that suppurating charnel pit. Woe betide those unfortunate enough to encounter upon a night of fogs on Dartmoor *such phantasms of the boggy depths.'*

There was for a time silence and Mr Hawtry, satisfied with his recital of The Lost Prisoners of Princetown that he fully intended to publish, sat back and awaited our approval. A train whistle blew; at this altitude our carriage was engulfed by low-lying cloud as the engine rounded a sharp bend, continuing its progress up onto the high moors.

'Is there some deep moral to this prisoner business? Am I missing the punchline?' enquired Holmes, knocking out his briar-root pipe. 'Really, Mr Hawtry, if you must compile a penny pamphlet on ghosts and hauntings, do try to think of something half intelligent to put in it, old chap.'

'But, Holmes,' said I, rather aggrieved by the insinuation. 'Mr Hawtry is reporting the facts as related to him locally.'

'The peasants in this region of pre-history provide a wealth of superstitious folklore, much of it passed down from generation to generation,' Mr Hawtry emphasised, unaffected by Holmes' stinging criticism. 'We are, gentlemen, approaching the Burrator and Sheepstor Reservoir to our right,' the local historian cheerfully directed our attention to the window.

'I think it's about time we opened that refreshment hamper attained at Exeter Central. I'd quite fancy a beaker of tea and a beef and mustard sandwich. Wiggins, old lad, be a good fellow and pour from the flask, would you,' asked Holmes.

Whilst we spread our eatables upon the cloth-covered seat, the train continued north, following the meandering railway across the moors, the gradient becoming ever more steep, until we eventually approached the raised heights of Princetown, by which time it was dark and snowing heavily.

★ ★ ★

Departing the ticket hall at Princetown Station, I perceived we were now present at the highest town in England. The cold could not be more piercing; patchy exigencies of snow accumulating upon the roofs and pavement, settling on the lamp-lit street as we trudged towards our intended hotel, Mr Hawtry leading the way with his umbrella held aloft.

Once we were assembled in the foyer, Mr Bonington the manager of the Rowes Duchy informed us that under Holmes' guardianship a Mister Seward had himself arrived that afternoon and been assigned a very pleasant pre-booked single room. Once our own room numbers were allocated, keys passed over the reception desk and the visitors' book was signed, we were duly directed by the clerk to the comfortable lounge where we could relax before dinner.

A blaze of green yule logs burned and sizzled in the grate of a stone fireplace, the mantelshelf decorated by festive evergreens and candles. Before this were placed about a semi-circle of enormous sofas with a densely tinselled and baubled Norwegian spruce dominating the bar. Electric brass lamp standards effused a soothing glow, pleasing to the weary traveller, and I felt at once welcomed and in a cordial setting.

At our approach, a painfully thin, emaciated individual rose from one of the comfy sofas. Seward, on first impressions, looked sly and unkempt, but of course he was older and more mature than when I last knew him as a boy. However, a chirpy cheeky grin and that thatch of pure blond hair were unmistakable and after polite if formal greetings, we each in turn shook him by the hand.

As a doctor, at one glance at his sallow complexion, I recognised the symptoms of inflammatory congestion. God knows the moist and gloomy air of the moors would not have been conducive to his health these last five years, for his lungs were weak, and he would have likely developed respiratory problems.

Seward smoked a hand-rolled cigarette while clutching a pint pot of foamy beer. He seemed overwhelmed to receive Holmes' kindness and delighted to see us, but nonetheless slightly drunk.

'I got yer letters, sir,' he expostulated,

'an' 'ere I is, straining at the bit, to get at me warehouse job at the East India. Gord bless yer, Mr 'Olmes. An 'ere's 'Wiggy' too, lookin' like a proper swell. The army suits yer. I wouldn't be no use 'cept as a private digging latrines, you a posh officer, all la-de-dah like.'

'A cadet training to be an officer at Sandhurst,' the young man corrected, strangely wary of his encounter with one of the long disbanded 'Baker Street Irregulars' and not appearing the slightest nostalgic nor in the mood for sentimental banter either. 'We'll have a little chat later, Barnaby. Lots to catch up on, haven't we.'

'Yeah, you'se 'n' me goes back a long way. Good ole pals, ain't we, 'Wiggy'? Any 'ow, I got me a pretty little wallpapered room with a nice gas fire upstairs that's much preferable to another night spent in one of them bloody awful cells. Truth be told, I'll be more than glad to see the back of Dartmoor, Mr 'Olmes, an' blessedly 'appy to board the train to Exeter.'

The ex-con let out a raucous cough

and I witnessed one of his all too frequent choking fits, which made me more determined than ever to give him a thorough check-up when we reached Marylebone, and additionally seek a specialist opinion.

Dinner proved somewhat of an ordeal. Slurring his speech and obviously the worse for wear, Seward, newly let loose on the outside world, could be forgiven for certain aspects of his behaviour, but what was inexcusable were his crude reminiscences of prison life, which I found particularly galling. Wiggins, who was sat across the table from him, looked as though at any time he might lean over and punch the other squarely in the face, so annoyed was he becoming at the boorish litany of uncouth prison behaviour and jokey indiscretions then being loudly alluded to. Despite this, Sherlock Holmes kept up a good-natured rapport, even on occasions guffawing at Seward's dullard humour.

During our meal, I occasionally waved at Mr Hawtry sat at the other end of the dining room with the chairman of his society, a Major Churchward. After our long journey down to the West Country and travelling on one of the remotest branch lines in England, we were for an early bed and thus with good cheer ascended the staircase from the lobby and each went to our appointed room, aware that it had been snowing since our arrival at Princetown and, according to Mr Bonington, was several inches thick in places.

I went to sleep with the conviction that however much I disliked the fellow, as a doctor I must do everything in my power to relieve Seward's chesty condition.

★   ★   ★

The following morning, the 24th December, heralded a bitterly cold and wintry day. Glancing out of the window in the foyer, I was dazzled by the sheer brightness. The long night had seen extensive falls of snow and it now lay crisp and thick on the ground, with very little traffic in evidence or persons caring to venture abroad. Above the surrounding moorland and the distant peaks, a leaden sky promised still further heavy snow showers to come.

Joining my companion Mr Sherlock Holmes — who was already attacking his ham and eggs with gusto in the dining room — and helping myself to coffee, I was curious when Mr Bonington came hurrying across looking most perturbed and officious. Leaning over our table he said in barely a confidential whisper, 'I hate to be the portent of such sadness, gentlemen, but your protégé, that is Mr Seward, has just been found by one of my staff lying in bed. He is most unfortunately not breathing, having passed away during the night. We have a routine that will be implemented so as not to worry or else disturb guests at the Rowes Duchy. The body will be carried down the back stairs and discreetly dealt with by a local undertaker, Mr Newcombe, who will arrive round by the kitchen entrance in an ordinary delivery van so as not to cause undue morbidity or attract attention. Doctor Watson, might I ask you to go upstairs and confirm a diagnosis? I believe Mr Wiggins is shaving and will be down presently.'

'Certainly,' said I. 'I shall be right up.'

'Well, my dear Watson,' remarked my colleague, helping himself to toast with a keen appetite. 'That's a turn-up for the books. Of course, I was expecting him to be murdered though it will be a somewhat challenging and most edifying task to find out exactly how it was done and by whom.'

'Holmes,' I felt compelled to remark, astonished by his lack of emotion, his stony indifference, 'you suspected this all along. Seward was very ill, you know.'

'The major point is this: the Putney case has yet to be resolved, and Mrs Lampton's precious emeralds, worth millions in sterling, which she coverts above all else, above insurance payouts, have still to be recovered. The wide-held suspicion, and this was held by the Lampton family at the time of the trial, was that Barnaby Seward knew where they were and that the gems were in his possession on the night of the house burglary when the gang split up. There were two days unaccounted for before his arrest. Easily enough time to conceal the hoard, so that after serving a prison sentence they might be collected and cashed in. Both the insurance company and I were convinced on his release from prison he would lead us to the trove and now he is dead, by Henry, he shall likewise prove most beneficious I think.'

'But five long years in Dartmoor,' I implored.

'Bah, once a 'bad penny' always a 'bad penny', Watson. Seward was a deceiving, violent and wholly ruthless crook. He possessed not a sliver of intention to reform. Once he had returned to London, he should have gone back to his old haunts in the East End and, after a decent interval, cash in on the stolen booty. My approach to the prison governor, my letters of support, he knew would quicken his release date as it did by several months.'

'But I thought you cared deeply for his welfare, his rehabilitation into society?'

'Me! My dear Watson, what do I care for a juvenile lout who smashed two persons over the head with a jemmy and left one of them half blinded for life, besmirching the name of 'The Baker Street Irregulars'. I personally wanted him hanged and at the time appalled he received only five years on Dartmoor. No, the 'good Samaritan act' was a mere fabrication developed by myself and the insurance company. Should we recover the missing jewels, I will receive a generous payment from Mrs Lampton's solicitor. The emeralds were a family heirloom and of great sentimental worth, so this is what must be forthwith promoted.'

'Well, where do we start?'

'Did you perchance observe a stuffed worm, a cloth draught excluder placed outside the door to number 7E? A puerile discrepancy, but worth debating.'

'I did not; perhaps a waiter or bell boy upon Mr Bonington's instruction put it there to help keep Seward's room warm.'

'Perhaps, although surely a draught excluder is provided for each guest inside the room to place along the bottom of the door at their own leisure. I noticed none, but 7E had one uniquely outside the door, as I discovered when I poked my head out at half past twelve after a last pipe before bed.'

Briefly nodding a greeting to Mr Hawtry and Major Churchward on the stairs, we passed along the corridor and quietly entered Seward's hotel room, number 7E.

A generous bribe in the form of a coin to the senior housemaid in attendance was well appreciated and, presuming us 'wanting to be left alone for a while to deal with our grief', she hurried off.

My companion, totally indifferent to Seward who lay sheeted on the bed, lost no time and at furious pace began examining every nook and cranny of the room.

'The fireplace is, you will observe, boarded up to accommodate the gas heater, no access to a chimney. What do you make of Seward, his pallor looks a bit questionable, as does that half empty mug on the bedside cabinet containing a suspicious sediment.'

'He appears to have died quite

naturally in his sleep, no evidence of a struggle. Bar a proper autopsy, I can't say for definite he was deliberately murdered.'

'But you can't rule out poisonous fumes.'

'Not at all.'

'That dratted draught excluder, that stuffed cloth worm, prevented any air from escaping, creating in effect a sealed chamber.'

'The gas fire you infer is the culprit, whether by being faulty or deliberately turned on at the tap, a flow of gas was allowed to fill the room by an intruder.'

'An intruder certainly, bent on asphyxiating Seward while he slept. A seamless method of dispatch, but no mention was made by Mr Bonington of a smell of gas.'

'Who then was this mysterious intruder, Holmes?' I asked.

'Most likely the same person who brought the ex-convict his bedtime drink of cocoa dosed with enough medicinal powders to ensure he lapsed into unconsciousness, a state of deep sleep, and who later quietly and unobtrusively re-entered the room and managed to murder him by the fatal inhalation of poisonous vapour while he still slept, thereafter making a meticulous search of his belongings. Most assuredly a female member of staff who works at the Rowes Duchy, an efficient lady very clued in as to her part in the crime. The gas fire is, I think, inconsequential. Ah, just step this way dear boy, across to the dressing table.'

I replaced the sheet over Seward's face, and did as my friend asked. Upon the top of the dressing table, marring the exquisite rosewood finish, was a discernible crescent shaped blemish, a scorch mark.

'The heated metal base of a spirit lamp for making tea,' I suggested, although I certainly was not provided with a similar in my room.

'What we are beholden to consider, Watson, is that such an obviously unsafe, inefficient methylated device should never under normal circumstances be permitted that marks an expensive piece of hotel furniture in this way. And anyhow, the dressing table should have been at once removed by staff to be repaired by a proficient cabinet maker. We can therefore deduce the mark is recent, so far undetected by housemaids systematically cleaning the rooms. There is no spirit lamp in my room!'

'Nor mine, but you're close on something, Holmes.'

'I am. You are no doubt familiar with the 'all-vaporising fumigator', my dear Watson?'

'You must enlighten me further, Holmes,' I answered.

'Likened to a spirit lamp in certain respects, the fumigator protects plants and flowers grown under glass from pestilence,' said he. 'There is a little container brim full of meths, into the neck of which is wedged a wick. After being lit, a metal guard is placed over the flame and, atop of this, a copper cup containing pure liquid nicotine. Once heated, the nicotine boils and emits a vapour fatally poisonous to humans — and most certainly to Barnaby Seward. It is widely advertised in gardening periodicals, growers' guides and so forth.'

'That should explain the absence of a smell of gas, although surely nicotine would leave a detectable odour?'

'My own conclusion is that later, upon discreetly re-visiting the room during the early hours while the guests in the hotel still slept, time enough for the fumigator to have burnt down before removing the deadly device and the cloth draught excluder, our intruder was careful to open the windows wide to allow fresh air to circulate and freshen up the atmosphere. That done, she of course withdraws to the staff quarters.'

'Holmes, you excel yourself! Hence, no one person entering the room should become the least suspicious.'

'Correct, Watson — 'death by natural causes'. Now I think I am myself deserving of a significant dosage of nicotine poisoning, so let us bid a fond adieu to our reclining corpse and re-join guests downstairs to enjoy an after breakfast pipe to mull over our options.'

In the foyer, I informed Mr Bonington I was of the opinion Seward had died from natural causes and that a local medical practitioner should no doubt share my prognosis. The mortuary arrangements and swift removal of the body were hardly our concern, and I was sure Mr Bonington and the staff at the Rowes Duchy would prove efficient in this matter. A large, rather daunting notice pinned to the cork board informed guests that trains would, for the foreseeable future, be no longer departing Princetown station due to snow drifts on Dartmoor blocking the line. Our travel arrangements for that afternoon must necessarily be curtailed, and it appeared we would be staying at the hotel over Christmas. Another point of interest, however, was the form of conversation being imparted by our elderly local historian and the promising officer cadet.

'Mr Hawtry, could you change the topic, I am becoming somewhat unsettled by this talk of the spirit's survival.'

'Why, Mr Wiggins, there is nothing remotely to feel ashamed of. It is the most natural progression.'

'Well, 'Wiggy',' said I, laughing, 'I've yet, in all my long experience as a medical practitioner, to see a certified corpse sit up and expound on philosophy. Once you're dead, you're dead, old chap.'

For the first time in our acquaintance-ship I found a serious side to Mr Hawtry for he tut-tutted and admonished me on the spot.

'Doctor Watson, the body is set in clay but the spirit most assuredly remains. I propose I chat with Major Churchward, our leader, and tonight when we have our meeting in the long room I shall make a point of asking for guidance. Spirits are often confused at the time of passing over and remain earthbound.'

'You're conducting an eve of Christmas séance, I take it?' said Holmes, under-standing the import of Hawtry's remarks better than I. Lighting his pipe with a match, he continued. 'Your society's psychical and you and your fellowship are of a mediumistic turn.'

'A private affair, I'm afraid, otherwise I should have invited you all to sit in. We shall amongst other things be discussing the society's finances and members' personal details so we are conducting our Christmas Eve séance behind closed doors.'

★　★　★

Christmas Eve was certainly surprising as it was remarkable. I recall vividly the bustle incurred for an after dinner tickets-only choral concert: sofas and chairs in the holly-bedecked hotel lounge being rearranged, tables were stacked to one side by waiters as guests re-seated themselves in order to appreciate a string quartet, and a choir of local ladies were singing most boisterously, 'fa la la la la la la la la'.

Wiggins, being his own man, had that afternoon, while enjoying an impromptu snowball fight in the hotel grounds, met by chance a Miss Collins, and the couple, I am delighted to report, soon became inseparable and were enjoying each other's company, after dinner, smoking a cigarette at a table. Holmes showed great interest in the psychic society and was of a mind to penetrate their meeting. The fact we were not permitted to participate and that the séance was being held behind closed doors acted like a red rag to a bull so far as my colleague was concerned.

By enquiring of a waiter, it soon became apparent that a side door existed with access to the long room used for tea trolleys during the interval. This led from the kitchens and we were thus able, by keeping the door ajar a few inches without ourselves being observed, to watch and hear tolerably well the séance then in progress. Of note there were only a trio of participants round the table: Major Churchward, Mr Hawtry, and a woman I had seen briefly handing out room keys at the reception desk. Each of the psychic society members bathed in the subtle glow from a green shaded desk lamp, the light of which gleamed upon several hung, framed etchings depicting Devon country pursuits, together with a section of polished oak panelling gracing the walls of the long room. This perceptive trio were alert to every nuance of the glass tumbler as it skimmed around the table from alphabet card to card spelling out a response to their urgent entreaties.

'Once more for the twentieth time of asking, where are the emeralds, Seward, we can make death on the astral planes extremely unpleasant if you persist to prevaricate. Mr Churchward is familiar with both the Egyptian and Tibetan Book of the Dead, having spent much time in Nepal, India and the Far East, and as a medium and widely read scholar of mysticism, he is not to be trifled with. None of us will tolerate untruths or alphabet waffle,' Mr Hawtry warned, like the others keeping his forefinger firmly oppressed on the upturned base of the glass as it sped around the polished surface of the table. A terrible and strange light gleamed from his eyes, an expression of malignancy and cruelty, so unlike the friendly and open countenance I remembered.

'We say it again, Seward, where are they? What became of the emeralds?' snapped the woman, losing patience.

Incredibly, I saw a luminescent face trapped, imprisoned like a goldfish in a fairground bowl, but to this effect squirming on the inside of the glass séance tumbler, mouthing desperate pleas, but words not discernible to living ears. The glass paused at various alphabet letters until an intelligible message was spelt out, occupying some twenty minutes, after which, suddenly Mr Hawtry, in a state of great excitement, jumped up from his chair holding up a piece of turn-off notepaper.

'We have it! Leave the séance, pack up the cards, Miss Whitehead. Major, it's spelt out here: '*The emeralds were broken from the settings and crowns then thumbed into oily, pliable putty affixing a pane of glass to the cast iron lantern of a gas lamp, the third along Albion Street near the Norwegian Seamen's Church in Rotherhithe.*''

'We shall be on the first train out of here. Well done, Mr Buss, and you too, Miss Whitehead. Our deception worked perfectly and we now have the opportunity of recovering the emeralds and disposing of them on the continent to a wealthy buyer. Our plan was a success and we may now adjourn to the lounge to enjoy the rest of the concert.'

Without preamble, we crept past the kitchens and, using the back stairs, were soon ensconced in Holmes' hotel room. 'So,' said my colleague, settling himself in an armchair and crossing his long thin legs, reaching for his Cherrywood pipe and charging it with the oily black shag he preferred. 'Our bogus psychic society shall be bound for the next train out, will they, while we, my dear Watson, shall be leaving the hotel almost immediately. Wiggins, having been smitten by Cupid's arrow in the form of Miss Delphinia Collins, I should hasten to say, had best remain. London must be achieved that much quicker, as indeed Rotherhithe.'

'Holmes, have you entirely lost your reason? Inclement weather and the geography of this desolate landscape are surely against us. No roads should be passable for a horse and carriage and I've no need to remind you there are ten and a half miles of solid granite betwixt

Princetown and Yelverton and, that said, due to the snow, are there actually any trains running to Tavistock and beyond?'

'Despite our unfavourable first impressions of Yelverton, the G.W.R. remains the most resilient and formidable railway company in the land. We shall make it a priority on our way up onto the high moors to firstly enquire at Princetown station the latest word on the train situation. The G.W.R., of course, runs a near-normal weekday service upon Christmas day, according to my Bradshaw.'

'You intend us to walk,' said I incredulously, 'ten and a half miles in deep snow.'

'I am shortly to procure from a downstairs cupboard a quantity of loosely stored tennis rackets, my dear Watson. By diligent use of a ball of twine and lengths of bandage we shall be in possession of the finest, rarest quality show-shoes in the whole of England. By the by, I recall reference to a Mr Buss, the fellow who duped us so convincingly with his alias 'Mr Hawtry, the fussy, lovable, old local historian'. That would be Chillingford Buss, an accomplished dealer and cutter of fine gemstones living in Amsterdam.'

★   ★   ★

What relief, there we were happily smoking our pipes, in a warm compartment of an engineer's train integrating a large steam crane and snow plough engine, trundling along, making excellent progress across the moors. The snow, it must be mentioned, had been successfully cleared by a number of these train arrangements, but the weather would have the final say, for more blizzards and widespread drifting were expected, leaving all the hard work and snow ploughing redundant by morning when the Princetown to Yelverton branch would be once more blocked and closed to trains. But the welcome news for us at least was that, although of a reduced service, we would be able to catch a connecting train to Tavistock and thence a near as dammit normal service was running to London-Paddington for Christmas day.

How peculiar that as Christmas day waned into Boxing day, and a blanket of snow carpeted the once marshy land of Rotherhithe with its thriving shipbuilding and commercial dock systems, we were to be found in dark and chilly Albion Street. Sherlock Holmes was wrestling at the top of a portable steps leaning against a gas lamp, working with a well-honed chisel at the old hard putty keeping in place one of the glass panes of the cast iron lantern at the summit, while I remained keeping my hand steady on the steps to help prevent wobbling, while additionally keeping my eyes peeled for any roving constable. A rather cracked and chipped panel was passed down and laid carefully flat on a strip of blanket, and then began the recovery — one dirtied and opaque emerald after another, more akin to bits of gravel dropped into the proffered Gladstone bag, and once Holmes was satisfied there were no more to cleave out of the putty I duly passed up the square of glass and, craning my neck, observed my companion make a fairly good job of guiding it into place, thereafter applying a dough of fresh putty round the edges.

We returned to our digs at Baker Street that early dawn, and ate a somewhat belated, spoiled Christmas dinner prepared much earlier by Mrs Hudson, but were gratified to learn in the morning broadsheets that abominable weather continued to affect the West Country, cutting off whole areas of Devon and making travel impossible.

Acknowledgements

Thank you to the team at Book Guild Publishing for their help in producing this book. Also to Roger Johnson, Amanda Payne, Sylvia Bedford and Helen.

The characters created by Sir Arthur Conan Doyle are used by kind permission of Jonathan Clowes Ltd, on behalf of the administrator of the Conan Doyle copyrights.

We do hope that you have enjoyed reading this large print book.

Did you know that all of our titles are available for purchase?

We publish a wide range of high quality large print books including:

Romances, Mysteries, Classics
General Fiction
Non Fiction and Westerns

Special interest titles available in large print are:

The Little Oxford Dictionary
Music Book, Song Book
Hymn Book, Service Book

Also available from us courtesy of Oxford University Press:

Young Readers' Dictionary
(large print edition)
Young Readers' Thesaurus
(large print edition)

For further information or a free brochure, please contact us at:
Ulverscroft Large Print Books Ltd.,
The Green, Bradgate Road, Anstey,
Leicester, LE7 7FU, England.
Tel: (00 44) **0116 236 4325**
Fax: (00 44) **0116 234 0205**

FROST LINE

Ardath Mayhar and
Mary Wickizer Burgess

A helpless woman is attacked in her home by a ruthless gang of murderers and thieves searching for her brother's valuable gun collection. They fail in their mission, and now they're coming back to finish the job — this time determined to leave no eye witnesses alive. Sheriff Washington Shipp must use all his instincts and expertise to track them down before they can strike again. But one of the criminals, more dangerous than all the rest, is leaving a trail of bodies across Louisiana — and Wash may be next in line . . .

LORD JAMES HARRINGTON AND THE CHRISTMAS MYSTERY

Lynn Florkiewicz

It's Christmas, and James and Beth are preparing for Harrington's festive dinner and dance. This year, famous diva Olivia Dupree is singing, a wedding is taking place, and they're hosting a reunion of Pals — ex-army comrades from the Great War. When Olivia falls ill and claims she's been poisoned, James puts his sleuthing hat on. But things take a sinister turn when a further attack occurs. What links the two victims? James must race against time to stop multiple murders taking place.

THE FRIGHTENED MAN

Gerald Verner

Samuel Coyne sends his ward Diana to enlist detective Paul Rivington as a bodyguard because three attempts have been made on his life. Although he denies knowing the attacker's motive or identity, he has erected elaborate defences around his house. Paul arranges for his brother and partner Bob to take on the job. Later, Bob captures an intruder on the grounds, who recognises Coyne as somebody he calls Kilroe. Surprisingly, Coyne lets the man go, not wishing to prosecute. Then they discover that Diana has mysteriously disappeared . . .

AMERICAN LEGIONNAIRE

John Robb

Amid the burning sands of the desert, the French Foreign Legion is constructing a new fort at Vateau — deep in the territory of El Dowla, ruthless leader of the Bormones, in constant struggle with France for control of the region. He aims to strike hard at the half-built stronghold before it is finished. Meanwhile, among the legionnaires sent out to protect Vateau is an American named Dice Regan — who has a very personal score to settle with El Dowla . . .